THE
LIBRARIANS
AND THE
LOST LAMP

THE
LIBRARIANS
AND THE
LOST LAMP

GREG COX

TOR

A TOM DOHERTY ASSOCIATES BOOK
NEW YORK

THE LIBRARIANS AND THE LOST LAMP

Copyright © 2016 by Electric Entertainment

All rights reserved.

A Tor Book
Published by Tom Doherty Associates
175 Fifth Avenue
New York, NY 10010

www.tor-forge.com

Tor® is a registered trademark of Macmillan Publishing Group, LLC.

The Library of Congress Cataloging-in-Publication Data
is available upon request.

ISBN 978-0-7653-8407-2 (hardcover)
ISBN 978-0-7653-8408-9 (trade paperback)
ISBN 978-0-7653-8406-5 (e-book)

Our books may be purchased in bulk for promotional, educational, or business use. Please contact your local bookseller or the Macmillan Corporate and Premium Sales Department at 1-800-221-7945, extension 5442, or by e-mail at MacmillanSpecialMarkets@macmillan.com.

First Edition: October 2016

Printed in the United States of America

0 9 8 7 6 5 4 3 2 1

THE
LIBRARIANS
AND THE
LOST LAMP

1

MacFarlane's Brewery was located in an out-of-the-way corner of Old Town, several blocks away from the more touristy stretches along the city's Royal Mile. The sooty brick building and its towering chimneys dated back to Victorian days. A rich, malty smell leaked from the cracks in the ancient masonry, and a chill autumn wind carried the intoxicating aroma down a dark, empty street to where Flynn Carsen stood watching. It was well after three in the morning and the brewery was closed, but that didn't matter to Flynn. He wasn't looking for a drink.

Not that I couldn't use one, he thought. *Considering.*

A lanky, boyish-looking fellow in his early thirties, he contemplated the brewery while a chilly breeze rustled his unruly brown hair. The night was cold enough that his breath misted before his lips. He tugged a rumpled trench coat tighter around his body and found himself pining for, say, the sultry warmth of an Amazon rain forest while he considered his next move. He had come straight from the Writers' Museum on

Lawnmarket, only a brisk walk away, where an unauthorized, after-hours visit had revealed that somebody else had gotten to a certain rare manuscript before him. Flynn was pretty sure he knew who had beaten him to the punch—and where they had probably gone to roost.

Duncan MacFarlane was the eccentric owner of the brewery and something of an avid collector in his own right. He and Flynn had been competitors of a sort, both in the pursuit of the same lost manuscript, but Flynn represented the Library, which had a legitimate interest in acquiring said manuscript for the good of all humanity. MacFarlane had his own personal agenda, which was what *really* had Flynn worried.

If that manuscript contains what I think it does . . .

Fearing that time was running out, Flynn snuck down a murky alley to find a side entrance to the brewery labeled "Employees Only." It was locked, of course, but he didn't let that stop him. Lock-picking was just one of the many useful new skills he'd acquired over the last couple of years. It was funny; there had been a time, only a few years ago, when he would have never dreamed of breaking and entering, but that was before he'd become the Librarian. Things were different now. *He* was different now. When you ventured into lost tombs and buried temples on a semiregular basis, breaking into a Scottish brewery barely warranted a shrug.

And, with any luck, there were fewer bottomless pits and booby-traps here.

Despite the cold nipping at his fingers, he picked the lock after only a couple of tries. Glancing up and down the alley to make certain that nobody was watching, he tugged open the door and quietly slipped inside the building, grateful to get out of the harsh weather. A large, ground-floor storeroom greeted him. Rows of tall wooden shelves were packed with aromatic bags of grains, malts, and hops, creating an even more pungent atmosphere than the one outdoors. More bags were piled high atop wooden pallets. A parked forklift waited to transport the heavy bags as needed. Humming ventilators kept the storeroom cool and dry.

Flynn gave the looming shelves only a passing glance. What he was looking for was unlikely to be stored there.

The clatter of heavy machinery, chugging away despite the lateness of the hour, led him into an automated bottling area. Glass bottles, tinted brown to protect the beer from the pernicious effects of sunlight, were carried along mechanized conveyor belts to be filled, capped, labeled, boxed, and unloaded at a rate of hundreds of bottles a minute. A separate assembly line did the same with large metal kegs intended for pubs all over the city and beyond. Stainless steel pipes ran along the ceiling, transporting the foamy beer from the vats, copper kettles, and tanks on the upper floors of the brewery. Insulated steam pipes connected with massive industrial boilers elsewhere in the building. The rattling bottles made quite a racket, making it *almost* too hard for Flynn to hear himself think.

And thinking was what Flynn did best.

Despite the urgency of his quest, he took a moment to admire the operation and the history behind it. Edinburgh had a long and illustrious heritage when it came to brewing beer; at one time, over a century ago, over forty such breweries had burnished the city's reputation for fine beer. Indeed, the city had once been nicknamed "Auld Reekie" thanks to the vast quantities of smoke produced by those breweries' many coal-burning furnaces and boilers. Moreover . . .

Stop that, Flynn chided himself. His brain was a Library in its own right, packed to overflowing with obscure and esoteric information, but now was not the time to go leafing through his mental card catalog. He needed to stay focused on the task at hand. He glanced around, wondering which way to go. A sign reading "Testing Area" caught his eye and interest.

That sounds promising.

Retreating from the mechanized clamor of the bottling room, he entered a small chamber that resembled an old-fashioned high school chemistry lab—or maybe the set of an old mad scientist movie. Laboratory glassware, including a wide variety of flasks, beakers, graduated cylinders, petri dishes, retorts, and test tubes, was arrayed atop stained slate counters, alongside old-school Bunsen burners and heating plates. Shelves held bottles and jars of reagents.

"Okay, this is more like it," Flynn muttered, even as his heart sank. He feared the lab had not just been used to test new strains of yeast or the specific gravity of some new decoction. *Oh, Duncan, what have you been up to?*

Sure enough, closer investigation revealed a stack of yellowed papers strewn across one counter. Flynn's heart sped up as he raced to inspect the documents, which were handwritten in fading ink. He instantly recognized the cramped, hurried handwriting, which belonged to one of Edinburgh's most illustrious native sons: Robert Louis Stevenson, author of *Treasure Island, Kidnapped,* and *The Strange Case of Dr. Jekyll and Mr. Hyde.*

Along with its beer, Edinburgh was also justifiably proud of its literary history. There were monuments and memorials to Stevenson all over the city, while the Writers' Museum, which Flynn had just come from, boasted an outstanding collection of artifacts and memorabilia once belonging to the likes of Sir

Walter Scott, Robert Burns, and Stevenson. Flynn hastily flipped through the loose pages to confirm what he already suspected, deftly deciphering Stevenson's scrawled prose:

At last the time had come to prepare the potion. I measured out a few minims of the red tincture, according to the process described previously, and added, in proper succession, those specific powders which I had taken such care to obtain. The mixture, which was at first of a crimson hue, began to darken, while foaming and emitting a noxious vapor until the compound changed to a dark purple. Trembling, I lifted the glass to my lips. . . .

"Whoa," Flynn murmured, experiencing a thrill of discovery despite the more ominous implications of the manuscript's presence in the lab. *This is it*, he realized: Stevenson's *original* draft of *Jekyll and Hyde*, long believed to have been destroyed by the author himself.

History claimed that Stevenson had burned his first draft back in 1885, because his wife, Fanny, had found it too horrific and not morally uplifting enough. But rumors had persisted over the years that Stevenson had not truly destroyed that early draft, only hidden it from the world, concealing clues to its location in the pages of his later books. For the last week or so, Flynn had been following a winding (and exhausting) trail that had led from Stevenson's mountaintop grave in Samoa to the author's former residences in Hawaii, New York, San Francisco, and London to, finally, the city of his birth—and a secret compartment hidden in Stevenson's first writing desk.

Too bad MacFarlane had gotten to it first.

If only I hadn't missed that connection at Heathrow, Flynn thought, *and Charlene hadn't insisted I fly commercial.*

The Librarian in him winced at the sight of the precious manuscript strewn all willy-nilly across the messy lab counter. Hastily gathering together the fragile pages, he tried to handle them as gently as he could manage, time allowing, and placed them in an airtight, acid-free plastic wrapper before tucking the package into a well-worn leather satchel slung over his shoulder by a strap. Then he took a closer look at the work area, hoping against hope that he wasn't too late to keep matters from escalating.

Please tell me he didn't mix the elixir yet.

But the evidence argued against that wishful thinking. An electric heating plate still felt warm to the touch. Broken glass crunched beneath his shoes. Dirty beakers and flasks gave off a distinctly chemical aroma that didn't smell remotely like beer. More like sulfur and brimstone, actually.

"Oh, crap," Flynn said. Having secured the manuscript, he was tempted to turn around and call it a day, but he knew in his heart that his job wasn't done yet. Librarians did more than collect and catalog lost documents and relics; they were also responsible for keeping certain ancient knowledge and artifacts out of the wrong hands—and dealing with the fallout when things went awry.

No matter how dangerous that could get.

"Duncan?" he called out. "Duncan MacFarlane? Are you still . . . you?"

No one answered, but Flynn knew he couldn't leave the brewery until he found out how far MacFarlane had gone. Exiting the laboratory, he set out to search for the reckless brewer, who was possibly still lurking somewhere else on the premises. He sighed wearily at the prospect of exploring the huge, five-story building from top to bottom, while keeping a careful eye out for MacFarlane, who was quite possibly not himself at the moment.

Why couldn't this be a micro-*brewery instead?*

"Mr. MacFarlane?" he shouted. "This is Flynn Carsen. I think we need to talk!"

Abandoning the ground floor, he climbed a wrought-iron spiral staircase to the upper levels of the brewery, checking them out one at a time. Gravity, which was used to transfer the brews-in-progress from one stage to another, dictated the layout of the brewery, so that Flynn found himself traveling backward through a vertical labyrinth of bubbling vats of fermenting liquid, antique copper boilers, and stainless steel tanks, all connected by a bewildering array of pipes and valves. Some of the pipes were labeled "Hot Liquor" and "Cold Liquor," but Flynn knew that the "liquor" in question was just water used in the brewing operation. Gas flames heated the huge copper kettle on the second floor, keeping the unfermented wort at a slow boil, using the same process employed by Victorian brewers over a century ago.

It was an interesting place and, ever curious, Flynn wished he had time to take a proper tour, but first he needed to find MacFarlane, who was nowhere to seen. Flynn was starting to wonder if he was wasting his time when, wearily climbing the stairs at a steadily decreasing pace, he heard laughter coming from just up ahead.

No, he corrected himself. *Not laughter.*

Cackling.

"Okay, that can't be good." He knew cackling when he heard it, particularly of the diabolical variety. *Is there such a thing as a* non-*diabolical cackling?* he wondered briefly, while reaching the top floor of the brewery and bracing himself for the worst. "Why is this never easy?"

Huge stainless steel mash tuns, where the malted barley and water were first mixed together and heated with steam, dominated the floor of the chamber. An elevated metal catwalk, overlooking the operation, stretched dozens of feet above Flynn's head. Another burst of maniacal laughter drew his gaze upward and he glimpsed a misshapen figure scurrying atop the catwalk. Heavy footsteps echoed loudly overhead.

"Mr. MacFarlane?"

"MacFarlane?" a mocking voice answered him. "No, MacFarlane isn't here anymore. Only Hyde!"

A hunched, vaguely simian figure shambled out from behind a metal sluice feeding one tun, stepping into the moonlight from a nearby window. Coarse, wild red hair and muttonchops matched his bushy eyebrows. Bloodshot eyes, nearly as red as his shaggy mane, bulged from their sockets. A sloping brow and prognathous jaws made him look more like a missing link than the actual Missing Link, whom Flynn had run into in Tanzania last Thanksgiving. A pair of lower incisors protruded from his mouth like tusks. An ill-fitting white lab coat looked one size too large for the stunted figure, which clasped a bubbling flask in a hairy, gnarled fist.

Needless to say, this was not what MacFarlane usually looked like.

I was afraid of this, Flynn thought. "You just had to try the elixir, didn't you?"

As Flynn had suspected, the *real* reason Stevenson had hidden his first draft and rewritten his book to be more "allegorical" was because that early version had contained the actual secret formula for Doctor Jekyll's infamous potion, which Stevenson had stumbled onto in his peripatetic travels around the world.

"And why not?" the creature on the catwalk replied, still retaining his thick Scottish accent. "What better way to throw off the stifling restrictions of morality and let loose my true self. I've never felt more free, more liberated!" He capered like a deranged monkey atop the catwalk. "And now I will share me wicked bliss with the world!"

He held up the flask, which was bubbling over with a frothing purple potion. Flynn realized with horror that Mac-Farlane—or rather his bestial alter ego—intended to contaminate the brewing mash with Jekyll's elixir. Judging from the size of the immense steel tun, Flynn estimated that they were looking at approximately eight hundred barrels of beer, soon to be bottled, kegged, and shipped to pubs all across Scotland and the rest of the world, which meant thousands of Mr. and Mrs. Hydes running amok, with even more to come if Mac-Farlane kept at it and produced more of the elixir. History's most monstrous beer bash would cause chaos and carnage across the globe.

"Hold on!" Flynn said. "That doesn't strike me as good idea."

MacFarlane glared down at him from the catwalk. "Ye cannae tell me what to do. Who do ye think ye are anyway?"

"The Librarian," Flynn said.

The creature's beetled brow furrowed in confusion. "A librarian?"

"No," Flynn corrected him. "*The* Librarian."

For over two thousand years, ever since the days of the first great Library in Alexandria, a Librarian had protected the world from dangerous secrets and magical relics that needed to be stored away until humanity was ready for them, which was quite possibly never. Flynn was hardly the first Librarian, and wouldn't be the last, but he was the one and only Librarian at present, and stopping a deranged brewer from turning thousands of thirsty beer drinkers into monsters fell squarely within his job description.

Easier said than done, of course.

"No matter!" MacFarlane snarled. "No one can stop me now!"

He poured the contents of the flask into the sluice leading down into the tun, where it joined the heated water and grains being mashed together in the tank. A scruffy hand slammed down the lid of the tank and dialed up the heat.

"And that's just the first batch!" he said, cackling. "I will flood the world with my divine concoction . . . and unleash the beast within us all!"

"Uh-uh," Flynn said. "The world doesn't need those kinds of spirits."

His keen eyes spotted a valve at the bottom of the tun. Rushing forward, he grabbed it with both hands and twisted it counterclockwise. *Lefty-loosy, righty-tighty*, he reminded himself as he strained to open the valve. The stubborn metal resisted him at first, but a good kick loosened it up.

"No!" MacFarlane cried out in rage. "Ye cannae do this. Ye have no right!"

"Got to disagree there. The way I see it, this falls squarely within my job description." The valve opened, and the tainted mash gushed from the tank, spilling onto the floor. He scrambled backward to avoid being knocked off his feet by the flood. A sticky, sugar-rich solution flowed across the floor. Flynn gasped in relief as he saw the contaminated mash vanishing into drains on the floor. That was one batch that wasn't going to ruin anybody's disposition.

"Damn ye!" MacFarlane smashed the empty glass flask against a railing, turning its wide end into a jagged weapon. Spittle sprayed from his lips. "Ye'll pay for that, ye meddling bibliophile! I'll mix yer blood and brains into me next brew!"

Springing from the catwalk, he grabbed onto the overhanging pipes and came swinging down at Flynn, who retreated toward the stairs. MacFarlane's feet slipped on the wet floor, but he managed to hang onto his balance and keep from falling flat on his face. The near spill did not improve the monster's mood.

"Come back, ye craven vandal!"

Brandishing the broken flask, MacFarlane loped after Flynn, splashing through puddles of spilled mash. His nostrils flared. Drool dripped from his lips. His dirty lab coat dragged through the mess.

"Maybe another time," Flynn shouted back, "when you're not under the influence!"

Flynn raced down the stairs, taking the steps two at a time. He was a scholar, not a brawler, so a strategic retreat struck him as the better part of valor in this instance. Past run-ins with unscrupulous treasure hunters, well-armed mercenaries, and the occasional mythological beast had toughened him up to a degree, but he still preferred to use his brains rather than fists or guns. He had the manuscript, and he'd foiled MacFarlane's scheme; that was enough for tonight. Now he just needed to get out of here in one piece. He could regroup and figure out how to deal with MacFarlane's transformation later.

The elixir had to wear off eventually, right?

Reaching the ground floor, Flynn glanced back over his shoulder to see MacFarlane gaining on him. The harsh fluorescent lights of the bottling room reflected off the jagged edges of the broken flask. MacFarlane cackled in anticipation of turning Flynn into fresh haggis. Librarian or not, Flynn found himself wishing momentarily that Stevenson had burned his manuscript after all.

"Hold on there," he said to MacFarlane. "Maybe you should sober up a bit before you do something we'll both regret."

MacFarlane chortled at the very idea. "Me mind has never been clearer." He backed Flynn up against the churning conveyor belt. Freshly filled bottles rattled along toward the labeling machine. "No regrets, no guilt . . . NO MERCY!"

He lunged at Flynn, who dropped to his hands and knees and scurried beneath the conveyor belt before jumping to his feet on the other side. Taking a leaf from MacFarlane's book, he snatched a bottle from the machinery and hurled it at the mad brewer like a missile. The bottle smashed against MacFarlane's chest, staggering him and driving him backward. Snarling in fury, MacFarlane tossed the broken flask at Flynn, but his throw went wild and missed Flynn's head by six inches or so. It crashed into the machinery behind the endangered Librarian.

"Bah!" MacFarlane spat. "I'll throttle ye with me bare hands if I have to!"

Flynn believed it, but he wasn't about to give MacFarlane an opportunity to carry out his threat. Keeping the transfigured brewer at bay, he flung bottle after bottle at the creature, as the conveyor belt supplied him with a seemingly endless supply of missiles. Bottles shattered loudly, one after another, causing the whole room to reek of spilled beer. Flynn thought it smelled like survival.

Until MacFarlane shut off the power.

Crouching low, the crazed science experiment loped across

the room to a control panel mounted on an exposed brick wall. His hairy hand flung a switch, and the entire assembly line ground to a halt.

So much for that bright idea, Flynn thought.

Hurling the last few bottles to slow MacFarlane down, Flynn darted across the sudsy floor to the storeroom beyond. Glancing around for the exit, he noticed the waiting forklift— and the towering piles of hops and grains stacked high atop the pallets.

On second thought, maybe he didn't need to leave Mac-Farlane running berserk. . . .

"Where are ye, meddler?" MacFarlane charged into the storeroom, murder in his bloodshot eyes. Rage contorted his already seriously unattractive countenance. His knotted fists swung at his sides. "No more of yer bloody interference. I've got some serious brewing to do!"

"Not without Stevenson's recipe you don't," Flynn shouted from the cab of the forklift. "And you're not going to go prowling through the city, either."

He fired up the forklift's engine and hit the gas. The loading truck surged forward, slamming into a huge pile of bagged hops, which toppled over onto MacFarlane, burying him beneath their weight. The startled monster only had time to let out a single howl before vanishing under the avalanche.

Not quite how Hyde was vanquished in the novel, Flynn thought, *but if it works* . . .

Flynn engaged the brakes and clambered out of the forklift. He cautiously approached the fallen bags, hoping that the collapse had only taken MacFarlane out of commission, not killed him. A muffled groan coming from beneath the strewn bags raised Flynn's hopes, and, straining his muscles, he shifted the bags to uncover MacFarlane's head, while leaving the rest of the bags to weigh the lunatic down, just in case he still had some homicidal mania left in him.

"MacFarlane?"

The stunned monster was out cold, but that wasn't all. Flynn watched in amazement as MacFarlane's bestial face began to melt and dissolve back into its original configuration. The jutting brow and jaws and tusks retracted, while the bristly red hair and eyebrows receded to a less frenzied state. Streaks of gray infiltrated the man's lank ginger tresses. Within seconds, the monster's atavistic features had given way to the blander, much more unassuming face of Duncan MacFarlane, hopefully for good.

Is that it? Flynn wondered. In Stevenson's book, it had taken repeated doses of the elixir before Jekyll started turning into Hyde spontaneously, without the aid of the potion. So, in theory, MacFarlane shouldn't be able to transform again without the formula in the manuscript. *Here's hoping that wasn't something Stevenson added in the rewrite.*

Stepping away from the unconscious brewer, who was probably going to have a monster hangover when he came to, Flynn checked to make sure the stolen manuscript was still tucked away safely in his satchel before contemplating the brewery itself. As far as he knew, he had disposed of the only batch of contaminated product, but could he be absolutely sure of that? It seemed a shame to let the rest of the brewery's refreshing output go to waste, but . . .

He took out his phone and dialed 999, which was the Scottish equivalent of 911.

"Hello," he said once someone picked up at the other end of the line. "I'd like to report a public health issue. I have reason to believe that the MacFarlane Brewery has been contaminated with . . . toxic fungus. You might want to have the health inspectors check things out." Another thought occurred to him. "And, oh, you might want to send an ambulance right away. I'm afraid there's been something of an industrial accident."

He hung up quickly before anyone could press him for details, and headed for the exit. He needed to make tracks before anyone showed up to investigate, but first he scribbled a sign on the back of a shipping invoice and taped it to the front door.

CLOSED—DUE TO HEALTH CONCERNS.

"That should do it," he said, stifling a yawn. "All in a day's work."

It was time to go home.

2

One of the world's great research institutes, housing more than six million books and twelve million documents, the New York Metropolitan Library was Flynn's home away from home. The landmark building, with its elegant brick and marble façade, looked out over a spacious plaza in midtown Manhattan, which was guarded by a pair of dozing marble lions. Wide steps led up to the library's grand entrance, which was supported by towering Corinthian columns. A banner stretched above the entrance advertised a new exhibition on King Arthur and the Knights of the Round Table.

Hah, Flynn thought, glancing up at the banner. *If only we could reveal the full story there. . . .*

Jet-lagged and dog-tired, he passed through a bronze front door into the library's magnificent marble entry hall, which was flanked by a sweeping double staircase leading upward. Flynn recalled standing in an endless line on the left staircase on that fateful day, only two years ago, when he had answered a mysterious invitation to apply for a "prestigious position" at the library. Little had he known at the time that his life was about to change forever and that the world was infinitely stranger and more fantastic than he ever could have imagined. Before then, he had been a professional college student, accumulating degree after degree—twenty-two in all—while studiously avoiding going out into real world. Sometimes he wondered what he'd be doing now if he'd blown off that interview.

Something safer, probably, but a lot less interesting.

Most visitors headed up to the Main Reading Room on the third floor, but Flynn veered off to drop into a spacious, sparsely furnished office that always struck him as being several times bigger than it needed to be. A woman was seated at a large, hand-carved mahogany desk at the far end of the office. She looked up from a ledger as Flynn entered.

"Oh, you're back," Charlene greeted him coolly. An unsmiling, thin-lipped woman of a certain age, she fit the stereotype of the stern, humorless librarian much better than Flynn did. She wore a pair of tortoiseshell glasses and a severe expression. Strawberry-blond hair was fading to gray. "I was wondering what was keeping you."

Flynn was used to her brusque manner by now. He'd stopped taking it personally . . . mostly.

"Good morning to you, too," he said, yawning. He had come straight from JFK International Airport after catching a red-eye flight from Heathrow. He couldn't wait to crash at his modest bachelor apartment in Brooklyn, but first he wanted to get the long-lost Stevenson manuscript safely stowed away in the Library, which had *much* tighter security than his apartment building. Heck, the Library's security made Fort Knox seem as safe as a convenience store at three a.m. It was one of the most impenetrable places on Earth.

Removing the manuscript from his satchel, he plopped it

onto Charlene's desk. "Mission accomplished," he bragged. "The first draft of *Dr. Jekyll and Mr. Hyde*, safely under wraps."

"I prefer the musical version," Charlene said, unimpressed. She shifted the manuscript out of the way, to maintain the neatly arranged order of her desk, and held out her hand.

"Receipts?"

Flynn rummaged around in his pockets. "Hang on. I'm pretty sure I've got them in here somewhere."

"Don't let me rush you," Charlene said dryly. "In the meantime, you owe $1.62 in library fines."

"Fines? What for?"

"That *Traveler's Guide to Hawaii* you checked out a few weeks ago. It's four days overdue."

Flynn vaguely remembered losing the book in question while escaping an erupting volcano in Sumatra. "That was work related."

"Submit an expense report," she said, unmoved. "Itemized, of course."

"Seriously?" Flynn hadn't slept in hours, thanks to a crying baby on his flight and a snoring tourist from New Jersey in the seat next to him; the last thing he needed right now was Charlene nickel-and-diming him as usual. "We're an age-old, secret organization guarding some of the great treasures of the world. Can't you loosen the purse strings once in a while?"

"Oh, yes," she replied archly, "why don't I just pawn the Ark of the Covenant for petty cash? Or hawk Pandora's Box on eBay or Craigslist?" She peered at him over her spectacles. "You know better than that. Large expenditures attract unwanted scrutiny, sometimes from the wrong quarters. And careful bookkeeping is the key to a well-run organization."

"So you've told me," Flynn said wearily, too tired to argue

the point one more time. "Look, I'll pull together those receipts after I've had a few hours of shut-eye."

"I've heard that before," she scoffed. "Oh, Judson wants to see you. Something's come up."

Flynn groaned. "Can this wait, Charlene? I *really* need to get some sleep."

"Well, I suppose I *could* tell him that you came all the way into the Library but couldn't be bothered to swing by long enough to check in with him. . . ."

"Okay, okay," Flynn said, giving in. "Which way?"

"I believe he's in the Large Collections Annex, tending to odds and ends," she said. "Don't keep him waiting. None of us are getting any younger, you know."

Flynn was tempted to ask Charlene just how old she really was, but he decided against it. He started away from her desk, but he only got a few steps before she called him back.

"Not so fast." She indicated the manuscript resting atop her desk. "Aren't you forgetting something?"

Flynn reclaimed the package and stuck it back into his satchel before exiting the office. A short hike brought him to a deceptively normal-looking reading room, where two stone-faced guards were posted to either side of a well-stocked bookcase. Telltale bulges beneath the guards' jackets suggested that both men were more heavily armed than you'd expect at the average library.

"Hi, Bud. Hi, Lou," Flynn greeted the guards, who let him approach the bookcase, where he casually tugged on a leather-bound edition of Shakespeare's *A Midsummer Night's Dream*, just as he had the first time he'd come this way, right after being selected as the new Librarian. The motion activated a hidden mechanism that revealed a secret vestibule behind the bookcase, facing a concealed elevator. The two guards stepped

forward in lockstep, and each inserted a key into a slot on opposite sides of the elevator door. They turned them simultaneously, as though following nuclear launch protocols.

As Flynn understood it, the Pentagon had gotten the idea
from the Library.

The elevator opened to admit him, and he settled in for the
long ride down to the actual Library, which was buried deep
below the public library. Tired as he was, the trip seemed to
take even longer than usual, but at last the elevator dropped
him off outside two frosted-glass doors. He slid back a wall
panel to expose a hidden touchpad. Running on autopilot, he
keyed in the password, and the doors swung open automatically on pneumatic hinges.

Home sweet home, Flynn thought. *More or less*.

Stone steps, carved out of the very bedrock and guarded
by a pair of golden lions matching the marble felines up top,
led him into a vast, cavernous chamber. Dark wooden shelves
and wainscoting lined the walls, while row after row of glass
display cases held some of the long-lost wonders of the world:
the Spear of Destiny, the Philosopher's Stone, da Vinci's secret diaries, a crystal skull from lost Atlantis, and many other
marvels and relics. The *real Mona Lisa* hung upon one wall,
not far from the actual Shroud of Turin. A unicorn neighed
somewhere in the depths of the Library, impatient for his
daily portion of virgin oats and olive oil. Vaulted barrel ceil-
ings stretched high above Flynn's head.

The Library, Charlene had once told him, was always as big
as it needed to be, and the awe-inspiring view before him was
only the proverbial tip of the iceberg. (The actual tip was on
ice in a special refrigerated vault elsewhere in the Library.)
Even after two years, Flynn was still stumbling onto new
sections of the Library that he had never discovered before.

At times he wondered if he would *ever* uncover all the mysteries filed away in the Library.

He had barely gotten a few steps into the stacks when a shining silver sword came whistling toward him, propelled by some unseen force. Sighing, Flynn ducked beneath the fifth-century English blade, which proceeded to dance around him expectantly. The fact that the sword was floating of its own accord, without anyone wielding it, did not faze him.

"Hi, 'Cal," he greeted the fabled sword of King Arthur. "I'm happy to see you, too."

Excalibur feinted at him playfully.

"Sorry, pal. I'm too tired to duel right now."

Under other circumstances, Flynn might have borrowed another sword from the Library's extensive collection of antique weapons and enjoyed a vigorous bout of fencing with Excalibur, but not when, as presently, he was dead on his feet. Instead, having anticipated this encounter, he fished a small rubber ball from his pocket and hurled it away from him with as much force as he could muster.

"Fetch!"

Excalibur gleefully chased after the bouncing ball, taking off down a seemingly endless corridor. With any luck, that would keep the sword occupied long enough for Flynn to make his way to the Large Collections Annex. A shortcut through the Hall of Fame, which was lined with painted portraits of all the previous Librarians, dating back to antiquity, brought him to an even more capacious chamber stuffed with oversized relics too big to fit comfortably within an ordinary bookshelf or display case. Noah's Ark loomed ponderously over the collection. The Fountain of Youth gurgled nearby. Flynn eyed the sparkling waters wistfully. He was thirsty from his walk, but not enough so to risk ending up in kindergarten again. He had graduated from *See Spot Run* a long time ago.

He found Judson inside H. G. Wells's celebrated Time Machine, a fabulous steampunk contraption of polished brass and oiled red leather, shaped roughly like an hourglass. The device flickered in and out of the present before powering down and settling into today. Judson climbed stiffly out of the Machine, which continued to tick away like a grandfather clock. He smoothed out the creases in his conservative black suit.

"Welcome back," he greeted Flynn, somewhat more warmly than Charlene had. "Excalibur has been missing you."

He was a short, soft-spoken man whose doleful, hangdog features belied his amiable manner. A bald pate and sagging skin betrayed his considerable age, although Flynn sometimes suspected that Judson was far older than he looked. A slight stutter made him seem deceptively mild-mannered and unassuming, but Flynn knew from experience that the old man was much sharper and more resourceful than he let on.

"Going somewhere?" Flynn asked, indicating the Time Machine. "Or -when?"

"No, no, not at all." Judson shook his head. "At my age, I much prefer to stay put in the here and now. I just had to re-set the Machine back from Daylight Saving Time to Eastern Standard Time; otherwise it starts losing time . . . literally."

Flynn took his word for it. "Charlene said you wanted to see me?"

"In a moment." Judson nodded at Flynn's heavy satchel. "Is that it?"

"You bet." Flynn delivered the manuscript to his mentor. "And don't ask me what I had to go through to get it."

Judson sniffed the air. "Do I smell . . . beer?"

"Probably," Flynn admitted. "I didn't really have time to take a shower before catching my flight."

"I, I see," Judson said, although his bemused tone and expression said otherwise. "In any event, congratulations on another job well done." He hefted the manuscript. "I look forward to shelving this in the Lost Drafts and Apocrypha Collection, next to Shakespeare's *Love's Labour's Won* and Aristophanes's *Women in Tents*."

Flynn's eyes widened at those tantalizing titles, which set his Librarian's heart racing. He made a mental note to check out those volumes *after* he got a little sleep.

"No problem, but if that's all—"

"You've returned just in time, Flynn. There's a situation in the Middle East that ought to be looked into."

"The Middle East?" A whine crept into Flynn's voice. "Judson, I just got back from Scotland. . . ."

"A lovely country. I hope you enjoyed the trip." He tucked the manuscript under his arm and strolled out of the annex into an adjacent section of the Library. "But I'm afraid the world didn't stop turning while you were gallivanting about the Highlands, and a Librarian's work is never done."

Tell me about it, Flynn thought.

He trailed after Judson, only to be interrupted by Excalibur, who caught up with him at last, the rubber ball proudly impaled upon its tip. The animated sword hovered before Flynn, eagerly wagging its blade.

"Again?" He plucked the ball from the sword. "Okay, just one more time."

He gave the toy another good toss, sending Excalibur zipping after it, before following Judson into a smaller chamber lined with yet more bookshelves, where Flynn was only mildly surprised to find Charlene waiting for them. He felt both out-numbered and ambushed.

"Okay, I'll bite," he said. "What's up overseas?"

"While you were away," Judson said, "the Baghdad Museum of Arts and Antiquities was robbed by unknown parties. It's unclear at this point who is responsible or what they were after, but there's reason to suspect that the Forty might be involved."

Flynn gave him a puzzled look. "The Forty?"

"As in the Forty Thieves." Judson pulled a dusty copy of *The Arabian Nights* off a shelf and laid it down atop a wooden table. He flipped through the pages until he reached an engraved color illustration of Ali Baba hiding from the blood-thirsty thieves whose treasure he had stolen from a hidden cave. Knives drawn, the Thieves scowled murderously, intent on revenge. "In reality, it's a centuries-old criminal syndicate that past Librarians have clashed with more than once, albeit a bit before your time. They haven't been heard of since they tried to get their hands on the Jewel of Seven Stars back in 1903, and I'd hoped they had finally died off, but I now fear that was just wishful thinking."

"What makes you think this Forty outfit is involved in the Baghdad heist?" Flynn asked. "I hate to say it, but looted historical sites and museums are old news in the Middle East at this point, what with the wars and political instability in the region. It's a shame, but I'm not sure where we fit in."

Judson looked at Flynn. "Are you familiar with the House of Wisdom?"

"Of course," Flynn replied, vaguely insulted by the query. "During the Golden Age of Islam, from roughly the eighth to the thirteenth century, the House of Wisdom was the greatest library in the known world, attracting scholars from all across the map to Baghdad, which, at the time, was the undisputed center of power, wealth, and learning in the medieval world. Alas, the House of Wisdom was sacked in 1258 during a Mongol invasion, causing many rare books and documents to be lost forever."

"*Supposedly* lost," Judson corrected him. "The invasion was instigated, at least in part, by the Forty to give them the opportunity to raid the House of Wisdom for the secrets it held, but the Librarian at the time managed to keep them from obtaining anything *too* dangerous—although, yes, some of the House's most priceless volumes did go missing in the process." Judson shook his head woefully. "Call it a hunch, but this business in Baghdad feels uncomfortably familiar. The thieves went straight for archives, bypassing more valuable artifacts and treasures, as though they were searching for ancient knowledge, not riches. That sounds like the Forty to me, and Baghdad used to be their home base, back in its glory days."

"I don't know," Flynn said. "No offense, but that sounds like a stretch to me."

"Perhaps," Judson said. "I could be wrong. I probably am. But we can't afford to take the chance. Even if the Forty aren't back in the game, *somebody* raided those archives, and, as you should know by now, the secrets of the past can often pose a serious threat to the present . . . if they fall into the wrong hands. In a worst-case scenario, we could even be talking about—"

"The fate of the world," Flynn supplied, knowing the spiel by now. "I get it, really I do. It's just that I was hoping for a little time off before embarking on another globe-trotting trek into possibly mortal danger."

"And I was hoping that my next blind date would turn out

to be Antonio Banderas," Charlene said sarcastically. "Tough. We don't always get what we want." She handed him a coach-class airline ticket. "Your flight leaves from LaGuardia in three hours. If I were you, I'd get going."

Flynn bowed to the inevitable. If he hurried, he might be able to manage a shower and a change of clothes before high-tailing it to the airport. New York to Baghdad was at least a twelve hour trip, so maybe he could catch *some* sleep on the way there.

Or catch up on his reading at least.

"Good luck," Judson said. "But watch your back. The Forty weren't just thieves; they were murderers and cutthroats. If they're back in business, they'll stop at nothing to achieve their ultimate goal . . . whatever that might be."

"You heard him," Charlene added. Just for a second, a flicker of what might actually have been genuine concern softened her pinched expression. "Be careful, and don't forget—"

"My receipts," Flynn said. "I know, I know."

He sighed in resignation. Times like this, he wished he weren't the only Librarian.

This job was too big for just one person. . . .

3

❈ *2016* ❈
Ten years later
Portland, Oregon

Magic is real, Colonel Eve Baird thought. *Just look at this place.*

Tucked away under the south end of a lofty suspension bridge crossing the Willamette River, in what appeared to be an unremarkable gray utility building, the Library's Portland Annex was much more impressive on the inside than on the outside. Antique electric lights cast a warm, gentle glow over the Annex's ground-floor office, which had a certain timeless charm that was distinctly at odds with the building's weathered stone exterior. Sturdy wooden bookcases were crammed with worn volumes on everything from stamp collecting to cutting-edge string theory. An old-school card catalog ran along one side of a sweeping staircase leading up to the mezzanine overlooking the office. A large inlaid compass symbol decorated the hardwood floor. Side doors magically linked the Annex to the rest of the Library, with its innumerable galleries and collections, while the frosted-glass "Back Door" led to, well, most anyplace she cared to imagine, as well as a few destinations beyond imagining.

Baird surveyed the familiar scene from her desk, where she had been carefully reviewing the Library's security systems and emergency action plans. A statuesque blonde whose supermodel good looks came in third to her top-flight military training and no-nonsense attitude, she preferred to leave nothing to chance when it came to guarding the Library, its inventory, and its agents. Granted, the deceptively cozy-looking Annex was a far cry from the hostile war zones and rogue states she'd once frequented as part of an elite NATO counterterrorism unit; you'd never guess that she was often dealing with far more dangerous weapons of mass destruction these days.

Magic is real and *frequently deadly*, she reminded herself for the umpteenth time. *And maybe someday that won't sound quite so crazy to me.*

Over a year had passed since the Library had recruited her as a Guardian, making her responsible for the well-being of three newly minted Librarians. The Portland Annex was already starting to feel like her home away from home, but the whole magic-and-monsters thing still took some getting used to. Yawning, she stretched at her desk to keep from getting stiff.

She could have used a good workout. Ever since that weird "time loop" business at DARPA, things had been quiet—maybe too much so for her tastes. Where had all the troublesome dragons and golems gone? Surely there had to be some long-lost magical relic they should be tracking down?

Two of her new charges, Jacob Stone and Cassandra Cillian, were seated at the cluttered conference table in the middle of the main office, across from Baird's own desk. Typically for Librarians, they were taking advantage of the downtime to catch up on their reading. Cassandra, a petite redhead with a penchant for short skirts, knee socks, and frilly collars, was avidly devouring some abstruse mathematics text as though it were the latest bestselling thriller, while periodically peering up at swirling patterns and calculations that only she could see, thanks to her peculiar gifts. Her slender fingers traced equations in the empty air. Baird had stopped trying to figure out what Cassandra was seeing. Chances were, she wouldn't understand it anyway.

Sitting opposite her, Jacob Stone looked as rugged as Cassandra looked dainty and delicate. Scruffily handsome, in a country-western kind of way, he leafed through a lavishly illustrated coffee-table book on pre-Columbian cave paintings while scribbling notes on a yellow legal pad, no doubt in preparation for writing a learned monograph on the topic. A rumpled plaid shirt, faded jeans, and work boots belied his status as a world-class expert on art and architecture, with numerous publications under a variety of pseudonyms. As every Librarian knew, you couldn't always judge a book by its cover.

Worryingly unaccounted for was Ezekiel Jones, self-proclaimed man of mystery and master thief. Baird wanted to think that Jones was behaving himself, but she knew better.

Try not to end up on a most-wanted list, Jones, she thought. *Just this once.*

"Seriously?" Stone reacted indignantly to something in the book he was perusing. His gruff voice held more than a hint of Oklahoma and the rough-and-tumble oil yards where he had once labored. "You call those Aztec fertility symbols? Any fool can tell that they're obviously Toltec in origin."

"Obviously," Baird said dryly.

Stone looked up from his book. "Say, didn't you and Flynn

explore a buried Toltec temple a while ago?" He turned the book toward her. "You remember seeing anything like these petroglyphs when you were there?"

" 'Fraid not," she replied. "I was too busy running from molten lava and a bad-tempered feathered serpent to check out the finer points of the decor."

The discussion drew Cassandra out of her private reverie. "Speaking of Flynn, have you heard from him recently?"

I wish, Baird thought. "Last I heard, he was in Nepal, or maybe Tibet, doing his own thing . . . as usual."

That last part came out a bit more acerbically than she had intended. Although she liked Flynn, and found him oddly attractive, his tendency to run off half cocked and on his own drove her nuts sometimes. Used to being the only Librarian at large, he wasn't exactly a team player, which was something of a sore spot between them. For all she knew, he was knee-deep in a new adventure right now, flying solo, which was apparently just the way he liked it.

"Sorry," Cassandra said sheepishly, as though fearing she had inadvertently crossed a line. "I didn't mean to pry."

"It's all right, Red," Baird assured her. "Flynn is a big boy. He can take care of himself."

"One would assume so," Jenkins said, strolling into the office from an adjacent reading room. A dapper, silver-haired gentleman who was older, by centuries, than he appeared, he had been looking after the Annex for longer than Baird knew or wanted to think about. He placed a neglected copy of Cagliostro's personal diary back on a bookshelf, precisely where it belonged. "Not that Librarians are always the most prudent of individuals. In my extremely extensive experience, their erudition is consistently beyond dispute, but their common sense? Well, that's another matter."

A pair of frosted-glass doors swung open, admitting a breeze and Ezekiel Jones. The cocky young thief sauntered into the Annex bearing a pink cardboard box and an infectious grin. A wiry man in his early twenties, he had dark hair, mischievous eyes, and designer clothes that had probably been shoplifted from only the most fashionable outlets. His stylish wardrobe contrasted sharply with Stone's more blue-collar attire, and put Baird's own workaday clothes to shame as well. As a rule, she preferred to dress for practicality, as in a white button-down shirt and trousers.

"Miss me?" An Australian accent betrayed his Down Under roots. An irrepressible smile lit up the room. "What am I saying? Of course you did. I'm Ezekiel Jones. Who wouldn't miss my delightful company?"

"Everybody you've ever ripped off?" Stone said sternly, like an older brother addressing a wayward younger sibling. "Where'd you get off to anyway? Monte Carlo? The Riviera? Fort Knox?"

Baird eyed the box apprehensively. *Please let that not be the Crown Jewels, or a priceless Picasso.*

"Nah," Ezekiel said. "Voodoo Doughnuts. Just up the road from here."

Cassandra's large eyes widened even more than usual. "Doughnuts?"

"Portland's best." Ezekiel placed the box down on the conference table and flipped its lid to reveal a mouthwatering selection of gourmet doughnuts. "Feast your eyes, and then just feast in general. The doughnuts are on me."

Baird stepped out from behind her desk to investigate, drawn in part by the tantalizing aroma of the deep-fried treats. She had to admit, they did smell tasty.

"That's very generous of you, Jones. Uncharacteristically so, in fact." She regarded him suspiciously. "I don't suppose you actually *paid* for these doughnuts?"

"You're joking, right?" He scoffed at the very notion. "I need to keep in practice, after all. You wouldn't want me to get rusty."

"Heaven forbid," Jenkins said archly. "But perhaps, Mr. Jones, you could kindly refrain from placing your ill-gotten refreshments on top of these private love letters between Napoleon and Josephine, detailing the actual circumstances of his exile on Elba?" He sighed theatrically as he extracted several yellowed sheets of paper, each carrying a faint whiff of French perfume, from beneath the doughnut box. "And to think this used to be such a quiet, contemplative environment, before it turned into a children's playhouse."

Baird was used to such grumbling by now. She and her freshly forged team of Librarians had set up shop in the Annex at a time when the rest of the Library was lost between realities. Jenkins had already been a fixture at the Annex, along with the card catalog and desks, and had stayed on for the duration, despite his frequent sighs, disdainful sniffs, and sarcasm. Baird suspected that his high-handed curmudgeon routine was at least partly an act.

"I don't know," she said. "Sounds to me like you're protesting a bit too much. Are you sure you don't actually enjoy our company?"

"Quoting the Bard, are we, Colonel?" Jenkins placed the Elba correspondence in a desk drawer, safely away from icing and sticky fingers. "Why don't you leave Shakespeare on the shelf and join your ravenous colleagues in their sugar spree?"

"Like you've never indulged your own sweet tooth," Ezekiel teased him. Claiming the biggest, frostiest, most lavishly sprinkled doughnut for himself, he took an enthusiastic bite and smacked his lips afterward. "Now that's what I call a treat for the taste buds. Almost as delicious as those gold-flecked Swiss chocolates I nicked in Dubai last Easter from a certain overfed oil baron who, frankly, could stand to lose a few stone." He licked some icing from his nimble fingers. "Come on, mates. Dig in."

Stone shrugged. "Don't mind if I do."

A raspberry jelly doughnut met with his approval. "Whoa. That's positively sinful." He stepped aside to let Cassandra get at the doughnuts. "Step right up, Cassie. You've got to get in on this action."

She contemplated the all-too-tempting spread. "Well, maybe just one. . . ."

"Only one?" Ezekiel asked in disbelief. "Live a little, Cassandra. What have you got to lose?"

An awkward hush fell over the office as his careless remark landed with a thud, reminding everyone present of the grape-sized brain tumor that threatened to make Cassandra's life a short one. An abashed look came over Ezekiel's face as he grasped what he'd said. It wasn't often that his trademark self-regard slipped, but this was one of those times.

"Um, I didn't mean it like that. It just slipped out. . . ."

"It's okay," she replied. "You don't need to walk on egg-shells around me. None of you do." She boldly plucked a triple-chocolate doughnut from the box and bit into it lustily. "And you're right. Life is too short not to indulge yourself sometimes."

"Roger that," Baird said, hoping to break the tension. "Dibs on the deluxe apple fritter doughnut."

Before she could snag her enticing prize, however, the Clipping Book grabbed her attention instead. Laid open atop its stand on the table, the magical scrapbook thumped momentarily as an unseen force turned its pages to reveal a couple of fresh news clippings that hadn't been there before.

"Heads up, people. Seems we've got a new mission on our hands."

The Clipping Book was the Library's somewhat anti-quated way of alerting the team to events that required their attention. A collection of newspaper articles pasted in an old-fashioned scrapbook, such as were once used in news-paper offices before the digital era, the Clipping Book's se-lections seldom spelled out exactly what kind of preternatural unpleasantness they could expect to encounter, but the mere fact that the clippings had magically appeared in the scrap-book indicated that there was more to the story than met the eye.

"Thank heavens," Jenkins said. "Some peace and privacy at last."

"Don't count on it," Baird said. Jenkins rarely ventured into the field with them, but that didn't mean she didn't need him holding down the fort here at the Annex—and providing them with crucial intel as needed. "All hands on deck, includ-ing you."

"Of course, Colonel. I'm at your disposal."

"You bet you are."

Along with their Guardian, the Librarians gathered around the Clipping Book to see what new mystery had presented it-self. Baird quickly scanned the headlines:

LOCAL MAN WINS MILLION-DOLLAR JACKPOT.
LOTTERY WINNER IDENTIFIED AS VEGAS RESIDENT.

The team crowded one another to read the clippings, with only Jenkins staying aloof. A quick skim revealed only that one Gus Dunphy of Las Vegas, Nevada, had recently won a big payout in a state lottery. A black-and-white photo showed a grinning Dunphy accepting an oversized check the size of small billboard. That in itself didn't raise any red flags for Baird; people *did* win lotteries without magical assistance, and Dunphy looked like a thoroughly average, unassuming type.

But if the Library thought it was worth checking out . . .

"Aces," Ezekiel said. "We're going to Vegas."

"So it seems," Baird agreed. "Get your game on, everyone. I want to be in Sin City in thirty minutes, tops."

With their snack break cut short, she reached for the apple fritter doughnut, only to find it curiously missing.

"Hey, what happened to my doughnut?"

Jenkins wiped a crumb from his lips with a silk pocket handkerchief.

"I'm sure I have no idea," he said.

4

❊ *2016* ❊
Las Vegas, Nevada

"Let your love be tender, let your love be true," the Elvis said. "By the power invested in me by the great state of Nevada, and your own burning hunk o' love, I now pronounce you—"

The door to the wedding chapel slammed open, accompanied by a blinding flash of bright white light, and the Librarians (and Guardian) rushed into the aisle, which was decked out with flowers, garlands, and an excess of twinkle lights. Instrumental versions of the King's greatest hits played softly in the background. Resplendent in rhinestones, the Elvis paused in his pronouncement, while the bride and groom, who were wearing matching Graceland T-shirts and blue suede shoes, turned to gape at the new arrivals. Stone realized at once that they were intruding on some rather less-than-solemn nuptials.

"Don't mind us," he said. "Carry on . . . and congratulations."

The Back Door of the Annex could magically lead to most any other door on the planet, but dialing up the correct destination was something less than an exact science. Getting the right city was as easy as pie; guessing precisely which door in that city you might emerge from was more of a gamble.

Which, this being Vegas, was only fitting.

"Sorry for the interruption," Baird added. "We'll be going now."

The team retreated from the chapel with all due haste, exiting the building to step out onto a sunlit sidewalk somewhere along Las Vegas Boulevard. Palm trees sprouted beneath a bright blue sky, while the temperature was a good deal warmer than it had been in Portland, even though they were still in the same time zone. Low-rent strip malls, fast food joints, and a pawn shop indicated that this stretch of the boulevard was not exactly at the heart of the famed Vegas Strip, with its celebrated casinos and mega-resorts. Stone figured that was just as well; they weren't here to party.

"An Elvis wedding?" Ezekiel snickered in amusement. "Talk about retro. What century do they think this is, anyway?"

Stone bristled. "You got something against the King?"

"Hey, I'm sure he's great, if you like moldy oldies that your grandparents used to make out to."

Stone couldn't believe his ears. "You've got no respect for the classics, you know that, man?"

"Too busy being on the cutting edge, I guess." Ezekiel grinned at Stone. "Send me a telegram from Backwardsville when you get a chance."

"I think it's sweet," Cassandra said, "that the happy couple obviously have so much in common."

"Assuming that they didn't just meet in a bar two hours ago," Ezekiel added, smirking. "I mean, this *is* Vegas."

"Don't be so cynical," she chided him.

"Don't be so naïve," he shot back playfully, "or this town will eat you alive."

"That's enough, all of you," Baird said, playing den mother as usual. "Let's stay focused on our mission. Jones, did you manage to track down Dunphy's home address?"

"Easy-peasy." He consulted his phone. "According to the local DMV database, he lives on the outskirts of town, about"—he switched to another app—"sixteen miles from here."

Stone wished the Back Door could have gotten them a little closer to their final destination. "Guess we need to hail a cab."

"A cab?" Ezekiel scoffed. "You really do need to get with today, mate." He keyed a new command into his phone. "Uber is where it's at these days."

"Just get us there, Jones," Baird said. "The easiest way possible."

"Leave it to me," he said confidently. "But you're paying."

A crowded car ride brought them to a dingy trailer park, far from the glitz and excess Vegas was famous for. Rusty mobile homes, in varying states of repair, squatted along both sides of pitted blacktop roads. Drying laundry hung on clotheslines. Barbecue grills, toys, and cheap plastic playground equipment littered patchy brown lawns. Weeds and potholes infested the pavement. A chained mutt growled at the Librarians, who took in the run-down neighborhood.

"Not exactly where you'd expect to find a guy who just won a million dollars," Baird observed.

Stone shrugged. "Guess his luck changed."

"See, that's just wrong," Ezekiel objected. "Picking out random numbers doesn't require any smarts or skill or daring. You want a million dollars, you ought to go about it the right way."

"By stealing it?" Cassandra guessed.

"Naturally." Ezekiel gave her a puzzled look. "How else?"

Stone let that one pass. "The real question is whether Dunphy's big win was really just a stroke of luck, or if he owes his change of fortune to some kind of magic instead?"

"Like a rabbit's foot," Cassandra speculated, "or a four-leaf clover?"

"Kind of early for Saint Patrick's Day," Baird said, "but I'm guessing it's something like that. The Clipping Book wouldn't have sent us here otherwise."

Locating the correct trailer took a few inquiries, but they soon approached a beaten-up aluminum trailer that had clearly seen better days. Rust discolored its once-shiny exterior. Duct tape patched cracked windows or covered them altogether. Weeds infested the lawn, which needed mowing.

"I'm going to go out on a limb," Stone said, "and predict that Dunphy has upgraded his living situation since winning the lottery."

"You're probably right," Baird said, "but we've got to start somewhere."

She walked up to the trailer and knocked on the door. "Mr. Dunphy? Anybody?"

"If you're looking for Gus," a raspy voice interrupted, "you're fat outta luck. He skipped out a couple days ago, without even saying good-bye."

The voice came from an older woman reclining in a lawn chair outside the trailer across the street. Her wizened features reminded Stone of a Rembrandt painting, although none of Rembrandt's models had been taking a drag on a cigarette while soaking up the sun. Dunphy's neighbor had a silver beehive hairdo that would have done the Bride of Frankenstein proud, a tank top, shorts, sandals, and pink sunglasses. An open can of beer sat within easy reach atop a plastic cooler next to her chair.

Stone and the others strolled over to talk to her. "Thanks for letting us know, ma'am. I don't suppose you know where we might find him?"

"Who's asking?" She held up her hand to fend off any replies. "Wait, let me guess." She lifted her shades to reveal canny brown eyes that looked the team over. "Bill collectors? Loan sharks? Ex-wives? Girlfriends? Distant relations looking for a handout?"

"Nothing like that, ma'am," Stone said. "We're . . . Librarians."

The woman blinked in surprise. "Come again?"

"He has a number of books overdue," Cassandra offered by way of explanation. It wasn't the most far-fetched excuse they'd ever volunteered for snooping around where they didn't belong. Not by a long shot.

"Is that so?" the woman said. "Never took Gus for much of a reader."

"How *would* you describe him?" Baird asked, fishing for intel. "If you don't mind me asking, Miss . . . ?"

"Call me Naomi," the neighbor answered. "Everybody else does." She took another drag on her cigarette. "Guess you'd call Gus a confirmed gambler, and not a very good one, honestly. Strictly small time and always in hock to somebody. Then again, he *did* win that lottery, so who am I to talk?"

"Any chance he left a forwarding address?" Stone asked.

"Not that I know. Like I told that other crew, he put this place in his rearview mirror the minute he got that big payout. Can't say I blame him, really."

Stone's ears perked up. "Other crew?"

"Yeah. Some Arab fellas just came looking for Gus yesterday, along with this bossy looker who was way out of Gus's league, frankly, and had something of an attitude. I told her and her boys just what I'm telling you, that Gus had high-tailed it out of here in search of greener pastures, and that I never expect to see his sorry mug again." Naomi shook her head. "Some people get all the luck."

"Don't they just." Stone glanced back at Dunphy's trailer. "You think it would be okay if we poked around a bit, just to try to figure out where Gus might have gotten to?"

"Because of those library books," Cassandra added. "There's a waiting list, you see, of people just dying to read those books. . . ."

Enough is enough, Cassie, Stone thought. *No need to lay it so thick.*

"Go ahead." Naomi shrugged. "No skin off my nose."

A baby wailed inside her trailer, calling her from her chair. She stubbed out her cigarette and rose creakily to her feet. "Now if you don't mind, I've gotta see to my grandnephew."

"Understood, ma'am," Stone said cordially. "Thanks again for your assistance."

"Coming all this way for library books," she muttered, shaking her head. "Now I've heard everything. . . ."

She vanished into her trailer, leaving the team free to talk openly among themselves.

"Seems like we're not the only people looking for Dunphy," Ezekiel said. "Who do we think that other crew is?"

"From the sound of it, it could be anybody," Stone said. "Nothing like a million bucks to bring plenty of interested parties out of the woodwork: creditors, scam artists, you name it."

A worried expression came over Cassandra's face. "You think we have competition?"

"Too soon to tell," Baird said. "This other crew could just be after Dunphy's money, not anything magic. Heck, we don't even know what we're actually looking for yet, let alone if somebody else is after it."

"My money's on a lucky horseshoe," Ezekiel said. "What with Gus being a gambler and all."

"I'll take that bet," Stone said. "Baird's right. It could be anything. A lucky coin, a crystal ball, a deal with the devil, or something else entirely."

Ezekiel grinned. "Care to make it interesting?"

"Wow," Baird said, rolling her eyes. "One hour in Vegas and you're both infected with gambling fever."

Stone shrugged. "Nothing wrong with a friendly wager." He smirked at Ezekiel. "Twenty bucks says it's *not* a horseshoe."

"You got yourself a bet, mate. Better keep a twenty handy."

"Well, leave me out of it." Baird sighed impatiently, like a harried schoolteacher trying to ride herd on a passel of unruly kids on a field trip. "Maybe we can get on with our investigation?"

"Any time," Stone said.

They headed back to Dunphy's trailer. Baird nodded at the closed front door.

"Time to work your magic, Jones. Get us into this trailer."

"A tragic waste of my talents." He reached for the door handle. "I could break into this tin can with both eyes closed and one hand tied behind my—"

The door swung open easily.

Stone was impressed. "Smooth work, man."

"It wasn't me." Ezekiel sounded vaguely disappointed as he fiddled with the handle. "This lock has already been jimmied, and not by an amateur."

Stone scowled. "Not sure I like the sound of that."

"Me neither," Baird said, drawing her gun. "Watch yourselves."

They cautiously entered the darkened trailer, with Baird

taking point and clearing the corners. Stone flipped a light switch, but nothing happened. He guessed that power had been disconnected and drew back some window curtains instead. Sunlight invaded the trailer, revealing that parties unknown had already ransacked Dunphy's former residence. Closets, cupboards, and drawers had been emptied, their contents carelessly dumped onto the floor. Unpaid bills, most labeled "FINAL NOTICE," littered the main living area, next to an overturned wastebasket. Plywood and laminate had been peeled off the walls in search of concealed hiding places. Even the mattress in the sleeping compartment had been sliced open and rifled through. Handfuls of cheap foam padding were strewn about the room.

"Somebody's tossed the place," Stone said. "But looking for . . . what?"

"Good question." Baird put away her gun. "On the bright side, it definitely looks like we're onto something. This is suspicious, or promising, or maybe promisingly suspicious."

Ezekiel surveyed the mess disdainfully, as though he didn't see anything worth stealing. "You think it was that Middle Eastern crew the old lady mentioned?"

"Possibly," Baird said. "But what were they looking for, and did they find it?"

"The only person who might know that is Dunphy," Cassandra said. "Too bad we don't know where he disappeared to."

"Are you kidding?" Ezekiel asked. "You don't need to be Sherlock Holmes—or our old friend Moriarty—to figure that out. This is Vegas. Where else would a diehard gambler who has just come into money go?"

"The Strip," the other Librarians realized in unison.

"Took you long enough." Ezekiel beamed in anticipation. "Viva Las Vegas."

5

※ *2006* ※

Six thousand miles, seven time zones, and more than twelve hours after departing the Library and New York City, Flynn arrived in Iraq. Dust, heat, and swaying palm trees greeted him, but there was nary a genie or flying carpet to be seen. The twenty-first century had been hard on Baghdad. Three years into the American occupation, the former home of the House of Wisdom was still effectively a war zone, torn apart by insurgency, strife, and a devastated infrastructure. An armored vehicle, along with an armed military escort, was required to travel safely from the airport to the fortified Green Zone in central Baghdad, which was pretty much the only secure part of the city. Peering out through the tinted, bulletproof windows of the airport shuttle, Flynn caught glimpses of a city under siege. Military helicopters buzzed overhead, while US troops and tanks patrolled the streets. Years of tanks and mortar shells had pitted the city streets, making for a bumpy ride through heavy traffic.

It was a far cry from the Baghdad of the Golden Age, hundreds of years ago, when the city had been a center of science and learning known throughout the civilized world for the quantity and quality of its libraries, where scores of dedicated scholars and scribes had devoted themselves to preserving, translating, and building upon the accumulated wisdom of ancient Greece, Persia, China, and India. Under the reign of such legendary caliphs as the great Harun al-Rashid, Baghdad had shone brightly while Europe was still mired in the Dark Ages. Gazing soberly out the window, Flynn felt a pang in his heart, remembering the city's glorious past and contributions to civilization. It was hard to imagine the likes of Sinbad or Aladdin swashbuckling through the war-ravaged Baghdad of today.

But perhaps the Forty Thieves were still at work?

Even gaining access to occupied Iraq was tricky these days, but Charlene had managed to pull the necessary strings to get Flynn a visa. In theory, his visit to Baghdad was part of the ongoing effort to recover precious antiquities and documents that had gone missing during the looting back in 2003, in the early days of the invasion. As cover stories went, it was a pretty good one; it made sense that an expert from the New York Metropolitan Library might be involved in the recovery effort. Flynn hadn't even needed to fake his credentials.

For once.

Fortunately, the Baghdad Museum of Arts and Antiquities was located in the Green Zone, so Flynn didn't have to worry about navigating the unsecured streets, where a lone American librarian might easily find himself in trouble. After passing through a series of gates and checkpoints, Flynn's transport dropped him off outside the museum. Clutching his solitary suitcase, he abandoned the air-conditioned comfort of the shuttle to step out into the overpowering heat and sunlight. Blinded by the sudden glare, he stumbled onto the sidewalk before remembering the sunglasses tucked into the front pocket of his safari jacket. He fumbled blindly for them.

"Mr. Carsen?"

An attractive woman, about Flynn's age, was waiting for him at the curb. Curly brown hair framed her face. Conservative Western attire, of a professional nature, looked good on her.

"That's me," he answered. "But, please, call me Flynn."

"Dr. Shirin Masri," she said, introducing herself in flawless English, albeit with an appealingly exotic accent. "I'm the curator of the Rare Documents Archives here at the museum. I was told to expect you."

Her neutral tone made it unclear if she was happy about this or not. Dark brown eyes looked Flynn over skeptically. They were nice eyes, he noticed, and more than a little distracting.

Uh-uh, he cautioned himself. *Keep your mind on the business at hand.*

"Thanks for meeting me." He held out his hand, while trying to smooth a stubborn cowlick back in place with his other hand. "My apologies if I seem a bit discombobulated, what with the twelve-hour flight and all. Jet lag cramps my style, I'm afraid."

She shook his hand, holding it not a moment longer than necessary.

"I'm not sure you needed to come all this way. I've already spoken with the authorities about the recent theft." She eyed him quizzically. "You're with the New York Metropolitan Library, or so they tell me?"

"That's right. Part of a new task force investigating black-market trafficking in rare manuscripts and relics."

"I wasn't aware of any such task force," she said.

"Well, we're more interested in results than publicity." He wiped his brow, which was already perspiring in the heat. "Any chance we can move this discussion indoors? I haven't quite adapted to the climate yet."

"Of course," she said. "Come with me."

His luggage rolled and bounced on a paved walkway as she guided him into the museum, which, like the city itself, had seen better days. Armed guards were posted at the front entrance, which was possibly a textbook case of closing the barn door after the horse had already been rustled. A sign out front indicated that the museum was presently closed to the public.

"We've been closed since the looting a few years ago," Shirin explained, "while trying to reconstruct the collection." Frustration tinged her voice. "We were on the verge of reopening when *this* happened."

"I'm sorry," Flynn said sincerely as they entered the building. Stark white walls strived not to compete with the ages-old artifacts and statuary on display. Glass display cases held souvenirs from thousands of years of recorded history. "Do the authorities have any idea who is responsible?"

"If they do, they haven't told me."

Crime-scene tape still sealed the lobby of the museum. A chalk outline on the floor reminded Flynn that, according to what he'd been able to learn about the burglary on the plane, at least one security guard had been killed by the thieves, his throat cut quickly and efficiently sometime during the heist. He gulped at the thought, while noticing that Shirin averted her eyes from the outline.

"Tariq Hassan," she said quietly. "He was a good man. Honest and incorruptible."

"I'm sure he was," Flynn said. "I'm sorry . . . again."

"Not your fault," she said, shrugging. "But thank you."

Passing by galleries of ancient statuary, tapestries, and relics, which had apparently gone untouched by the thieves, they arrived at Shirin's office in the Archives section of the museum. A plethora of volumes and scrolls were stacked in the corners of the office, waiting to be reshelved. An overturned bookcase needed to be righted. A spinning fan struggled to combat the heat and stuffiness; apparently the museum's air conditioning was another casualty of war.

"Here we are," she said. "Sorry about the mess. We're still picking up the pieces after the robbery." She sat down behind a cluttered desk, whose disorganized state would probably have given Charlene a heart attack. "Take a seat . . . if you can find one."

Rooting around, Flynn found a chair buried beneath a pile of books. He cleared it off before sitting down. The cramped, overstuffed office offered barely more leg room than the plane had.

"Don't get too comfortable," she said impatiently. "No offense, but I can't really spare you much time right now. Like I said, I've already spoken with the local authorities, and, as you can see, I've got plenty of work to do putting things back where they belong."

"I understand," he said, getting down to business. "So I'm told the thieves targeted the Archives specifically. Do you have any idea of what they were after?"

"Well, I'm still in the process of conducting a thorough inventory to determine exactly what might have been taken and what was left behind, but . . . yes, at least one item has gone missing," she said bitterly. "A very rare and precious item."

"And that would be?"

"Possibly the oldest existing edition of the *Kitab Alf Layla Wa-Layla*, or, as it's known in the West, *The Arabian Nights*, or *One Thousand and One Nights*. This particular copy dated back to the eighth century, which makes it a good century older than any other version in existence."

"Whoa," Flynn said, impressed. "In Persian or Arabic?"

He was aware that that no complete edition of the *Alf Layla*, containing all 1001 tales, was known to exist and that the very origins of the book were obscured by the mists of time; as he understood it, current scholarship held that the celebrated Arabic version had been based on an even earlier Persian chronicle long lost to history. Subsequent translations and variations, including the early French and English editions, had taken the collected stories even further from their roots, to the extent that there was no definitive version of the text, only countless variations comprised of different combinations of stories. There were practically a thousand and one versions of *One Thousand and One Nights*.

"Ancient Persian," she said. "A sixth-century Farsi script, to be exact. I had only recently stumbled onto the volume while cataloging a treasure trove of old documents captured from one of Saddam's palaces." Her eyes lighted up at the memory. "You can imagine my excitement when I realized what I had discovered. Mind you, I'm not saying that it was the *original* text, said to be penned by Scheherazade herself, but it was older and more authentic than any other surviving copy of the *Alf Layla*. I was in the process of translating it when—"

She gestured at the messy aftermath of the robbery.

"This whole travesty makes me sick to my stomach, not to mention mad as hell. I really wish you could help me, Mr. Carsen, but I'm afraid that one-of-a-kind copy of the *Alf Layla* has been lost again, perhaps forever this time."

"Never underestimate a determined Librarian," he said, while wondering how the thieves had found out about the book in the first place. "How many people knew about your discovery?"

"I'd mentioned it to a few of my colleagues and fellow curators," she said, shrugging. "It never occurred to me to keep it a secret. In retrospect, that might have been a mistake."

"You can't blame yourself. It's not your fault that some bad people got wind of the book's existence. You were just doing your job."

"I suppose," she said, sounding unconvinced. "But speaking of my job, I really do need to get back to it." She stood up behind her desk, as though to signal that the interview was over. "I'm sorry you came all this way for nothing."

I wouldn't say that, he thought. If nothing else, he had discovered what the thieves had absconded with, even if he still wasn't quite sure if this was a matter for the Library. A unique, centuries-old edition of *The Arabian Nights* was undoubtedly a priceless item, well worth stealing, and its theft a genuine loss to legitimate scholars and historians, but he wasn't convinced that this was "fate of the world" territory. Sometimes a museum heist was just a museum heist.

"I'm staying at the Tigris Hotel, at least overnight." He handed her a business card with his cell phone number on it. "If you think of anything else . . ."

"Don't get your hopes up, Mr. Carsen. The *Alf Layla* is gone, and, frankly speaking, I doubt that the New York Metropolitan Library can do anything about that. This was, by all indications, a professional operation, executed with merciless precision. I suspect you're out of your league."

Flynn shrugged.

"You'd be surprised."

The Tigris Hotel catered to visiting American contractors and consultants. Like much of the Green Zone, it was an oasis of air conditioning and steady electricity amid the privations of war-torn Iraq. Exhausted by his nonstop journeying, Flynn barely registered the relative comfort of his accommodations before collapsing onto the bed with his clothes on. He was out like a light within seconds.

But that didn't necessarily mean that he was off the job.

Dreaming, he found himself wandering through a crowded outdoor marketplace in the long-lost Baghdad of *The Arabian Nights*. Bearded men wearing turbans and robes haggled over fine goods, spices, and produce from all across the known world: silk and paper and porcelain from far-off China, coconuts and sandalwood from India, grain and linen from Egypt, perfumes from Arabia, succulent fruits from Persia and beyond, all brought to Baghdad by countless caravans and sailing ships. The mouthwatering aroma of cooking fish and lamb competed with the smells of myriad spices wafting on the breeze. Gleaming palaces and mosques, topped by gilded onion domes and towering minarets, climbed toward the sky, in contrast to the humble beggars pleading for alms in the streets and alleys. Mules and camels made their way through the packed buyers and sellers, transporting yet more wares to the market. Money changers converted silver Persian dirhams for gold Byzantine denarii and vice versa, bridging East and West. A storyteller held a small crowd transfixed by tales of doomed lovers, capricious genies, and fiendish ghouls waiting in the wastes for unwary travelers. Veiled women peered out from behind the filmy curtains of gilded palanquins born on poles atop the shoulders of brawny servants. Glancing down, Flynn saw that he was dressed like a Hollywood version of Ali Baba or Sinbad, complete with an embroidered vest, silk pantaloons, and a sash around his waist.

Yep, he thought. *I'm definitely dreaming.*

Roaming idly through the colorful scene, he paused before a small bookshop tucked away in a side street. A pair of gold-tinted bookends on display at the front of the shop caught his eye; fashioned in the shape of twin lions, they looked like miniature versions of the sculpted golden felines guarding the entrance to the Library back in Manhattan. He pushed forward through the crowd to get a better look, only to step into a fragrant heap of camel dung.

"Watch your step," a familiar voice warned him, a moment too late. "Oh, never mind."

"Judson?" Flynn turned to see his mentor standing nearby, clutching the reins of a particularly cranky-looking camel. A traditional Arab robe was draped over the former Librarian's slight form. "What are you doing here?"

"I, I'm not doing anything," Judson stammered. "This is your dream, isn't it?"

"So I thought," Flynn replied suspiciously. This wasn't the first time Judson had appeared to him as a dream or mirage. "You ever going to tell me how exactly you pull off stunts like this?"

"I'm sure I don't know what you mean, Flynn. I'm undoubtedly just a figment of your subconscious, talking back to you." He glanced with distaste at Flynn's soiled boot. "But, just for the sake of argument, if I *was* here talking to you for real, what would you have to tell me? Have you learned anything more about that robbery at the museum?"

"Possibly," Flynn said, maintaining a safe distance from the camel. Even in a dream, he didn't feel like getting bitten. "I spoke with the curator of the Archives, and she mentioned that one particular item had apparently been stolen by thieves."

He quickly filled Judson in on what Shirin Masri had told him about the lost copy of the *Alf Layla*.

"Oh, dear," Judson said, sounding distinctly troubled by the news. The worry lines on his face grew even deeper than usual, and he shook his head gravely. "That's, that's very troubling to hear. I was afraid it might be something along those lines."

"How come?" Flynn asked. "I mean, *The Arabian Nights* is just a collection of folk tales." He regarded Judson curiously. "Isn't it?"

" 'The Goose That Laid the Golden Eggs' is a folk tale," Judson reminded him, "but I still have to clean out its coop every morning. There's more truth to the old myths and legends than today's modern world wants to admit, and that applies to the Thousand and One Tales of Scheherazade as well, particularly in their original tellings."

Flynn could believe it. If there was one thing he'd learned as the Librarian, it was to check his twenty-first-century skepticism at the door when it came to fantastic stories from bygone days. If the Sword in the Stone and the Medusa's Head were real, why not the myriad wonders of *The Arabian Nights* as well?

"All right," he said. "Assuming the bad guys had a reason for stealing the *Alf Layla*, besides it being priceless and all, what's their endgame? What are they really after?"

"What the Forty have always been after, since the sacking of the House of Wisdom more than seven hundred years ago," Judson guessed. "Aladdin's Lamp."

"Aladdin's Lamp!" Flynn could not contain his excitement. "That's for real?"

Judson gave him a look.

"Never mind," Flynn said sheepishly. "Of course it is. So what's the actual scoop on the Lamp? Are we talking wishes, a genie, the whole nine yards?"

"Pretty much," Judson said. "Aladdin's Lamp is arguably the most powerful magical relic described in *The Arabian Nights* and the most dangerous . . . in more ways than one."

Flynn wasn't sure what Judson meant by that. "Okay, I can see why letting the Forty gain control of a wish-granting genie would be bad news for everyone else, but is there another downside I'm missing?"

"Very much so," Judson explained. "As unfortunate as it would be if the Lamp fell into wrong hands, the greater threat is the Djinn trapped inside the Lamp. Djinn are spirits of fire, and not necessarily friendly ones. Every time the Lamp is rubbed and a wish is granted, it imparts energy to the confined Djinn, who will eventually grow strong enough to break free of the spell binding him to the Lamp." Judson shuddered at the thought. "Aladdin's Lamp has been missing for centuries. There's no way of telling just how fragile the Lamp is at this point or how many more wishes it will take to shatter it, releasing the Djinn for good."

"Which would not be a happy ending, I take it?"

"Hardly. Djinn are capricious, often vindictive entities. They lack imagination, which is why they rely on human beings to make wishes for them, but they bitterly resent humans for the same reason. And this particular Djinn, the one confined in Aladdin's Lamp, is more vengeful than most." Judson's voice took on a forceful tone, losing its characteristic stammer. "Whatever you do, Flynn, no matter how tempting, you must *not* rub the Lamp. Remember that."

"Got it," Flynn said. "So we have no idea where the Lamp is hiding these days?"

"The final resting place of the Lamp has been a mystery for ages, which is where I fear Dr. Masri's stolen copy of the *Alf Layla* comes in. None of the previously known translations of *The Arabian Nights* reveal where the Lamp ended up after Aladdin's time, but perhaps an even earlier version, closer to the original source of the legend—"

"—might contain a clue on where to find the Lamp," Flynn said, getting the picture. "Sounds to me like maybe I need to talk to Dr. Masri again, and find out if she managed to translate the Aladdin story before the book was stolen."

"I'd do that," Judson advised. "Preferably before the same idea occurs to the Forty."

Flynn winced at the thought of the ruthless thieves targeting Shirin Masri.

"I can't stress how important this is, Flynn. You cannot let the Forty obtain Aladdin's Lamp, or allow the Djinn to break free of the Lamp. Both prospects are, well, alarming to the extreme."

"Message received," Flynn said. "Loud and clear."

"Glad, glad to hear it. We're counting on you, Flynn. And, oh, one more thing."

"Yes?" Flynn asked.

"Watch out for the camel."

Too late! The camel spat in Flynn's face, spraying him with gloppy green drool.

"Aaagh!" Flynn woke with a start, wiping his face frantically, only to find it mercifully free of camel drool. Sitting up straight in his hotel room, he needed a moment to reorient himself as the sights and sounds and smells of medieval Baghdad receded and reality snapped back into place. A digital alarm clock informed him that it was late afternoon, local time.

But though the dream was already fading in his memory, the gist of his "conversation" with Judson stayed with him.

Aladdin's Lamp. A vengeful genie. The Forty.

And Shirin.

I need to get to her, he realized, *before anyone else does!*

6

❈ *2006* ❈

The Barani Street market was still going strong as Shirin made her way home from the museum. Rows of open-air stalls hawking everything from books to fabrics to spices lined the narrow avenue, while more shops occupied the maze of surrounding streets and alleys, many of which didn't even have names. Merchants called out to passersby, extolling their wares. The tantalizing aromas of coffee, black pepper, cardamom, nutmeg, cumin, ginger, cloves, and other spices wafted through the air. Concrete barriers at both ends of the street were an unpleasant reminder of the realities of modern-day Baghdad. Shirin enjoyed browsing in the market on her way home most afternoons, but remained alert and on guard for any possible threats. You couldn't be too careful these days.

"Fresh spices! Best prices!" a merchant called out to her from his stall. Brightly colored heaps of powdered spices created a festive display. "Paprika! Turmeric! Saffron!"

Enticed by the vibrant colors and smells, Shirin paused to inspect the spices. There was a curfew in effect after sundown, but she figured she still had time to do a little shopping and make it home before dark. She put down her battered black attaché case, tucking it between her feet for safekeeping. Come to think of it, she was running low on nutmeg. . . .

Distracted, she let her guard drop a moment too long.

"Don't react. Don't say anything," a husky female voice whispered in her ear as a figure came up behind her and pressed the tip of a knife of against her ribs. "You're coming with us, Dr. Masri."

Despite the heat, Shirin felt her blood freeze. She had no idea who was holding the knife, and she was afraid to look back over her shoulder, but all at once she was in mortal danger. If only she had gone straight home after work, or paid more attention to her surroundings . . . !

First the robbery at the Archives, she thought. *Now this.*

"There's a car waiting at the north end of the street, beyond the barricades," the other woman said. "Come quietly, and you won't be harmed."

Shirin doubted that, but she saw no choice but to comply. There was a black-market cannister of Mace in her pocket, but it might as well have been on the other side of the Persian Gulf for all that she could reach it before her captor slid the blade between her ribs. She started to turn away from the spice stand, wondering if she would live to see tomorrow.

"Dr. Masri," another voice called out to her. "Fancy meeting you here."

To her surprise, Flynn Carsen stepped out in front of her, blocking her path. Beneath a traditional white headscarf, the well-meaning American wore an open, guileless expression, clearly oblivious to her plight. Shirin wasn't sure whether to be grateful for the interruption or alarmed by his interference. Her situation was dire enough without a loose-cannon librarian complicating things.

"Mr. Carsen," she said, doing her best to keep a quaver out of her voice. "I didn't expect to see you here."

"Well, I guess it's true what they say. Everybody comes to the Barani Street market." He nodded at the figure behind her. "Who's your friend?"

"Nobody in particular." The mystery woman discreetly prodded Shirin with the knife. "But we really must be going."

"What's the rush?" Flynn seemed in no hurry to move along. "We haven't even been properly introduced." He held out his hand. "Flynn Carsen. New York Metropolitan Library."

"You're a long way from home, Mr. Carsen," the woman said, not volunteering her own name. "And, if I may say so, perhaps out of your element. The streets of Baghdad are not always safe for lone Americans, not in these troubled times."

Glancing around, Shirin saw that the conversation was indeed attracting attention from the merchants and shoppers crowding the marketplace. Suspicious, even hostile glares turned in their direction. Again, she wasn't sure if that was a good thing or not. She suspected that her would-be kidnapper was not appreciating this kind of scrutiny.

"Thanks for the warning," Flynn said. "But how could I resist checking out this market while I was in the vicinity? I just had to soak up the atmosphere, you know? Check some of the local color." He gawked like a tourist at the bustling market all around them. "Did you know that this was one of the very first paved streets in the city, and that there's been a public market on this site since at least the late Abbasid period back around seven fifty AD or so?"

Further up the street, where the knife-wielding woman had been steering Shirin, three grim-faced men began to shove their way through the crowd toward them. Indignant protests greeted their progress. Shirin recalled that the other woman had spoken of "we" before. She guessed that the other kidnappers were growing impatient, which could put Carsen in serious jeopardy as well.

I can't let that happen, she thought. *It's not his fault that he's in the wrong place at the wrong time.*

"It's good to see you again, Mr. Carsen, but—"

"Flynn," he corrected her. "Please."

"All right, *Flynn*." She saw the other kidnappers drawing closer and realized that she needed to get rid of Flynn before he became a target, too. Her mouth felt as dry as the desert. "But my . . . friend . . . is right. We really need to get going. Perhaps some other time?"

"Careful. I'm going to hold you to that," he began, only to be distracted by the spice merchant's wares. "Hey, is this turmeric?" He scooped up a big handful of bright orange powder. "Wow. You never see anything this fresh at the supermarket back home." He held up his palm to show the woman behind Shirin. "I mean, look at that color—"

Without warning, he blew the powder into the woman's face. She sputtered and coughed as the spice hit her like a face full of tear gas. Seizing the opportunity, Shirin elbowed the woman in the gut, causing her to stagger backward, gasping for breath. Shirin felt the knife tip pull away from her and sprang forward in the opposite direction, practically colliding with Flynn.

"Looked like you could use a hand," he said, over the spice dealer's strident protests. He grabbed her hand and pulled her away from the stand. "Quick! Come with me. I've done this kind of thing before."

She stared at him incredulously. "You have?"

"Trust me."

Shirin didn't think she had much choice. She started to go with him, then remembered something important.

"My briefcase!"

"Leave it," he said, tugging on her.

"Not a chance!" She pulled her hand free and darted back toward the case, which was still resting on the pavement in front of the spice stand. She grabbed it by the handle, relieved that it hadn't gotten displaced in the confusion. No way was she leaving the case—and its contents—behind.

"Stupid girl! You should have run while you had the chance!"

For the first time, Shirin got a look at her attempted abductor, although the other woman's irate face was obscured by tears, snot, and spice. Shirin got a quick impression of a twentyish young woman wearing a traditional black cloak and headdress. Kohl-lined eyes and a golden nose stud adorned her natural beauty. She lunged at Shirin with her knife held high.

So much for taking me alive. . . .

Years of living in a combat zone had honed Shirin's reflexes and taught her how to defend herself if she had to. Thinking fast, she swung the briefcase up to deflect the knife attack, then kicked the other woman in the knee, causing her to stumble backward, cursing.

You had that coming, Shirin thought. *Witch.*

"Wow," Flynn said, reappearing at her side. "Remind me not to get on your bad side."

Shirin would have liked to get a few more licks in, but she knew they couldn't linger. Glancing north, she saw the woman's accomplices getting nearer. The murderous looks on their faces left no doubt whose side they were on.

"We have to go," Shirin warned Flynn. "There are more of them."

"You mean those bruisers heading toward us?" he said without looking. "Already on my radar."

He took hold of her hand again and they made tracks toward the southern end of the market, away from the on-coming kidnappers. The bustling crowd impeded them, so that Shirin felt as though she was swimming up the Euphrates against a heavy current. She held on tightly to her attaché case with her free hand, terrified of losing it in the crush. She could only pray that the tightly packed throng was slowing their pursuers as well.

"Excuse me!" Flynn shouted, in alternating English and Arabic. "Coming through!"

They had almost reached the end of the street when Shirin spotted four more men, looking equally hostile, pushing their way through the crowd toward them. One of them pointed at Shirin and shouted to his accomplices. "There she is! Don't let her get away!"

She and Flynn came to an abrupt halt, briefly causing a pedestrian traffic jam. Looking behind her, she saw their original pursuers gaining on them. They were less than half a block away and eating up that distance quickly. Any hope of escape was fading fast.

"How many of these goons are there?" she asked out loud.

"Best guess?" Flynn replied. "Forty, tops."

His glib reply caused her to stop short and stare at him in bafflement. "Huh?"

"Granted," he said, elaborating, "I suppose that not all of the Forty are muscle. That number is bound to include bosses, spies, smugglers, safecrackers, assassins, and other criminal types. Maybe even an inside man—or woman—at your museum. Which probably cuts down on the number of personnel actually employed in a simple kidnapping operation like this. . . ."

She couldn't believe he was babbling like this—in full paragraphs, no less—while they were running for their lives. She looked about desperately for another escape route.

By now, the commotion was beginning to register on the crowd around them. Worried shoppers, not entirely sure what was happening, clutched their burdens close to them and tried to distance themselves from Flynn and Shirin, at least as much as possible amidst the press of the crowd. Wary shop-keepers looked on with concern. Braver souls raised their voices in objection to the scowling kidnappers rudely forcing their way past the shoppers. A foolhardy young man, inspect-ing a display of pots and pans, refused to get out of the way and was roughly shoved aside, smashing into the stall. Copper and cast iron clattered onto the pavement, adding to the clamor.

At least they're not opening fire, Shirin thought. *Maybe to avoid attracting the US patrols and helicopters?*

But the men were still closing in on them. Shirin extracted the Mace from her pocket, but she doubted it would do much good against an entire gang of kidnappers. She and Flynn were outnumbered and underequipped.

"They're all around us," she whispered. "They're not going to let us get away."

"Maybe, maybe not." Flynn tightened his grip on her hand. "Stay close."

"Wait. What are you going to do?"

Instead of explaining, he cupped his other hand around his mouth like a megaphone and shouted a single word in decent Arabic:

"BOMB!"

Pandemonium erupted in the marketplace. Frantic vendors and pedestrians stampeded away from Flynn, bowling over the goons who had been converging on him and Shirin. For a moment, she feared that she had merely traded being kidnapped for being trampled, but, letting go of her hand, Flynn grabbed her by the waist and swung her up onto the table in front of a coppersmith's stall, away from the panicked mob. Dislodged pots and pans clattered noisily onto the pavement as he sprang up after her.

"Keep your head down," he advised, as they dived into the stall, which had already been abandoned by some terrified vendor. They crouched down behind the upset display, taking refuge in the stand. "But be ready to run when I say so."

She gaped at him again, trying to make sense of what was happening.

"What kind of librarian *are* you?"

"The kind who ends up in this sort of fix more often than you'd think." He poked his head up long enough to peek at the street. Agitated voices and pounding footsteps implied that the panicky exodus had yet to abate. "The market's clearing out fast. We're not going to be able to hide here for long, since I don't think we can count on your 'friend' and her colleagues to give up anytime soon."

Shirin saw his point. She didn't want to get stuck in an empty market with nobody but the kidnappers, who were surely still after them. "My apartment is only a few blocks away."

"Forget it," he said, shaking his head. "That's the first place they'll look for you, if they haven't got it staked out already. Same with the museum."

"What about that hotel where you're staying?"

She wasn't in the habit of visiting strange men's hotel rooms, but she was willing to make an exception in this case. Her life—and her work—were more valuable than her reputation.

"That's no good, either," he said. "They may be onto me already . . . or will be soon."

Shirin didn't understand any of this. " 'They'?" she echoed. "Who are 'they' anyway?"

"The Forty Thieves, presumably. Out for Aladdin's Lamp."

Her jaw dropped. Of all the answers and explanations possible in these turbulent times, that was probably the last thing she'd expected to hear.

"You can't be serious. That's just . . . insane."

"Do I seem crazy to you?" he asked. "On second thought, don't answer that." He began to creep out from behind the stall. "Anyway, we can talk about that later. Right now we need to get you away from the Forty."

He indicated an alley opening across the street. "I don't suppose you know where that goes?"

"No, not really." She spent most of her time commuting between her office and her apartment; she didn't pretend to know every back alley and side street in Baghdad. She wasn't sure anybody did. "I'm sorry."

"We'll have to risk it anyway," he said. "You ready to make a run for it?"

She swallowed hard and made sure she still had a tight grip on her case, which she was not letting out of her sight again. "I think so."

"Good," he said. "Go!"

Breaking from the shelter of the stand, they dashed across the now empty street into the waiting alley. She thought at first that maybe they were free and clear, but then she heard a furious female voice cry out: "Over there! After them! Kill the man, but leave the woman alive . . . if you can!"

Shirin didn't find that particularly encouraging.

Dashing through the narrow alley, which was barely wide enough for them to pass through side by side, they found themselves in a bewildering labyrinth of unmarked streets and alleys. Heaps of rubble littered the streets. Stray dogs, rooting in the trash piles, barked and fled from their approach. Shirin heard sirens in the background along with the whirr of vigilant Black Hawk helicopters.

"Maybe we should try to connect with the security forces?" she suggested.

"Or not," Flynn said. "To be honest, I'm not in a big hurry to explain why I started a bomb scare in a historic market. And we don't really have time to be detained by the authorities, not if we want to beat the Forty to the Lamp."

The Lamp, she thought. *Aladdin's Lamp*.

"Please tell me you didn't just say what I thought you said, because I really don't want to think that I'm trusting my life to a lunatic."

"What can I say?" he said with a shrug. "If it's any consolation, you're not the first woman to feel that way. . . ."

They came to a dead end and had to double back to an intersection that was partially blocked by loose debris. Shouts and pounding steps echoed through the warren of dusty alleys surrounding them, so that it sounded as though the kidnappers were around every corner.

What was it that Flynn had said about there being forty of them?

"Spread out!" shouted the woman with the knife, possibly from less than a block away. "Find them, or there will be hell to pay!"

Flynn glanced up and down the alley ahead, clearly uncertain which way to go. Shirin knew how he felt. Another dead end could be the death of them.

"Any suggestions?" he asked.

"I'm afraid not. Too bad we don't have Aladdin's Lamp after

all," she quipped, trying to keep her spirits up. "We could just wish ourselves to safety."

"That would be a *very* bad idea," he replied, seemingly in all seriousness. "Trust me."

Hearing bodies approaching from the left, they ran right. Shirin's heart pounded along with her feet as they raced blindly down yet another nameless side street. The sun was sinking in the sky, and people were retreating indoors in anticipation of the curfew. She envied them for actually having somewhere safe to go.

We can't just keep running forever. . . .

All at once, Flynn skidded to a halt, so abruptly that he yanked her backward like an anchor. Turning to see what the matter was, she found him staring, transfixed, at a run-down, hole-in-the-wall bookshop that looked as though it might have been there since the glory days of the caliphs.

"No way," he murmured. "It can't be . . . can it?"

Following his gaze, she saw that he was focused on a pair of shiny gold-colored bookends in the front window of the shop, fashioned in the shape of lounging lions.

"What?" she asked. "What is it?"

Was it just her imagination or were the footsteps behind them sounding louder and louder? She tugged on his arm, trying to get him moving again. "Come on, Flynn! They're getting closer!"

But Flynn seemed to have another idea in mind.

"I don't know about you," he said, "but I feel a sudden need for reading material."

Without bothering to explain, he dragged her toward the bookshop. She was half convinced he had lost his mind entirely, but she followed after him anyway.

What else was she supposed to do?

7

※ *2016* ※

Ali Baba's Palace was a deluxe new casino and resort nestled right on the Strip, the gaudy, neon-drenched stretch of Las Vegas Boulevard that pretty much defined Sin City as far as the rest of the world was concerned. Gold-tinted domes and minarets, glittering in the sunlight like a sultan's treasure, crowned the main casino, which was obviously going for an Arabian Nights theme. A long Persian carpet led from the sidewalk to the imposing Moorish arch where buff doormen sporting turbans, scimitars, and open vests "guarded" the palace. Live camels and actors dressed as Bedouins trudged through mock sand dunes on either side of the crowded walkway. Throngs of excited tourists, out for a good time, flowed in and out of the casino, nearly swamping Ezekiel and the others as they passed through the archway.

"All right," he said, grinning from ear to ear. "Now we're talking."

He was in his element. Easy money, fun, style, and a total lack of responsibility . . . who could ask for anything more?

"You sure this is the right place?" Baird asked him. "There's no shortage of ritzy casinos on the Strip, not to mention else-where in Vegas. The Bellagio, the Excalibur, the Luxor, et cetera. Plenty of places for Dunphy to gamble his new for-tune away."

"Please!" Ezekiel placed a hand over his heart, as though mortally wounded that she would even think to doubt him. "Trust me, I know the security systems of every big casino like the back of my hand." He flaunted his customized smart-phone. "Took me all of ten minutes to hack into their data-bases and find out that an Augustus Dunphy was checked into a penthouse suite here at Ali Baba's."

"Doesn't mean he's not cruising the Strip," Stone pointed out, "hitting all the other hot spots."

"True," Baird said, "but this is best lead we have at the moment. Good work, Jones."

"You expected anything less?" he replied. "This is Ezekiel Jones you're dealing with."

"So you keep reminding us," Stone said crankily.

Ezekiel shrugged off Stone's remark. Why shouldn't he show off how awesome he was? Modesty didn't become him.

Leading the way, he followed the crowd into Ali Baba's Palace, where some poor bloke dressed in a plush camel cos-tume greeted guests and posed for pictures; rolling his eyes, Ezekiel guided the others through the palatial lobby to where the spacious gaming floor offered no end of eye-popping di-versions and games of chance, all served up with a faux Arabian flavor. Slot machines, roulette wheels, and black-jack tables sprouted amidst the exotic decor. Cocktail wait-resses dressed like harem girls, complete with gauzy veils, wound sinuously through the packed casino, delivering drinks to the gaming tables. Flashing lights and ringing bells added to the hubbub and laughter, nearly drowning out the piped-in

Middle Eastern Muzak. Framed posters advertised an "adult" belly-dancing revue, playing twice daily.

"Oh, for Pete's sake," Stone grumbled. "Give me a break."

Baird glanced at him. "Something wrong?"

"Everything's wrong," he griped. "They call this an Arabian palace? Look at it: it's a mishmash of styles and designs from over six hundred years of Islamic art and architecture, and from all over the Middle East. They're jumbling early second-dynasty Umayyad motifs with late Abbasid refinements, thrown together completely at random." He pointed indignantly at a decorative tile banner curving above a nearby archway. "See, those are fourteenth-century Persian arabesques, but the intertwined calligraphy is early Arabic script—ninth-century gliding Kufic, to be exact—and complete gibberish to boot." He shook his head in dismay. "Unbelievable."

"Lighten up, mate," Ezekiel said. "It's a playground, not a museum."

"Yeah, yeah," Stone said irritably. "But they could at least try to be a bit more authentic when it comes to the decor and architecture. Would it have killed them to hire somebody who actually knew something about classical Islamic art and design?"

Ezekiel chuckled at how worked up Stone was getting about the phony Arabian trappings of the casino. It was funny how seriously he took his beloved art history jibber-jabber sometimes. "Kind of think you're missing the point here, mate."

"We're Librarians," Stone insisted. "We're supposed to care about this stuff." He looked to the third member of their trio, who had kept quiet up until now. "Back me up on this here, Cassie . . . Cassie?"

Concern crept into his voice, displacing exasperation, as

Cassandra was found to be transfixed by the overpowering sights and sounds of the casino floor, staring wide eyed at the garish spectacle. Her eyes were unfocused, her head swaying atop her slender neck. Her breathing quickened until she was almost hyperventilating.

"Patterns," she murmured under her breath, so that Ezekiel had to strain to hear her over the general clamor. "Patterns and probabilities. Too many probabilities . . . calculating odds, counting cards, double or nothing, let it ride. Einstein said that God did not shoot dice with the universe, but quantum theory begs to differ. Progressive slots build to exponentially bigger jackpots. Roulette wheels keep on spinning; the odds against correctly betting on a single number are thirty-five to one, but American wheels have a single zero and European-style wheels have two. Two of a kind, two pairs, too many games, too many ways to win or lose. . . ."

"Oh, crap." Ezekiel recognized the symptoms. "She's in meltdown mode."

Along with her brain tumor, Cassandra suffered from synesthesia, a condition that often caused her senses and synapses to get scrambled when she took in too much stimuli at once. She saw numbers as colors, smelled mathematics, and heard science like music in her ears. Auditory and visual hallucinations impinged on her senses, which were cross-wired to her photographic memory. At such times, she could get lost in her own rapid-fire calculations and streams of thought, resulting in a cerebral chain reaction that put her more or less out of commission. This hadn't happened in a while, however, and Ezekiel had thought she'd gotten the problem under control . . . until now.

"It's the sensory overload," Stone diagnosed. "All this glitz and gaming. She can't process it all."

Makes sense, Ezekiel thought. Casinos were supposed to be over-the-top and disorienting, the better to part you from your hard-earned cash. *No wonder Cassandra's blowing a fuse.*

"Can you talk her down?" Baird asked Stone urgently. "You've done it before."

"I'll give it my best shot." He took Cassandra gently by the shoulders and maneuvered himself so he blocked her view of the gaming floor. "Cassie? Cassandra? Listen to me. Just look at me and tune everything else out. You hear me?"

She blinked, as if she was trying to concentrate on what Stone was saying, but some sort of mental static was getting in the way.

"I'm trying, but . . ." She teetered unsteadily. Her eyes spun in their sockets, trying to take it all in along with whatever mathematical magic was going on in her brain. "Percentages, possibilities, profits and losses . . ."

"Never mind that. Just let it go. You can do it. I know you can."

Ezekiel wasn't sure about that. This was as bad as he'd seen Cassandra for some time. What if Stone couldn't snap her out of it?

Baird looked worried, too. "Maybe we should just get her away from here and come back later?"

"No!" Cassandra blurted. "I can manage. You don't need to coddle me. I just need a minute to get my thoughts under control." She closed her eyes and took a deep breath. "Focus . . . focus . . . focusing . . . the Clipping Book, Dunphy, from the Annex to the chapel to the trailer to here . . ."

Ezekiel rooted for her. *Come on, Cassandra. Shake it off.*

It took more than a moment, but she somehow managed to pull herself together. Her eyes opened and she exhaled as she looked at her teammates instead of the bedazzling bedlam of the casino. She still looked a little shaky, but better than before.

"Okay," she said weakly. "I'm back."

"You sure you're okay?" Baird asked.

"I think so," she replied. "Sorry about that. I just didn't expect it to be so . . . overwhelming."

"Don't beat yourself up about it," Stone said. "You're hardly the first person to lose their bearings in Vegas." He snorted at the glorious excess surrounding them. "You know what they say: what happens in Ali Baba's Palace stays in Ali Baba's Palace."

"Unless it ends up on YouTube," Ezekiel said to lighten the mood. "Not that Cassandra's spell was terribly view-worthy."

"Thanks," she said. "I think."

As ever, Baird tried to get them back on mission. "Any thoughts on how to find Dunphy in this mob scene?"

"We could just stake out his room," Stone suggested, "and wait for him to show up."

Ezekiel couldn't think of a more tedious prospect. The last thing he wanted to do in Vegas was camp out in a hotel corridor. Talk about a wasted opportunity, especially when he had a much better plan.

"Forget that," he said cheerfully. "I know just where to find him."

"And where is that?" Baird asked.

"Not playing the slots or anything penny-ante, that's for sure. He's living his dream here, being a high roller at last. He's going to go where the serious action is. High stakes, big players, lots of attention, the works."

"Which is?" Stone pressed him.

"Just follow me." Ezekiel set off across the floor of the casino, never doubting that the others would fall in behind him.

He strode briskly through the invigorating chaos and commotion, enjoying himself thoroughly. "I know exactly where to find him . . . or I'm not Ezekiel Jones."

––––––––––

Ezekiel's instincts proved correct, as he led them unerringly toward a raucous, high-stakes craps game that seemed to be attracting a whole lot of attention. Squeezing through a mob of whooping spectators, Baird spotted Dunphy seated at the table, blowing on a pair of dice. She recognized him at once from the photo in the news clippings. Dunphy was better dressed now, and he had a slightly better haircut, but he still gave off the air of somebody who spent too much time in casinos. An obviously fake spray tan suggested that he didn't get much sun in real life, and his designer clothes were already rumpled. He was a slight, scrawny fellow, with fuzzy red hair, googly eyes, and a weak chin, whose rather comical features were brightened by his beaming expression. He was obviously having the time of his life.

Just as Jones predicted, Baird noted. *I've got to give it to him: he knows his stuff, all right.*

A huge stack of chips rested in the chip slot in front of Dunphy, not far from a posted sign stipulating that the minimum bid at this table was a daunting twenty-five dollars. More chips were stacked on the green felt table, which was surrounded by a low padded wall. Giddy spectators cheered him on, while a skimpily clad server comped him to a free drink. He tipped her a green chip, while fiddling with a penny that he kept rolling back and forth between the fingers of his free hand.

"Let it ride!" the crowd chanted. "Let it ride!"

Dunphy grinned, basking in the spotlight. "What the heck? It's only money."

Tossing the dice with one hand, he bounced the dice off the far side of the pit. The audience and other players gasped in dismay as he crapped out by rolling a three. A dealer collected his previous winnings, but Dunphy shrugged off the loss. Wagering more chips, of recklessly large denominations, he rolled the bones again and came up with a winning seven. Cheers erupted as the dealer paid off.

"Now that's what I like to see!" Dunphy said.

Playing boldly and betting all over the board, while soaking up the adulation and attention of the crowd, he swiftly built up his winnings to where they'd been before—and then some. Dice bounced across the table. Brightly colored chips piled up before being exchanged for even higher value chips.

"Looks like his winning streak is still going strong," Stone said, "more or less."

Baird was reluctant to jump to conclusions. "Could be he's just on a roll. It happens."

"No, not like this," Cassandra said, frowning. Her eyes lifted upward, studying her invisible calculations. "He's not winning every throw, but he's still beating the odds to a degree that is statistically impossible, even allowing for random chance. The house, at the very least, should have an edge of 1.4 percent, so that the longer he plays, the more he should lose, and that edge goes way up the more aggressively he plays. Gus is betting recklessly, challenging the odds on every throw, but he's still winning like they're slanted in his favor."

"Check out that lucky penny he keeps fiddling with," Stone said. "Wanna bet that's our magic talisman?"

"Not necessarily," Ezekiel said. "Might just be his personal good-luck charm. Lots of gamblers have them."

"Then why are we here?" Stone said. "Admit it, Jones. You

were wrong about the horseshoe thing." He held out an open palm. "Pay up, man."

"Not so fast, mate. I'm not conceding defeat until we've confirmed that coin is the real deal."

"What else could it be?" Stone said. "Get real."

Baird intervened. "I can't believe I'm saying this, but I'm with Jones. We need to get an official ruling before we act on our assumptions." She backed away from the craps table. "You three keep an eye on Dunphy—and that penny—while I consult with Jenkins. Maybe he can shed some light here."

Retreating from the frenetic clamor of the gaming floor, she sought out a (relatively) quiet corner in which to make a phone call. An outdoor courtyard, adjacent to the gaming floor, offered a portion of peace and privacy and she dialed up the Annex on her phone.

"Colonel?" Jenkins answered immediately. "How may I assist you?"

She quickly filled him in on their investigation to date. "So are we on the right track here? Is there really such a thing as a lucky penny?"

"Absolutely. Pennies, silver dollars, doubloons, dinarii, drachmas, not to mention lucky socks, jewelry, and undergarments. Humanity has been using magic to try to manipulate the laws of probability since before we discovered fire, with profoundly mixed results. And the likelihood of such charms actually working has surely increased since wild magic was let back into the world."

Baird nodded to herself. Once upon a time, as she understood it, magic had been more or less confined to certain rare sites and relics, making it much less prevalent in modern times than in ages past, but then a diabolical secret society known as the Serpent Brotherhood had conspired to reactivate long-dormant ley lines and cause "wild" magic to flow unchecked back into the world at large, resulting in a huge uptick in magical activity and a lot more work for the Librarians. Maybe Dunphy's lucky penny had been kick-started by that worldwide influx of loose magical energy as well?

"Give it to me straight," she said. "How serious is this?"

"Well, I'd have to examine the coin personally to be certain," Jenkins said. *"But make no mistake, Colonel, tampering with Dame Fortune can have truly dire consequences, and not just for the foolhardy soul who is rash enough to attempt it. Our entire reality is based on probabilities, from the subatomic level to the odds of an asteroid not hitting our planet. Throw probability out the window, and you can potentially set off an avalanche of unlikely occurrences spreading far beyond the immediate orbit of Mr. Dunphy to affect all of Las Vegas and its environs, with catastrophic results."*

"But that's a worst-case scenario, right? What are the odds of things getting that bad?"

"Weren't you listening?" Jenkins said archly. *"The odds don't matter if chance itself is out of order. Even the most unlikely scenario can become likely if probability is taken out of the equation. Trust me on this, Colonel, Luck is anything but a lady. More like a two-faced trollop who will stab you in the back and break your heart when you least expect it."*

"Er, you're being metaphorical, right?" Baird asked.

"Am I?" he asked, deadpan.

8

Cassandra winced as Dunphy rolled yet another seven. Just watching him beat the odds over and over, in defiance of anything resembling elementary statistics, made her head hurt. There *had* to be magic at work; it was the only explanation that made any sense.

"Heads up, folks." Baird rejoined the team at the craps table, which was still drawing a large crowd of raucous onlookers. "I just spoke with Jenkins. We need to get our hands on that penny so that he can verify that it's our target."

"Leave it to me," Ezekiel said, confidently casing the scene. "I don't suppose anyone has a spare penny? I never bother with small change myself."

Stone fished a penny from his jeans. "Anything else you need?"

"A distraction would be helpful," Ezekiel conceded, "if not strictly required."

Stone glanced around the casino. "I could start a ruckus," he suggested, maybe a bit too readily.

"Slow down, cowboy," Baird said. "I know how much you enjoy a good brawl, but let's hold off on that option for the time being. I'd rather not bring hotel security down on us be-fore we even know for sure what we're dealing with."

"Spoilsport," Stone muttered.

"I've been called worse." She turned toward Cassandra. "What about you, Red? You up to trying to break the house?"

"I think so," Cassandra said. "But not at this table. The odds aren't playing by the rules here." She massaged her temples. "It's making my head spin."

"Fair enough," Baird said. "Choose your game."

Turning away from the craps game, Cassandra surveyed the gaming floor. The dizzying mix of noise, lights, and gambling threatened to overwhelm her again, but she forced herself to focus on the task at hand, tuning out any and all distractions. Odds and angles flashed before eyes, swirling in space like lu-minous sigils, shifting and recalibrating along with her racing thoughts. She waved her hands as though conducting an or-chestra, manipulating the hallucinatory symbols and equa-tions as needed. Hypothetical roulette wheels spun in the air. Imaginary piles of chips rose and fell according to the relevant ratios and variables. Synesthesia scrambled her senses, so equations sang like melodies in her ears and numbers tasted like . . . doughnuts?

"Games of chance, games of skill and chance, fifty-two cards in a deck, six sides on a die, six ways to roll a natural seven, eighty numbers on a keno card, but only twenty balls are drawn each game, two ones equal snake eyes, two sixes are called boxcars, the odds of rolling either are thirty-six to one." She started speaking faster and faster, almost breath-lessly. "*Baccarat* is the French pronunciation of the Italian word for zero, there are zero to thirty-six numbers on a stan-dard American roulette wheel, an ace is worth ten points except when it's only worth one. . . ."

"Cassandra?" Baird asked. "You okay?"

"I'm fine," she said, only slightly fibbing. To keep her brain from running amuck, she wiped each possible game from view before analyzing the next one. Games of pure chance, like keno or slots, were impossible to outwit; poker was as much about bluffing and body language as math; roulette wheels made her dizzy, and baccarat was just weird, but . . .

"Blackjack." She dismissed the orbiting visuals with a swipe of her hand. "A smart player can reduce the house edge to less than one percent. With my brain, I can do even better . . . in theory."

"Good enough for me," Baird said. "Get to it, girlfriend."

A high-stakes blackjack table was running not far from the crowd-pleasing action at the craps table. Taking a seat at the table, Cassandra gulped at the minimum bid. Hypothetical money was one thing. Actual cash, albeit transformed into shiny plastic chips, was something else again. It dawned on her that Jenkins had never really explained how the Library's finances worked or what the limits of their expense accounts were. . . .

Stone procured a wad of cash from an ATM. "You ever played this game before?"

"Not in practice, but I think I've worked out a system."

He snorted. "You and everybody else at this table."

"But I'm not everybody else," she reminded him.

"No, you're not." He backed off to let her get to it. "Go to town, Cassie."

She sat down at the table and exchanged a hundred dollars in cash for chips. It was a six-deck game, to discourage card counting, but the casino hadn't reckoned on Cassandra's special talent for visualizing odds and keeping track of what cards had already been played. Unknown to the dealer and other players, probability tables shimmered above the table, instantly updating themselves with every hand and guiding her play. She started small, making modest bets to get a feel for the game, but soon stared betting more aggressively, depending on the cards she was dealt. She could literally taste the odds in her mouth, hear them singing only to her. Her modest stakes began to build at a geometric rate, doubling, tripling, quadrupling. . . .

"Yes!" she blurted as the dealer busted, multiplying her winnings. "Chips ahoy!"

To her surprise, she found herself having fun. The thrill of victory settled her nerves and sent a rush of adrenaline through her veins. *I could get used to this.*

"Easy does it, gambling queen," Baird said, standing behind her. "Don't get carried away."

It was good advice; Cassandra could see now why some people got hooked on gambling, even if they couldn't play the odds as well as she could. She could only imagine how exciting it must be for people who couldn't predict if they were going to win or lose in the long run.

As she'd hoped, her winning streak began attracting more than its fair share of attention, luring people away from the craps table.

"Way to go, Red!" a random spectator cheered her on. "Keep it going!"

A gorgeous harem girl thrust an unsolicited martini into her hand. "On the house, sweetie."

"Um, thanks."

She hadn't felt this popular since that time an enchanted storybook briefly turned her into Prince Charming. She understood intellectually that the casino was plying her with booze in hopes of impairing her judgment and keeping her at the table long enough for them to win their money back, but she figured a sip or two couldn't hurt.

Like Ezekiel had said before, why not live a little?

Despite the occasional loss, her winnings accumulated rapidly, especially when she started doubling down and splitting her bets. "Blackjack!" she called out as she flipped over her cards to display a natural twenty-one consisting of a queen of diamonds and an ace of hearts.

Reminds of that time we ran into the real Queen of Diamonds, she thought. *Talk about a multifaceted individual. . . .*

"Excuse me, miss." A palace guard built like a bouncer squeezed through the crowd to reach Cassandra. "Perhaps you should collect your winnings and call it a day."

"Nope," Cassandra said. "I'm good."

The casino employee signaled the dealer to hold off. An edge crept into his voice. "I'd strongly advise you to reconsider, miss. You've had a good run. Don't push your luck."

He plucked the half-finished martini from her hand.

"Hey!" she protested. "I wasn't done with that."

"Oh, you're done," he said firmly. "Take the hint, why don't you?"

Cassandra wasn't sure how to respond. She realized, belatedly, that the casino had apparently decided to cut off her winning streak, but they couldn't just bounce her from the table, could they?

"What's your deal, man?" Stone challenged the guard, coming to her rescue. "Let the lady play if she wants to."

"Please stay out of this, sir," the guard said. "This is between the Palace and the lady."

"And, what if I want to make this my business?" Stone got up in the guard's face. "You got a problem with that, Ali Bubba?"

Baird shot him a cautionary look. "Stone . . ."

The guard scowled. "Don't make me evict you, sir. For the record, the management reserves the right to eject any player suspected of card counting."

"Card counting?" Cassandra asked incredulously. "With six decks in play? Do you even realize how ridiculously impossible that would be? I can run the numbers for you if you like. Six decks equals three hundred and twelve cards, which means twenty-four possible face cards, and approximately a one in a hundred chance of any particular value card turning up in any given hand, and—"

"Save it." Stone raised his voice so everybody in earshot could hear. "Don't shut her down. Let her play." He threw out the question to the spectators. "You all want her to keep playing, right? So let her play."

The crowd and the other players picked up the chant.

"Let her play! Let her play!"

Cassandra smiled slyly. This was working out even better than she'd hoped.

You wanted a distraction, Jones?

"Hey, what's going on over there?" Dunphy asked, noticing the commotion at the blackjack table, which was now drawing an even bigger audience than his craps game. "Where's everybody going?"

Ezekiel took advantage of the thinning crowd to ease up behind Dunphy. "Some gal is on fire playing blackjack. It's a pretty impressive run. You should check it out."

"Really?" Dunphy sounded curious. Still playing with his lucky penny, he stood up to get a better look, craning his neck to try to see over the heads of the crowd. "Good for her."

"Not that you aren't killing it yourself, mate." Ezekiel flashed the gambler his most winning smile. He held out his left hand, even though he was right-handed. "Put it here. Maybe some of your luck will rub off on me."

"Uh, sure, I guess."

Still distracted by the hoopla a few tables over, Dunphy popped the penny into his jacket pocket in order to shake Ezekiel's hand. The thief tried to not smirk too obviously.

"Excuse me, Mister Dunphy," the dealer asked. "Are you still betting, sir?"

Ezekiel wondered why the casino hadn't terminated Dunphy's winning streak yet. Maybe he was spending his proceeds on high-priced accommodations and amenities as quickly as he was raking it in? That penthouse suite didn't come cheap. . . .

"Hold your horses, Jerry," said Dunphy, who was apparently on a first-name basis with the dealer. His attention was split between his own game and the action at the blackjack table, so that he barely noticed Ezekiel at all. "Me and my chips ain't going nowhere."

"You tell him, mate!" Ezekiel threw an arm over Dunphy's shoulder and thumped him on the chest. "You're a real high roller, anyone can see that. You're calling the shots here, am I right?"

Like taking candy from a baby, he thought.

"Damn straight I am." He retrieved *a* penny from his pocket and blew on the dice in his other hand. "Just get a load of this."

"No need, mate. You've obviously got this covered."

Ezekiel sidled over to the blackjack table, where a squirming palace guard was facing a small-scale insurrection. Chants of "Let her play!" indicated that Cassandra had already generated her own fan club. Confident in his own awesomeness,

Ezekiel was perfectly fine with sharing the spotlight. He was just glad that Cassandra's brain hadn't short-circuited again.

He sidled up to Baird and slipped the *real* coin into her hand.

"Penny for your thoughts," he said. "No, don't tell me. You're thinking how truly grateful you are to have a world-class thief and pickpocket on your side."

"And a mind reader, too," she said dryly. "Amazing."

"I know!" he said, grinning. "Sometimes I even astound myself."

Baird leaned forward to whisper to Cassandra. "Objective achieved. You can call it quits now."

"Already?" Disappointment showed on her face. "But I was still winning."

"This is not the game that matters," Baird reminded her. "We have the penny. That's the important thing."

Cassandra sighed. "I know, I know." Generously tipping her dealer, she collected her winnings and stepped back from the table, to the audible dismay of the spectators. "Thanks for your support, everybody, but, on second thought, maybe I ought to take a break. Give somebody else a chance to win."

The besieged guard looked relieved.

"Want me to hold on to your chips, Cassandra?" Ezekiel asked.

"Thanks, but no thanks," she replied. "I'm sure I can find a good home for these winnings, like maybe a deserving charity or a cancer research project."

"Charity?" Ezekiel cast a longing look at her sizable collection of chips. "You know you're killing me here, right?"

"Sorry," she said. "It just wouldn't feel right to keep the money, considering."

Ezekiel shook his head. "Sometimes I just don't understand you people. . . ."

"Give it time," Baird said.

The team reconvened out in the courtyard, beneath the shade of a leafy palm tree. "Okay," Baird said. "Somebody needs to run this penny back to the Annex so Jenkins can check it out."

"I can do that," Cassandra volunteered. "To be honest, I could use a break from this casino."

"Works for me," Baird said. "In the meantime, the rest of us should probably keep an eye on Dunphy, just in case this isn't over yet."

"Speak for yourself," Ezekiel said. "I've done my part. You and Stone can babysit Dunphy now that we've stolen his mojo. Me, I can find better ways to amuse myself in Vegas."

"Such as?" Stone asked.

"I don't know. Gambling, partying, maybe a harmless little heist or two," Ezekiel said breezily. "As a reward for my valuable services, as it were. If you need me, you know how to reach me."

"Fine," Baird said, sounding unreasonably exasperated. "Take five. I'm sure we can manage without you for the moment. Just try to act like a Librarian, please."

Ezekiel took that as a green light to break rules and look for treasure. His grin broadened.

What was the point of visiting Vegas if you couldn't let loose a little?

9

Flynn pinched himself to make sure he wasn't still dreaming.

Unless his memory was deceiving him, the bookshop before them was identical to the one in his "dream," right down to the miniature gold lions in the window. That couldn't be a coincidence.

Could it?

Lacking any better ideas, he dragged Shirin inside the shop. A musty atmosphere, universal to used bookstores the world over, made Flynn feel strangely at home. Sagging bookshelves, crammed with everything from dog-eared paperbacks to leather-bound collector's editions, lined the walls, while more books were piled high on a rickety wooden table in the center of the cramped little shop. Rarer volumes were kept under glass at the back of the store, where an older woman, who looked to be in her eighties at least, sat behind a counter. The store was sparsely populated, with only a handful of prospective customers browsing the shelves. They cast suspicious glances at Flynn and Shirin as the pair hurried into the store, looking sweaty and disheveled, before turning their collective gazes back toward the shop's inventory.

"Can I help you?" the bookseller asked.

Despite her advanced years, her eyes appeared sharp and discerning. Silver hair peeked out from beneath a cotton head-dress. A shawl was draped over her bony shoulders. A pair of reading glasses dangled on a chain around her neck. She looked the newcomers over thoughtfully. Flynn got the distinct impression that she missed very little.

"Just looking." He kept one eye on the street outside the window while trying to act casual. Ordinarily, he would have liked nothing better than to kill time in a cool old bookshop, but not when a gang of irate thieves was out to kill him. He pretended to scan the shelves, while wondering if there was a back room or exit they could resort to if necessary. "We're not looking for anything in particular . . . Wait a second, is this actually the 1909 translation of Omar Khayyam?" He flicked through the pages excitedly, no longer feigning interest in the shop's inventory. "It is, with the original illustrations by Pogany!"

Not for the first time, Shirin eyed him as though he had lost his mind. "That's nice," she said, her voice strained, "but maybe you can curb your bibliophile tendencies for the moment? It's not like we don't have other . . . priorities . . . at present."

"Nonsense," the bookseller said. "There's always time to appreciate a good book." She nodded at Flynn with a knowing expression on her face and pulled a hardcover book out from under the counter. "Can I interest you in a deluxe edition of *A Midsummer Night's Dream*?" A smirk lifted her lips. " 'If we shadows have offended . . .' "

" '. . . think but this, and all is mended,' " Flynn said, completing the quote. Judson had tested him with the very same passage on the day Flynn first became the Librarian. He stared at the old woman in wonder and confusion, momentarily at a loss for words. "Who . . . how . . . ?"

"Everyone out," she said, raising her voice. "We're closed for the night." Emerging from behind the counter, she shooed the other customers toward the door. "Thank you for your patronage. Please come back tomorrow."

Shirin hesitantly moved to join the exodus, looking understandably reluctant to step outdoors again, where the Forty were presumably still searching for them. "All right. We're going. . . ."

"Not so fast. You two stay right where you are." Scooting the last of the other customers out of the shop, she locked the door and drew old-fashioned reed blinds down over the front window, concealing the interior of the store from view. "There, that's more like it," she muttered before turning back toward her bewildered visitors. "So, now that we have a little more privacy, you mind telling me who exactly is chasing you?"

Flynn remained flabbergasted by this unexpected turn of events. He suddenly understood how utterly baffled Shirin had to be feeling. "I don't understand. How do you know that?"

"Please." The bookseller chuckled, clearly amused by Flynn's reaction. "You think you're the only Librarian to pass through Baghdad in the last sixty years or so? Don't make me laugh. This is the cradle of civilization, the heart of ancient Mesopotamia. The Sumerians, the Akkadians, the Babylonians and Assyrians . . . the history of Iraq is the history of mankind. There are treasures here that predate most of the scrolls and relics in that big fancy Library of yours in New York City . . . and you can tell Judson I said so."

Flynn blinked in surprise. "Excuse me. Who are you exactly?"

"Leila Hamza at your service." Her voice was raspy, but

strong. "You wouldn't know it to look at me now, but I was quite the adventurer in my youth, and not a bad archaeologist if I do say so myself. I even took part in the ill-fated Nineveh expedition of forty-three, which was where I first crossed paths with one of your illustrious predecessors." A wistful tone softened her raspy voice. "The times we had. I could tell you stories, not all of them suitable for children. . . ."

Her voice trailed off, and her gaze turned inward as she seemed to lose herself in her memories. Flynn thought of the portraits in the Hall of Fame back at the Library. Who was the Librarian during the '40s again?

"So you know about the Library," he said, "and the Librarians?"

"Hard to forget," she said, returning to the present. "After what we went through at the Temple of Ishtar . . . well, let's just say I'm going to remember that even after I've forgotten my own name. And now here you are, another Librarian on another quest, or so I assume." She chuckled again. "Of all the bookstores in all of Baghdad, you had to wander into mine. What are the odds?"

Flynn doubted that mere random chance was involved. Judson could be cagey sometimes, and that had been a conveniently well-timed dream.

Not that he was complaining, mind you.

"Yeah," he said. "Go figure."

"Think of this as a safe house," Leila said, "if you need it."

"Thanks," Flynn said. "As it happens, we could use a place to catch our breath and regroup. You should know, though, that that there are seriously bad people on our tail, so you might be placing yourself in danger."

"I'm an eighty-seven-year-old woman living in modern-day

Baghdad." She shrugged. "This is the least I can do . . . for old time's sake."

Flynn figured she was more than old enough to make her own decisions, and, honestly, he and Shirin could use all the help they could get. "Fair enough. And don't think we don't appreciate your hospitality. I wasn't looking forward to camping out in a bombed-out ruin tonight."

Assuming we even manage to get away from the Forty, he thought.

"My lodgings are above the shop," Leila said. "They're not exactly as secure as the Library, but what is?" She put the copy of *Midsummer* back where it belonged. "Is there anything else I can do for you?"

Shirin, who had been taking in this entire conversation in perplexed silence, spoke up.

"Well, somebody could tell me what the devil is going on . . . if that's not too much trouble."

"Aladdin's Lamp? The Forty Thieves?" Shirin rolled her eyes. "You can't seriously expect me to believe all this storybook nonsense."

Flynn sighed, having anticipated this reaction. He and Shirin were sipping tea at the kitchen table in Leila Hamza's cozy second-floor apartment above the bookshop. A ceiling fan fought a losing battle against the heat, while Leila kept an eye on the street. He couldn't blame Shirin for being skeptical in this day and age. He recalled having a similar discussion with Emily Davenport in Morocco a few years back, before she saw for herself that magic was not confined to old myths and fairy tales, and before they ended up going their separate ways.

"Says the curator of the Baghdad archives," he pointed out, "and an expert on *The Arabian Nights*."

"So?" she shot back. "The *Alf Layla* is a classic work of literature, with deep roots in the history and folklore of the Middle East and India. That doesn't mean I believe it's literally true, any more than you believe in, say, the Tooth Fairy or Santa Claus."

"Well, funny you should mention that. It turns out that—"

"No! I don't want to hear it." Shirin clapped her hands over her ears. "This is insane!"

"Those kidnappers in the market didn't think so," Flynn said. "They took this seriously enough to try to abduct you, after robbing the museum earlier—and killing that security guard."

That gave her pause, but only for a moment. "Fine. You're all crazy, but you can't expect me to go off the deep end, too. Aladdin, Ali Baba . . . those are all just stories. Old stories, classic stories, but still just make-believe."

He wondered if maybe she was protesting a bit too much.

"So you've *never* believed in the tales? Not even a little bit?"

She didn't answer right away, staring into the murky depths of her tea instead. Now that they weren't running madly for their lives, he couldn't help noticing again just how attractive she was. *Watch it*, he warned himself. He'd mixed romance with work before, and the relationships had never worked out. He was in no hurry to get his heart broken again. *Remember Emily, and Nicole. . . .*

Shirin *was* gorgeous, though, and smart and resourceful.

Just his type, in other words.

"It's funny," she said finally. "When I was growing up, my mother used to tell me that we were descended from the original Scheherazade, the one who told all the tales to the sultan for a thousand and one nights. It was just a silly family legend turned bedtime story, of course, but it probably helped inspire my interest in ancient writings and the *Alf Layla* in particular."

"You see," Flynn pressed. "Maybe part of you has always believed . . . or wanted to."

"But that's just foolishness," she insisted. "This is the real world, a world of checkpoints and curfews. There's no room for fantasy anymore. Why would anyone want to kidnap me because of an old folk tale about a lamp and genie?"

"Probably because they needed your help with the translation," Flynn guessed. "You are the expert, after all, and the one who discovered the book in the first place."

"Then it's a good thing they didn't get my case." Shirin checked to make sure it was still resting on the floor by her feet. "If that's really what they're after."

Flynn recalled that she had risked her life to recover the case back in the market. She hadn't let it out of her sight since.

"What's in that case that's so important anyway?" he asked.

"My notes on the translation, naturally. Thank goodness I took them home with me the night of the robbery. They're all I have left of my work to date."

"You still have a copy of the translation?" Flynn's heart leaped in excitement. "You didn't mention that before!"

"A *partial* copy," she clarified. "And after what happened at the museum, I was being a lot more careful about what I revealed to, for instance, some random stranger who just got off a flight from America." Guilt washed over her lovely features. "I'm still kicking myself for not being more discreet about my discovery before."

Flynn felt for her, understanding that her whole life had turned upside down.

"I'm sorry you had to get sucked into this craziness," he said, "but I could really use your help—and those notes—to find the Lamp before the bad guys do. You don't have to come with me. Just point me in the right direction."

"Toward Aladdin's Lamp?"

"Exactly. Which, believe me, is more serious than it sounds."

Shirin lowered her head onto the table. "This is just a crazy dream, right? I'm going to wake up any minute now?"

"I'm afraid not," Flynn said. "But, if it's any consolation, I was just thinking the same thing not too long ago."

10

Marjanah's eyes were still burning from the turmeric that damn American had blown in her face back at the market. She'd taken the time to thoroughly scrub her face and rinse her eyes out after returning to their hideout in the Red Zone, but her mood had not improved. She wasn't sure what stung more, her eyes or the fact that she had failed in her mission to obtain Shirin Masri.

"Tell me more about this American meddler," her leader said.

The First of the Forty sat behind a desk, listening to her report on the botched operation. Only a single desk light illuminated the room, allowing him to keep to the shadows as he preferred. As his Second, Marjanah was one of the few members of the Forty who was allowed to see his unveiled face. Armed guards were posted outside the door to ensure their privacy.

"He identified himself as Flynn Carsen," she stated, "of the New York Metropolitan Library."

"A librarian?" The First leaned forward, bringing his face

into the light. A frown marred his distinguished features. His brow furrowed thoughtfully. "Or maybe *the* Librarian?"

"Perhaps." Marjanah chided herself for not considering that possibility before; well-versed in the Forty's long and storied history, including their past run-ins with the do-gooding Librarians, she understood why the First was concerned. "He didn't act like any librarian I've met before."

"I see," he said. "That complicates matters. Rather than take chances, I think we need to operate on the assumption that we now have competition in our quest, which makes it all the more imperative that we move quickly to translate the book and uncover any clues to the final resting place of the Lamp."

The stolen copy of the *Alf Layla* rested on the desk before him, flipped open to the story of Aladdin. A hand-colored illustration portrayed the mighty Djinn towering over Aladdin, who was clutching the precious Lamp while gazing upward at the freed giant in amazement. Marjanah could make neither head nor tail of the ancient Persian script on the fragile pages. She knew it was giving their best translators trouble, too.

"What of Dr. Masri?" he asked.

"She was last seen in the company of the librarian, fleeing the market."

Marjanah didn't mention that, in a moment of rage, she had attempted to stab the uncooperative curator. *But I still owe that sneaky witch for striking me*, she thought, *and I intend to collect that debt someday . . . when we have no further use for her.*

"Before they somehow eluded you and your men?"

"Yes."

The admission tasted like bile in her mouth, but there was no way to sugarcoat the truth. Shirin Masri was in the wind, at least for the moment.

"I have to say I'm disappointed," the First said, leaning back in his plush desk chair. "I thought I had done a better job of rebuilding the Forty after it had fallen into obscurity and irrelevance, but now I'm wondering if that was a waste of my time."

His words stung like a lash, but she didn't let it show.

"This was just a temporary setback," she promised. "We have spies and informers all over Baghdad, and lookouts posted outside all of the woman's usual haunts. She and Carsen won't be able to hide from us for long."

"I hope you're right," he said. "We have an opportunity to fully restore the Forty to its former glory and achieve ultimate power at last. And Dr. Masri could prove an invaluable asset to us, *if* you can manage to secure her without further delays or complications."

"We'll get her," Marjanah said. "And the librarian?"

"I'll do some digging into this Flynn Carsen person to see if I can confirm our suspicions. In the meantime, do *not* underestimate him again." He slammed the *Alf Layla* shut forcefully enough to make Marjanah jump. "Under no circumstances can we permit the Library to keep the Lamp from us. Are we clear on that, Second of Forty?"

"Yes, sir."

Along with the turmeric, this humiliating failure was Carsen's fault as well. She had a score to settle now, with both him and that troublesome curator. And if he was actually the Librarian . . . well, that would make her eventual revenge all the sweeter.

———

"There's something I've been meaning to ask you," Shirin said. "How did you manage to show up in the nick of time at the market anyway? Don't tell me that was just a chance meeting."

"Nope," Flynn answered. "I had gone back to the museum, hoping to catch you before you left for the day, when I spotted some suspicious-looking characters tailing you on your way home. So I followed them following you, keeping a low profile until it was obvious you were in trouble."

Makes sense, Shirin decided. In fact, it was probably the least crazy thing Flynn had said so far. That she was trusting her life to an apparent lunatic was . . . troubling. *Maybe he's just a little nutty where the old stories are concerned?*

Her partial translation of the *Alf Layla* was spread out over Leila Hamza's kitchen table as she and Flynn pored over her notes . . . in search of clues to the location of Aladdin's Lamp. The whole idea still struck her as ridiculous, but she had to admit that it felt good to be doing actual research again, as opposed to running from knife-wielding criminals. Studying ancient documents was more in her comfort zone.

"The odd thing about the Aladdin story," she observed, "is that it actually doesn't appear in any of the earliest editions of the *Alf Layla*. It was added by the first French translator, back in the early 1700s, who claimed to have heard it from a storyteller in Damascus."

"Added or restored?" Flynn asked.

"The latter, apparently. The fact that it appears in the eighth-century volume I discovered is proof that 'Aladdin and the Magic Lamp' *was* included in the earliest compilations of Scheherazade's stories, even if it fell out of favor for a few centuries."

Her heart ached again for the loss of the precious volume. There was no way she could share her conclusions with the world without the actual book as evidence. She'd be dismissed as a crackpot or worse.

"Interesting," Flynn said, "but what did the book have to say about what happened to the Lamp?"

"Nothing really." She leafed through the relevant pages again, while doing her best to remember exactly what the original Persian text had said. "The story simply ends with Aladdin living happily ever after, having triumphed over his enemies and been granted great wealth and success by the Djinn. There's nothing about what happened to the Lamp afterward." She shoved the pages away from her. "I'm afraid we've hit a dead end, Flynn. Even *if* the Lamp were real, and I'm hardly ready to concede that, there's nothing in this old version of the story that could help you find it."

Which means, she thought, *I'm being stalked by killers for no reason.*

"Let's not give up just yet." Getting up from the table, he paced restlessly around the small kitchen, so full of nervous energy that Shirin felt exhausted watching him. He scratched his head, having taken off his headscarf earlier. "Maybe we're missing something."

"I'm not sure what," Shirin said. "I've gone over the Aladdin pages over and over. There's nothing there."

Flynn's eyes lit up. "Maybe that's our mistake. Maybe we're zeroing in too closely on those particular pages and not seeing the bigger picture." She could practically see the wheels turning inside his brain. "What if we have to look at the forest instead of trees?"

"How do you mean?" she asked, confused.

"When in doubt, seek out the primary sources. That's one of the basic principles of solid scholarship, right?"

"Absolutely," she agreed. "But what does that have to do with—"

"You said that what you found was not the *original* edition of *The Arabian Nights* but simply the earliest known one," he interrupted her. "What if what we really need to find is the very first copy of the book, written by Scheherazade herself . . . and *that's* what will lead us to the location of the Lamp?"

"But Scheherazade—or 'Shirazad' as she's called in the older Persian accounts—is just a myth in her own right," Shirin protested. "And her famous tales are just stories within a story."

"That's what I used to think about Mother Goose, too," Flynn said, "until I learned better." He nodded at the pages strewn atop the table. "What did the stolen book have to say about Scheherazade's last days . . . and what became of her stories?"

Shirin remembered reading something about that before when she was working on her translation. Intrigued despite herself, she flipped to the end of her notes.

"According to this," she said, "Scheherazade lived happily ever after with the sultan, after telling him a story every night for a thousand and one nights. But when she finally passed away at a ripe old age, the only complete copy of the *Alf Layla*, written in her own hand, was buried with her in a secret tomb hidden from the world. All subsequent versions were penned by other hands, including those of her younger sister Dunyazade, who attempted to preserve them for posterity."

"That's it!" Flynn said excitedly. "If I can find the original edition, with all one thousand and one tales, maybe that will tell me what happened to the Lamp."

"Tell *us*," she corrected him. "Don't think you're leaving me out of this."

"But I thought you didn't even believe in this stuff?"

"I don't, not about the genie and the magic lamp and all

that. But if there's even a chance of proving that Scheherazade was an actual historical figure, and finding the original text of the *Alf Layla*, how can I pass up that opportunity? That would be an incredible, game-changing discovery . . . that would more than make up for losing that book from the museum."

Shirin still blamed herself for the theft of the ancient edition of the *Alf Layla*, but if she could locate an even older edition, maybe even the original text, that would make all this craziness worthwhile. It would be a discovery for the ages.

"Are you sure about that?" Flynn asked. "Not that I wouldn't appreciate your help, but . . . mortal danger, remember?"

"I'm already in danger," she reminded him. "If I'm going to be stalked by thieves and killers, I might as well try to get something out of it . . . and what could be more tempting than finding the lost tomb of Scheherazade? That's something worth risking my life for."

For a second, she flashed back to the bedtime stories her mother had told her so many years ago, about how Scheherazade, their supposed forebear, had cleverly kept the bloodthirsty sultan from executing her every morning, as he intended, by telling him a never-ending string of stories that always ended on a cliffhanger just as the sun was coming up, so that he kept her alive for yet another day in order to find out what happened next, and how she had kept this up for a thousand and one nights until he finally fell in love with her and spared her life forever. Even as a child, Shirin had always been impressed by Scheherazade's courage, ingenuity, and imagination; the mere possibility that she might have actually lived thrilled both Shirin, the serious historian and scholar, and the little girl inside her, who had listened enraptured to her mother's tales way back when.

"Okay," Flynn said. "Trust me, I know the feeling." He called her attention back to the pages on the table. "So does your translation offer any clues to exactly where Scheherazade was buried?"

"Let me see."

Her excitement dimmed as she reviewed the pages again, finding little concrete information.

"It's no good," she said. "The closest thing to actual directions is a statement to the effect that Scheherazade's tomb lies where the stories end, 'two hundred and eighty and four miles northeast, as an enchanted carpet flies, from the House of Wisdom, and two thousand seven hundred and nineteen miles from the fabled mines of King Solomon the Wise.' Which is no help at all, since nobody actually knows where King Solomon's Mines were, or whether they actually existed."

A grin broke out across Flynn's face. "That's what you think."

"Hold on," Shirin said. "Now you've got to be pulling my leg. You're not seriously telling me that you know where King Solomon's Mines are."

"Well, I know where they *used* to be," he replied. "They weren't in such good shape the last time I saw them." Ignoring her stupefied expression, he kept on thinking aloud. "Let's see, an Arabic mile, as used in the classical era, equaled approximately 1.2 modern miles, so the tomb would be roughly thirty-three hundred miles northeast of the Mines—which are outside Mombasa, by the way—putting Scheherazade's tomb somewhere in the mountains of northern Iran, which would have indeed been Persian territory back then. And we know where the House of Wisdom once stood, before the Mongol invasion, so now we just need to draw two straight lines from both sites and see where they intersect." His voice rose in excitement. "I need an atlas!"

He raced out of the kitchen to the landing at the top of stairs, leading down to the bookshop, where Leila was maintaining a lookout. Shirin hurried after him.

"Excuse me, Ms. Hamza?" he hollered down. "You don't have a good world atlas at hand, do you?"

"Quiet!" she said urgently. The elderly bookseller peered out through the blinds over the front window. "Someone's coming. Keep out of sight."

Shirin and Flynn retreated from the landing. "Pack up your notes," he whispered. "Quickly."

Her heart racing, she did as he instructed, hastily stuffing the loose pages back into her attaché case. At the same time, Flynn pulled a cookbook down from a shelf and started ripping random pages from it. Shirin stared at him in confusion. "What . . . ?"

"Just a precaution," he said. "Get ready to make a break for it."

Within moments, there was a pounding at the front entrance downstairs. "Open up!" a harsh voice demanded. "Let us in!"

"Go away!" Leila shouted back through the door. "We're closed!"

"We have reason to believe that you're harboring an American spy," the voice insisted. "Open up!"

"You're mistaken," Leila said. "There's nobody here but me and my books. Leave a harmless old woman alone, you scoundrels!"

Glass shattered loudly, followed by the unmistakable sound of intruders smashing into the bookshop. Leila cried out in protest.

"You can't do this! You have no right! I swear to heaven, there's no one here but—"

Her voice was cut off abruptly, as though by a knife or a noose. A loud thump sounded too much like a limp body hitting the floor. Shirin clasped her hand over her mouth to keep from gasping. She knew what she had just heard, even if she didn't want to accept it. Leila Hamza was gone.

It all happened so fast, she thought. *One minute she was alive, and then . . .*

"Search this place!" an all-too-familiar female voice ordered impatiently. "Find the Masri woman!"

Shirin recognized the voice. It belonged to the nameless kidnapper who had placed a knife to her ribs only hours ago.

"We have to go," Flynn said tautly. A pained expression betrayed his own dismay over Leila's sacrifice. Along with the torn pages from the cookbook, he snatched their teacups from the kitchen table and stuffed them into the pockets of his jacket. "Quickly, out the back."

Like many homes in Baghdad, the back of the building faced an inner courtyard. They rushed onto a small balcony overlooking the patio. Shirin peered over the railing; it looked like a sizable drop. "How are we getting down there?" she asked in a low voice.

"We're not." Flynn cupped his hands to give her a boost. "Up . . . onto the roof!"

Footsteps pounded up the stairs inside the building. Doors were thrown open noisily. Gulping, Shirin tossed her brief-case onto the roof and clambered up after it. She reached down to offer Flynn a helping hand.

"Just a sec." He rushed to the edge of the balcony and tossed the loose pages over the edge, so that they fluttered down onto the courtyard below. A moment later, he tossed the salvaged teacups over the railing as well. They shattered loudly against the brick floor of the patio.

"Listen!" one of the intruders shouted. "They're escaping out the back!"

With Shirin's help, Flynn scrambled up onto the flat, dusty roof of the building, only heartbeats before a couple of the intruders burst out onto the balcony. The men ran to the railing and stared down at the courtyard. "Look! They dropped some papers! Find them!"

Shirin held her breath, afraid to make a sound, as she and Flynn flattened themselves against the roof while the intruders ransacked the building searching for them. More men stampeded out into the courtyard and inspected the various gates and doorways leading away from the enclosed yard. Frightened neighbors slammed their windows shut and turned off their lights. A kidnapper scooped up the strewn pages and squinted at them in the dim light; he was in for a severe disappointment when he realized that they held only recipes and cooking instructions.

The woman from the market strode out onto the balcony, wearing a hooded black cloak. She threw back the hood to reveal short black hair with bangs. Her gold nose stud glittered in the night.

"Well?" she demanded. "Where are they?"

"We are looking, Second of the Forty," one of her men said, somewhat sheepishly. "But they may have eluded us again."

"Fools!" She slapped him across the face. "Our spies told us exactly where they might be found. How can you let them get away? You're a disgrace to the proud tradition of the Forty, all of you!"

The Forty? Shirin's eyes widened at the term. *As in . . . the Forty Thieves?*

Maybe Flynn was not quite as delusional as he'd sounded.

In years gone by, before the helicopters and flying mortar shells, the people of Baghdad had routinely slept on their roofs to escape the heat, but that had always required wetting the roof down first. Leila's roof was thickly coated in dust, which invaded Shirin's nostrils, tickling them. To her horror, she felt a sneeze coming on. She sniffled as quietly as she could, struggling to hold the sneeze in, but the harder she tried to contain it, the more intense the urge became.

I can't help it, she thought. *I'm going to sneeze.*

Flynn reached over and clamped his fingers over her nose. He shook his head while holding onto his own nose with his other hand. He shook his head to remind her that they had to remain totally still.

Like she didn't know that already!

They hid on the roof, spying on the murderous home invaders, for what felt like hours, but was actually only a few minutes. Sirens wailed in the distance, along with the whirr of an approaching Black Hawk helicopter. Shirin guessed that one of Leila's neighbors must have called the police.

The slapped henchman looked about nervously. "We must flee, Second of the Forty. We have attracted too much attention already."

She glared furiously at him, but did not dispute his conclusion. "Tell the men to keep searching every back alley and garbage heap until they find them! We need what's in that woman's brain, before I crack open her skull and spill it onto the ground."

Wheeling about, she stormed off the balcony in disgust, followed closely by her henchmen. Shirin heard them stomping down the stairs toward the street as their accomplices left the courtyard. Within moments, the assassins had fled back into the night.

"Wait," Flynn whispered, "until we know they're gone. Count to a hundred first." He adjusted his position slightly, settling in for the wait. "On second thought, make that five hundred. . . ."

"Okay," Shirin said, daring to breathe again. She was all for letting the mystery woman and her cronies get far away, especially after hearing that talk about having her skull split open. "But what are we going to do now?"

"That depends," Flynn said. "What's the best way to get to Iran from here?"

11

"Baird? Eve Baird?"

To her surprise, a voice addressed her by name. The voice sounded familiar, but she couldn't quite place it until she turned around to see a friendly face making its way through the crowd toward her. Even still, she couldn't quite believe her eyes.

"Krieger?"

Major Mark Krieger was an old army buddy she hadn't seen in years. His leathery features and cropped blond hair were familiar to her from any number of shared operations—and close calls—overseas. Easily as tall as her, with a reddish-blond crew cut and a strong, square jaw line, he was a career soldier whose military bearing gave away his background despite his civilian attire. A neatly pressed tan sport coat and khakis conveyed the appearance of a man at leisure. His left arm rested in a sling, wrapped in Ace bandages, which possibly explained why he was off duty at the moment. It had been fine the last time they worked together.

"In the flesh," he said, grinning. "Never thought I'd run into you at a Vegas casino."

"Roger that." Baird smiled back at him. "Last I heard you were stationed in Afghanistan."

"Got a little banged up during my last tour of duty," he said, displaying his injured arm. "Figured Vegas wasn't a bad place to recuperate, even if it did mean deploying to yet another desert." He chuckled at the irony. "But what about you? Rumor has it you opted out of Special Forces to go to work for . . . a library?"

Baird wasn't surprised to hear that talk of her career change was making the rounds. She imagined that many of her old colleagues were puzzled by the news.

"That's a long story," she said.

"I'd love to hear it." Krieger drew nearer. "You doing anything right now?"

"Not really," she admitted. Dunphy hadn't budged from the craps table, and they were still waiting on Jenkins's verdict concerning the stolen penny. Nor could she explain to Krieger that she was monitoring a suspected magic abuser. "Just soaking up the atmosphere, I guess."

"Sounds like you," Krieger said. "You never struck me as a gambler. You always preferred solid plans and preparation to taking unnecessary chances. Should have known I'd find you conducting reconnaissance."

You have no idea, she thought, keeping one eye on Dunphy. "You've got me pegged, all right."

"So you want to get a drink at the bar?" he asked. "Catch up a little?"

"I'd like to," she said sincerely. She and Krieger had been through some tough scrapes together and had saved each other's lives more than once, like that time their convoy got ambushed outside Kirkuk. "But . . ."

"But what?" he pressed. "You here with anyone?"

She glanced at Stone, who shrugged and gave her a nod. *I've got this* was his silent message.

"Just some . . . librarians . . . from work," she said, "but I guess I've got some downtime before I have to meet up with the others." She reconsidered Krieger's invitation. "Sure, why not? But the first round's on you."

"I wouldn't have it any other way." He started to offer her his wounded arm, but the sling got in the way. He circled around her to make his other arm available. "Sorry. Still not used to this thing. Blasted sling is seriously cramping my style."

"Who are you kidding?" she ribbed him. "We both know you never had any style to cramp."

Leaving Stone to keep tabs on Dunphy, she let Krieger escort her to one of the casino's many bars, a midrange watering hole called, appropriately enough, the Oasis. Despite the ubiquitous mock-Arabian decor, the bar offered a decent selection of American beers, including a few from Portland. They settled into a cushioned booth. A lattice screen offered a degree of privacy.

"To old times," Krieger said, raising a glass, "and even better days ahead."

Baird clinked her glass against his. "To old times and comrades-in-arms."

"So, about your current gig," he said. "How does a top-notch soldier like you go from hunting down terrorists and WMDs to doing security for a library?"

"The Portland Annex of the New York Metropolitan Library, to be exact." She couldn't tell him the full truth, of course, but she was prepared for the question now. "What can I say? I was ready for a change, and the library has some highly valuable assets that need guarding by someone who knows what they're doing."

"I'm sure," Krieger said. "But don't you miss the excitement of your old job?"

Memories of mummies, dragons, and alternate realities flashed through her brain, and she smiled slyly.

"Trust me, it's more exciting than it sounds. . . ."

———

"What the—?"

It took him a while, but Dunphy finally noticed that his lucky penny had been switched out somehow. His brow furrowed in confusion as he rooted through his pockets, dumping their contents onto the ledge on the outside of the craps table. Squinting at his loose change, he found a few more pennies, but not the one Ezekiel had filched. "Where in the world?"

On its way to the Annex, Stone thought. He kept watch over Dunphy from a discreet distance. *Where we'll hopefully get a ruling on that coin before long.*

"Is there a problem, sir?" the dealer asked.

"Yes . . . no . . . I mean, I guess not." Dunphy shrugged and got back to his game. "Just as long as these dice stay hot."

Funny, Stone noted. *He doesn't seem too alarmed over the loss of his allegedly lucky penny.*

The Librarian grew more concerned as Dunphy kept on winning, even with the wrong penny. Some sort of lingering side effect of the magic coin, or was there something else going on here? Stone was about to call in to the Library, to query Jenkins on the topic, when Dunphy crapped out at last, losing a good chunk of his winnings.

On second thought, maybe the effect of the coin *was* wearing off?

Again, Dunphy blew off the loss as though it was no big deal and he had every expectation of winning it all back eventually. He polished off another cocktail and passed the dice to the player on his left before pocketing the remainder of his chips.

"Gotta take a leak," he announced, relinquishing his spot at the table. "See you later, Jerry."

"I'm sure," the dealer said. "Take it easy, Mr. Dunphy."

Stone frowned as Dunphy strolled away from the craps table. Keeping tabs on Dunphy had just gotten a little more complicated now that the suspiciously lucky gambler was on the move, but Stone figured he could easily tail Dunphy on his own, particularly if the other man was just taking a bathroom break. It wasn't like Baird could follow him there, and only the Library knew where Ezekiel had gotten to.

Probably picking some deep pockets, Stone guessed. *Or just generally playing hooky.*

Exiting the gaming floor, Dunphy veered away from the more heavily trafficked regions of the casino to reach some restrooms tucked away inconspicuously in a side corridor. Stone groaned inwardly at the signs on the doors, which distinguished "Sultans" from "Sultanas," complete with cheesy turban and veil stencils to get the idea across. He waited outside and down the hall as Dunphy slipped into the little sultans' room. The way Stone saw it, he didn't need to stick *that* close to Dunphy.

Or did he?

To his concern, a pair of tough-looking customers followed Dunphy into the restroom, while a third man posted himself outside the door, suspiciously like a lookout. Wearing a black snakeskin jacket, the guy was built like a refrigerator, albeit one wearing a bad toupee. His sullen expression didn't exactly fit with the fun-and-games atmosphere of the casino. Stone's unease deepened as a random tourist, sporting a Celine Dion

T-shirt and a ponytail, approached the door and was turned away.

"Out of order, dude," Bad Toupee growled. "Move it along."

This was not what the baffled tourist wanted to hear. He fidgeted restlessly as he looked in vain for any signs to that effect. "Um, are you with the casino? 'Cause you don't exactly appear to be dressed the part. . . ."

"You deaf, buster?" Bad Toupee glowered at him in a very inhospitable way. "Take a hike."

The tourist gulped, getting the message.

"N-no problem. I'm going." He cast a lost, longing look at the men's room door. "Um, by any chance, do you know where the next closest restroom is?"

"Do I look like an information booth? Scram."

The tourist made himself scarce.

Probably a smart move, Stone thought. Whatever these guys wanted with Dunphy, they clearly didn't want to be interrupted, which probably meant that the gambler's luck was taking a serious turn for the worse. Stone covertly inspected the self-appointed sentry barring the door. Bad Toupee didn't look remotely Middle Eastern, like the crew that supposedly came looking for Dunphy at the trailer park, so who else was tailing him?

Only one way to find out.

Stone casually approached the men's room, acting as harmless as possible.

"Out of order," Bad Toupee said. "Take it somewhere else."

"Seriously, man?" Stone feigned discomfort. "'Cause this is kind of urgent, if you know what I mean."

"Not my problem. Beat it."

The guy's surly attitude made it a lot easier to do what came next. "Thanks for nothing," Stone grumbled. "You'd think a classy place like this would want to treat their customers more—"

A right cross to the jaw dropped Bad Toupee to the floor. His wig went askew.

"Sleep it off," Stone said, massaging his knuckles.

Leaving the stunned goon in the hallway, Stone slipped into the men's room, which was probably one of the few areas of the casinos that didn't have cameras watching everywhere— or so one would like to think. The sound of a toilet flushing helpfully drowned out the sound of his entrance, so he had a chance to check out the situation—which was pretty much as dire as he had expected.

Dunphy was face down in a toilet, getting an old-fashioned swirly. A burly tormentor, boasting a shaved skull with an eight ball tattooed onto it, held Dunphy's head down in the oversized handicapped stall, while his significantly smaller associate looked on approvingly. Stone guessed that the little guy, who wasn't getting his hands dirty, was the brains of the operation and most likely the boss. Wearing a six-gallon hat and a bolo tie, he snarled at Dunphy as the eddying waters drained and the big enforcer yanked Dunphy's head up by his hair. Idle hands shuffled a pile of chips that had probably come straight from Dunphy's pockets.

"Think you can cheat me, you red-headed moron? Well, you've got another thing coming."

Dunphy sputtered. "I swear, Rudy, this is just a misunderstanding. I didn't cheat nobody!"

"That's a load of bull and you know it. No one's that lucky!"

The door swung shut behind Stone, alerting them to his presence. Rudy looked both confused and annoyed by the new arrival, but more the latter than the former. He made a face as though he smelled something bad. "How the hell did you get in here?"

"Er, through the door?" Stone replied, all innocence. "Am I interrupting something?"

"None of your business, hayseed. If you're smart, you'll turn around and head back out that door."

"Whatever, man. I don't want any trouble." Stone milked his good ol' country boy routine for all it was worth. He started toward an adjacent stall. "I'll just take care of business and be on my way."

Leaving Dunphy for a moment, the big, bald bruiser got in Stone's face. "Don't think you're listening, pal. You need to hit the road, pronto."

"What's your problem?" Stone feigned confusion. "Your buddy outside said it was okay."

"He did?" Eight Ball looked puzzled for real. He looked past Stone toward the door, no doubt wondering how Stone had got past the lookout. "He tell you that?"

That was all the opportunity Stone needed. The veteran of more bar brawls than he really ought to admit to, he grabbed the enforcer by his lapels, swept his leg out from under him, and threw the guy sideways into an empty stall. Eight Ball crashed through the swinging metal door, and his butt collided with the toilet . . . hard. The door bounced halfway back into position.

"You okay, man?" Stone asked. "Think you slipped on a puddle there."

Livid with rage, Eight Ball sprang back to his feet and charged at Stone. "You're going to regret that, you—"

Stone kicked the door so that it swung back and smacked the goon in the face before he could make it out of the stall, knocking him back into the rear of the compartment. He slumped onto the toilet, the fight knocked out of him for the moment.

Eight Ball, corner pocket, Stone thought. *One more to go.*

"You stupid hick!" Rudy reached into his jacket, almost surely for a weapon, but Stone lunged at Rudy, body slamming into him and pinning his arm to his chest. The back of Rudy's head banged against a wall-mounted hand dryer, activating it. Hot air blew noisily from the unit as Stone grabbed Rudy's wrist and, twisting, relieved him of a Smith & Wesson pistol. He ejected the cartridge, almost as smoothly as Baird might have done, and lobbed the pistol into the nearest urinal, where it cracked loudly against the enamel. Rudy slid down the wall onto the floor, landing in a sitting position on the pseudo-Arabic tiles. His cowboy hat sat askew atop his head as he practically spat at Stone.

"You're making a big mistake, buster! You have no idea who you're messing with."

"Neither do you." Stone pocketed the cartridge, just to keep it out of the wrong hands, and tugged Rudy's hat down over his ears. "Would you believe this isn't even the first time I've busted heads in a men's room? I should really look at my life choices."

Dunphy gaped at him from the handicapped stall. "Who . . . why . . . ?"

"Later, man." Stone grabbed him by the collar and dragged him to his feet. "We've got better places to be right now."

Dunphy nodded, still looking understandably shaken. Stone hustled him out the door into the hallway, where a pack of senior citizens were clucking over the sprawled form of Bad Toupee. One of them cautiously prodded him with her foot, eliciting a low moan.

"Will you look at that?" Stone shook his head. "Some people just can't hold their liquor."

He figured that it was only a matter of time before the casino's own security staff showed up, so he hauled Dunphy out of the casino onto the sidewalk with all due haste. Oddly enough, as Stone knew from experience, local authorities were seldom keen on meddling Librarians disturbing the peace, and getting bailed out by Baird was not high on his to-do list.

"Thanks, buddy!" Dunphy said. "I owe you one, big time!"

Water dripped from his soaked red hair onto his shoulders. Stone was glad he'd managed to barge into the restroom before anything worse happened to their unlikely person of interest. Aside from possibly using magic to beat the odds at gambling, Dunphy struck Stone as harmless enough. Looks could be deceiving, especially where magic was concerned, but Dunphy wasn't exactly giving off a diabolical mastermind vibe. He seemed better suited to Gamblers Anonymous than the Serpent Brotherhood.

Then again, sometimes clueless amateurs, messing with forces they didn't really understand, could be more dangerous than an actual black magician or mythological creature. Like that well-meaning college student not long ago, the one who accidentally opened a doorway to another reality and sicced a hungry, tentacled monster on her campus. . . .

"We probably ought to stick to public places." Stone guided Dunphy toward an empty bus stop, planting him down on a bench, before pausing to take stock of the situation and look Dunphy over. "You okay, man?"

"Pretty much, I guess. Just a little rattled, you know." Dunphy wiped his brow and tried to slick his hair back into place. "Good thing you came along when you did."

"Glad to be of service," Stone said. "What was that all about anyway?"

"Bunch of sore losers, that's what. I cleaned Rudy out at a high-stakes poker game last night. He didn't take it well, accused me of cheating him somehow." Rudy shrugged. "Guess he holds a grudge."

That doesn't sound like the same crew who ransacked the trailer, Stone thought. Then again, a guy like Dunphy who had been winning big, and conspicuously so, was probably bound to attract the wrong kind of attention from more than one party. "Some people just don't like losing, which means they're probably in the wrong town."

"Ain't that the truth." Dunphy extended his hand. "Gus Dunphy, by the way."

"Jake Stone." He shook Dunphy's hand. "Glad I could play Good Samaritan for you. Guess anybody who wins big needs to keep looking over their shoulder around here."

Dunphy glanced around nervously, even though the passing crowds were ignoring them. "Yeah, you're probably right about that." His stomach grumbled audibly. "Say, Jake, I know a great steakhouse downtown. You want to join me, maybe watch my back? My treat, naturally."

Stone mulled over his options. Befriending Gus had not been part of the plan, but maybe he could work with this? He needed to stick close to Dunphy anyway.

"Sounds good to me. Let me just check in with my old lady." He stepped away from the bus stop and dialed Baird. "Sorry to interrupt your reunion with your buddy, but we've had some new developments."

He concisely briefed her on recent events, including the fracas in the restroom and his unexpected dinner invitation.

"Seems like I've ended up as Dunphy's temporary body-guard."

"There are worse ways to shadow him," Baird said over the phone. *"Do you need backup? I can cut things short here and rendezvous with you."*

"Nah. We're just going out for steak. I don't expect things to get hairy."

To be honest, a nice slice of rib eye was sounding pretty good.

"Okay. Just keep your eyes open and stay on your toes. Remember what Dunphy's former neighbor said about loan sharks, ex-wives, et cetera. Lots of people may want a piece of him, including any number of sore losers . . . or worse."

"Duly noted," Stone said. "I'll keep you posted."

Wrapping up the call, he returned to Dunphy, who looked visibly relieved to have him around.

"Everything cool with your lady friend?"

"You bet," Stone said. "So, you were saying something about steak?"

12

"Heads or tails?"

Jenkins flipped the purloined penny.

"Tails," Cassandra said, not entirely sure this was the most scientific way to test the coin, which landed heads up on the conference table in the Annex. "Does that count as a win or a loss?"

"Unlucky for you," Jenkins said, "but possibly lucky for me?" He flipped the penny again and got tails this time. "I must say, I'm not really observing anything remarkable about this coin so far."

Cassandra was reaching the same conclusion. She scanned the penny with a handheld magic detector that resembled a battery-powered egg beater with spinning silver globes at the end of the probes. A lighted display panel measured any unusual electromagnetic energies, but was failing to register any anomalies along both the conventional and paranormal spectrums. She recalibrated the device, which she had customized herself, to search for unlikely quantum fluctuations, which you'd expect if probability was being messed with, but struck out again.

"I know what you mean," she says. "I'm not detecting any supernatural emanations at all. And the composition of the coin is perfectly standard as well. 97.5 percent zinc and 2.5 percent copper . . . well, copper-plated zinc, to be exact."

"As one would expect from any US penny manufactured after 1982," Jenkins confirmed. He stopped flipping the coin and tallying the results long enough to consult a massive tome lying open on the table, which he had retrieved from the reading room earlier. He leafed through the book while examining both sides of the coin with a magnifying glass. "Hmm. Just as I suspected. Zumwalt's *Guide to Arcane Numismatics* has nothing to say about a 2003 copper penny minted in Denver displaying any special properties." He put down the magnifying glass. "Now if it had been an 1857 Flying Eagle penny from the secret mint in Baltimore that would be another story, but this, to all appearances, is a perfectly mundane piece of currency, of no particular distinction."

Cassandra scanned the penny one more time, looking for residual traces of manna or ectoplasm, but found nothing but greasy fingerprints. Nor could she spot any occult sigils hidden in the engraving.

"I'm striking out here," she admitted. "Could it be that we're on the wrong track?"

"That certainly appears to be the case." Jenkins closed the book on the matter, literally. "It seems Mr. Dunphy's lucky penny is nothing but a red herring as far as our investigation is concerned. If there is indeed a magical explanation for his improbable winning streak, it must lie elsewhere."

Discouraged, Cassandra put away her scanner. "So this has all been just a wild goose chase?"

"Not if the Clipping Book dispatched you there. More likely, you have simply taken a wrong turn." He stepped away

from the table. "Which reminds me, though, I need to collect some eggs from the Golden Goose. She gets cranky if her
nest gets too full."

Cassandra's eyes widened. "We have a goose?"

"Nothing you need concern yourself with this minute," Jenkins said. "You had best deliver the results of our analysis to
Colonel Baird and the others."

Cassandra sighed. Despite the brief exhilaration of her epic
blackjack run, she was in no hurry to return to Vegas, let alone
to inform the rest of the team that they were back at square
one. Pocketing the penny, she took the Back Door to Ali
Baba's Palace, Jenkins having fine-tuned the coordinates to
(hopefully) bypass the wedding chapel. A flash of light, along
with a crackle of eldritch energies, deposited her in a back-
stage dressing room crammed with Vegas showgirls getting
ready for a show. Sequined belly dancer costumes let Cassandra know she was in the right place, give or take a door. A
leggy brunette looked up from a lighted makeup table, where
she'd been applying her lipstick.

"You lost, babe?" She looked Cassandra over. "No offense,
but aren't you a little short for a showgirl?"

"I'm a Librarian," Cassandra explained. "And I'm only a
little bit lost. . . ."

Skorzeny's was a downtown steakhouse just a block or two off
the main action on Fremont Street. A far cry from the gaudy,
theme-park excesses of Ali Baba's Palace, it was an unpreten-
tious, old-fashioned eatery that wasn't pretending to be anything it wasn't. Exposed brick walls and wooden beams conveyed
a cozy ambiance, while cloth tablecloths and linens provided
a touch of class. Autographed photos of Frank Sinatra, Dean

Martin, Lauren Bacall, Sammy Davis Jr., and other legendary entertainers were framed upon the walls. Judging from the photos, the restaurant's decor hadn't changed much since the Rat Pack was in its prime. Classic crooners played softly over the sound system. A rolling salad cart went from table to table.

"Isn't this place great?" Dunphy asked, digging into his prime rib. "Real, old-school Vegas. Used to be a mob hangout back in the good old days. Everybody ate here: Bugsy Siegel, Meyer Lansky, that whole crowd. If you look close, you can still see a few bullet holes in the brickwork."

"I can believe it." Stone couldn't fault Dunphy's taste in restaurants. This place felt a whole lot more authentic than Ali Baba's, and the food was pretty good, too. He sprinkled some more black pepper over a thick rib-eye steak, cooked just the way he liked it. "So, you a local?"

"You bet," Dunphy said. "I've got Vegas in my blood. Couldn't imagine living anywhere else." He looked across the table at Stone. "Where did you say you were from?"

Stone hadn't, but saw no harm in volunteering the info. "Oklahoma, originally, although I'm working out of Portland these days." He took advantage of the opportunity to try to find out more about Gus. "You one of those Vegas high rollers you hear about?"

Dunphy lowered his voice and looked around warily.

"Can't tell a lie. I've been making out like a bandit since winning the lottery last week. Poker, craps, roulette . . . you name it, I've been winning big time. And no penny-ante stuff. We're talking real money here."

"Whoa." Stone made sure to sound suitably impressed. "So what's your secret, man, if you don't mind me asking?"

Dunphy hesitated before answering, taking a gulp from a beer bottle to buy time.

"No secret, really. You just gotta trust your instincts, you know, and go for broke when Lady Luck comes your way. Trust me, I was way overdue for a hot streak, but I stuck it out and look at me now."

Stone remembered the unpaid bills and past-due notices littering Dunphy's run-down trailer. Gus's luck had changed, all right, but he doubted his new buddy was being entirely straight with him. Maybe a few more beers would loosen his tongue?

"So that's all there is to it?" he asked. "Just seizing the day when you're on a roll?"

"Well, there's some skill involved, naturally." Dunphy puffed up his chest. "You need to have a clear head, steady nerves, and the guts to roll the dice in the first place. Gambling is just like life, if you think about it. It's all about—"

"Excuse me, gentlemen. Allow me to join you."

Without asking for permission, an attractive woman in a black turtleneck and slacks sat down at their table. Straight black hair and bangs matched the kohl accenting her eyes. A golden stud pierced her nose, while an exotic accent suggested that she was hardly native to these parts. A sly, somewhat icy smile told Stone at once that she was trouble.

Dunphy's eyes bugged out. He grinned as though he couldn't believe his luck. "Do I know you? Maybe from that pool party at Ali Baba's the other day?"

"Hardly," she said. "I'm here to make you a business proposition."

Stone had no doubt that this was the "looker with an attitude" who had come looking for Gus at the trailer park. What she wanted now was anybody's guess.

"What kind of proposition?" Stone asked.

She cast a disdainful glance in his direction. "I recommend

you stay out of this, Mr. Stone. Believe me when I say I have no great love for Librarians."

Stone sat up straight, going on full alert. The very existence of the Library was a deeply guarded secret. Only the most serious bad guys, like Delaque or Prospero, knew of them, let alone could identify them by name.

Forget local toughs like Rudy and his goons, he realized. *We're playing in the big leagues now.*

"Librarians?" Dunphy swung his gaze back and forth between Stone and the woman, understandably baffled. "You know each other?"

The woman shook her head. "Only by reputation."

"That puts you one up on me, lady," Stone said. "'Cause I don't have a clue who you are."

"Call me Marjanah, and please don't think of doing anything rash, Mr. Stone." She preemptively confiscated both men's forks and steak knives. "I assure you I'm not here alone."

Looking away from her for a moment, Stone surveyed the interior of the steakhouse. A quick sweep of the place confirmed that Marjanah had muscle loitering near all the exits, watching the dealings at the table intently. Stone counted at least four men, all of them radiating menace if you looked hard enough. A telltale bulge under the nearest thug's jacket made it clear that he was armed with more than just a surly expression.

Crap.

Stone suddenly wished that he had held on to Rudy's pistol. Not that he was all that eager to trigger a gunfight in a crowded restaurant, full of innocent diners; as a rule, he preferred to rely on his fists—and brains—to get out of a tough scrape. Firearms were for fighting genuine monsters, not human beings, even though the former had an annoying tendency to be bulletproof.

"Hey, what's going on here?" Gus picked up on the rising tension at the table. "Am I missing something?"

"As I said," Marjanah replied, "I have a business proposition." She smirked coldly. "Your life . . . for the Lamp."

Lamp? Stone thought, confused. *What lamp?*

This wasn't about the penny?

"Um, what lamp?" Dunphy nervously took a swig from his beer bottle, no longer delighted by their beautiful visitor's presence at the table. "I don't know anything about a lamp, although there's a nice home furnishings shop a few blocks from here, by the Greyhound station."

Wow, Stone thought. *He's an even worse liar than Cassandra.*

"Don't try my patience, little man." Marjanah scowled while toying with a commandeered steak knife. Contempt dripped from her voice. "You've had your fun with the Lamp, wasting it on petty diversions, but it's time to surrender it to those of us who truly appreciate its value. Enjoy your winnings and count yourself fortunate that there's no need for matters to get . . . messy."

"Messy?" Gus swallowed hard, going pale beneath his spray tan. "What do you mean by messy?"

Instead of answering, she helped herself to his steak, slicing off a big piece of pink meat, cooked very rare. She took her time chewing the morsel, letting Dunphy sweat and Stone ponder his next move.

"Ah, nice and bloody," she declared finally. "Just the way I like it."

"Really?" Stone asked. "Looks to me like it needs pepper."

She may have taken his cutlery, but Stone had palmed the pepper shaker while she was looking at Dunphy and furtively unscrewed the cap underneath the table. Before this could go too far, he threw the contents of the shaker into her face. She cried out furiously.

"No! Not again!"

Again?

Stone had no idea what she was referring to, but could live without an explanation. Tears streaming from her eyes, and sneezing uncontrollably, she slashed blindly at him with the knife, but he threw himself backward in time. Springing to his feet, he took hold of the tablecloth and yanked it off the table, spilling plates and food and drinks into her lap to keep her off her game.

"Kill him!" she shouted at her men. "Make him pay with his life!"

———————

Baird's phone chimed, alerting her to an incoming call from Cassandra.

"Excuse me," she told Krieger. "I need to take this."

Stepping away from the booth in the bar, she answered the call. "Cassandra? What's the verdict?"

"It's not the penny," Cassandra blurted. *"It's something else."*

That was not what Baird had expected to hear. "Such as?"

"I have no idea, and neither does Jenkins. We investigated the penny every way we could think of, but it still tested negative for magic. We've been looking in the wrong direction."

"Damn. Just when I thought this case was all but wrapped up," Baird said. "Where are you now? Still at the Annex?"

"No, Jenkins sent me back to regroup with you and the others. I'm in the hotel lobby."

"Great, I'll rendezvous with you there in a few minutes. Stone is kind of tied up right now, babysitting Dunphy, but see if you can get hold of Ezekiel. Tell him his play break is over. We need all hands on deck now, if we're starting from scratch again."

"*Got it,*" Cassandra said. "*See you soon.*"

Baird returned to the booth, where Krieger was waiting. "Anything serious?" he asked.

"Nope," she lied through her teeth. "But I'm afraid I'm going to have to cut this short. It's been great seeing you again, but some of my colleagues from the library are expecting me."

"Fair enough," he said amiably, displaying only a reasonable amount of disappointment. "So how long are you in town anyway? Maybe we can get together again at some point?"

"Hard to say." She sent him her contact info, phone to phone. "I'd like that, but we'll have to see."

"Eve Baird working without a plan?" He made a show of disbelief. "Now I've seen everything. Are you sure you haven't been replaced by your double from a parallel universe?"

Probably only a matter of time, she thought. "Negative. Just taking it easy, that's all."

"Well, don't let me monopolize you then. Go meet up with your friends, and don't worry about the tab. I've got it."

"Thanks. Next time's on me."

As if the bar tab were the only thing she had to worry about. . . .

———

Pandemonium erupted in the steakhouse as startled customers and waiters, who had been gawking at the juicy scene before—while trying to capture it on their phones as though it were a particularly dramatic episode of *The Real Librarians of Las Vegas*—panicked upon realizing that Stone and Marjanah were having more than just a highly entertaining spat.

Chairs toppled over and tables were abandoned. Frantic men and women shoved each other aside as they stampeded for the exits, obstructing Marjanah's men as they tried to converge on their targets, much to Dunphy's alarm and confusion.

"W-what's happening?" He stumbled away from the table, knocking over his chair. "Who are you people?"

Stone grabbed his arm. "Never mind that. We've got to get the hell out of here!"

"But—"

"Trust me, Gus. Your life depends on it!"

Dunphy hesitated for only a moment. Given a choice between a past rescuer and a snarly femme fatale who had just threatened to slice him up like a piece of undercooked meat, he nodded at Stone.

"Of all times to lose my lucky penny!" he moaned.

Eschewing the front door, Stone dragged Dunphy in the opposite direction as the fleeing staff and customers, heading toward the back of the restaurant instead. A member of Marjanah's crew, posted to block any rear exits, reached beneath his jacket for a weapon. Improvising, Stone seized an abandoned salad cart and propelled it at the thug with as much force as he could muster. The cart barreled into the bad guy, knocking him off his feet and into a table. Glassware crashed to the floor, along with a half-eaten meal for two.

"Don't forget your greens," Stone quipped.

Gunfire blared as another henchman opened fire, despite the panicky exodus jostling him. Missing his target, he hit a framed photo of Liberace instead, cracking the glass. Wild shots put fresh bullet holes in the old brickwork.

Just like old times, Stone thought. *The more things change . . .*

"Forget me, you fool!" Marjanah shouted at a third man who had rushed to her aid. Groping for a pitcher of water at a table, she tossed it in her face to rinse out her streaming eyes. She sneezed violently as she yelled at her minions. "After them, but leave the gambler alive! We need him to tell us where he hid the Lamp!"

Stone really wished he knew more about this Lamp business.

"Keep behind me," he hollered at Dunphy, for more reasons than one. He hadn't meant to use Gus as a human shield, but if it kept Marjanah's men from thinking twice about shooting at him. . . . "I can get us out of this, in theory."

The guy who'd been hit by the salad cart stumbled back onto his feet. Splattered with salad fixings, he chased after them and grabbed Gus by his collar. "That's far enough," he snarled, splitting out a stray spinach leaf. "When we get through with you two . . ."

"Gus!" Stone grabbed the back of an empty chair. "Duck!"

Dunphy obligingly dipped his head, and Stone swung the chair into the face of the crook, breaking the wooden legs right off the seat. Stunned, the man fell backward, losing his grip on Gus. Stone hoped the chair hadn't been part of the original furnishings.

"I say we skip dessert," Stone said. "How 'bout you?"

Gus nodded weakly.

They barged into the kitchen, where the terrified chef and staff were cowering on the floor, wisely trying to avoid catching a bullet. A sirloin steak was burning on the grill, which struck Stone as a damn shame. He snatched a heavy steel meat mallet from a counter.

"The basement?" he asked urgently. "Which way . . . quickly!"

The trembling chef pointed to a recess at the rear of the kitchen.

"Thanks!" Stone said. "Keep your heads down!"

Gunfire from the dining room peppered the kitchen in a surely unintended bit of poetic payback for what Stone had done to Marjanah. Shots rang off hanging cast-iron skillets. Frying pans and ladles clattered onto the floor, adding to the clamor. Stone ducked low as he made tracks across the kitchen.

"This way," he told Gus. "Hurry!"

"The basement?" Dunphy balked. "But we'll be trapped!"

"Not if this place is as authentic as you say it is."

Yanking open the cellar door, they scrambled downstairs to the basement, which was obviously being used as a storeroom. Harsh fluorescent lights lit up the cellar, exposing metal shelves stocked with ingredients and cleaning supplies. A refrigerated meat locker hummed. Kegs of beer were stacked in a corner. Grunting, Stone hastily rolled one of the heavy kegs in front of the door at the bottom of the stairs, creating a barricade.

"That should buy us a few moments," he said, stepping back from the door.

Dunphy didn't look reassured. "What good will that do? We're stuck!"

He pulled out a snazzy new smartphone to dial 911.

"Maybe not," Stone said. "Most of these old mob joints had secret tunnels and escape routes, just in case the cops raided the place or, more likely, a rival gangster came gunning for you." Stone hurriedly searched the cellar as he talked. "The basement is the obvious place to look for an underground tunnel, but where . . . ?"

A closet door, built into an exposed-brick wall, caught his eye. He raced over to take a closer look.

"Yes! This looks like part of the original construction, dating back to the late forties. The mortar appears to be a postwar blend of limestone and Portland cement, and this white

milk-glass doorknob with the brass rosette? Clearly the right
era as well."

Dunphy looked at him funny. "What kind of librarian are
you again?"

"The kind you need right now."

Stone tried the knob, only to find it locked. "Figures."

As much as he hated vandalizing the antique door and
knob, he pounded on the lock with the meat mallet until it
broke. The door swung open to reveal a ladder descending
into an unlit vertical shaft. Stone peered down into the shaft
but saw only darkness.

So what else is new?

"This is it," he said. "Our way out."

Gus hesitated. "But it's so dark. I can't see a thing."

Heavy bodies thumped against the basement door, only a
few yards away. Bullets blasted through the wooden door and
perforated the metal keg, causing beer to gush onto the floor.
Marjanah's irate voice could be heard above the gunshots.

"Stop them! I can't lose that Lamp again!"

Her men threw themselves against the door with renewed
force, forcing it open a few inches. The bottom of the keg
scraped across the floor.

"On second thought," Dunphy said. "But you go first!"

Whatever, Stone thought. Having worked laying pipe in the
natural-gas business before becoming a Librarian, he was used
to climbing down into holes in the ground. Taking the lead,
he clambered down the ladder before reaching solid ground
about twelve feet below. "So far, so good" he yelled to Dunphy. "Get a move on!"

That keg wasn't going to block the door forever.

Muttering unhappily to himself, Dunphy joined him at the
bottom of the ladder, which was lit only by whatever light

leaked down from the basement. Stone started to feel his way forward before remembering that his phone could be used as a flashlight. A bright white beam revealed a brick-lined tunnel stretching off to the right.

At least there shouldn't be any Bronze Age deathtraps, he thought, *or trapped Native American trickster spirits.*

"Run for it!" Stone ordered. "This is our way out . . . in theory."

He felt bad about running out on the bill and stiffing their waiter, but at least they were luring Marjanah and her henchmen away from the restaurant. He made a mental note to pop some cash in the mail—if he and Gus got away in one piece.

Shouts and commotion, echoing down from above, spurred their heels as the men dashed down the tunnel to who knew where. Stone estimated that the tunnel was at least sixty years old, which made it relatively new compared to some of the ancient tunnels and passages he'd explored as a Librarian, like the hidden catacombs beneath the Tiber, but he was in no position to be picky. Cobwebs hung like curtains, clinging to them as they barreled through them. A rat scurried out of their way.

"I don't like this!" Dunphy whined. "This is not what I wished for!"

Wished? Stone thought. *Just how literally does he mean that?*

The doorway to the basement crashed open loudly, giving him no time to quiz Dunphy on his remark. Their pursuers were bound to find the exposed ladder any moment now.

"Where does this go?" Gus asked anxiously.

"Your guess is as good as mine."

Fortunately the tunnel was only about ten yards long, so they soon came upon a second ladder leading up to a rusty metal door in the ceiling. Stone scrambled up the ladder, with

Gus right on his heels, only to find it bolted shut. He pounded on it with the mallet.

"Open up! It's an emergency!"

At first, he feared there was nobody on the other side to hear him. He shouted louder and kept on pounding for attention.

"Help us, please! It's a matter of life or death!"

For me, that is, Stone thought. Marjanah would want to take Gus alive in order find that Lamp of hers. "Open up!"

The ladder was up against a dead end, so there wasn't even a door for the Library to try to latch onto. He gripped the mallet, but he knew it wouldn't be enough to balance the scales against a band of determined gunmen. He was good in a fight, but not *that* good.

Just wish I knew what I was dying for. . . .

Then, just in time, he heard a bolt being drawn on the other side of the door, which swung upward to reveal a puzzled-looking teenager gazing down on them.

"Hello?" the acne-faced youth asked him. "Are you in trouble?"

"Not so much now." Stone hurried up the ladder into what appeared to be the basement of a cut-rate souvenir shop, stuffed with crates of Vegas-themed baseball caps, snow globes, postcards, calendars, playing cards, poker chips, and other knickknacks. He hauled Dunphy up behind him. "Thanks!"

"How'd you guys get down there?"

"Took a wrong turn." Stone bolted the trap door behind them. "But I wouldn't let anybody up after us, and you might want to vacate the premises. There's some not very nice people right on our tail. The kind with guns and knives."

"Whoa," the teen said. "You think I should call the cops?"

"Not a bad idea, but I'm afraid we can't stick around."

"We can't?" Gus asked.

Stone shook his head. "Not unless you want to explain to them about the Lamp."

That struck a nerve, even if Gus tried (and failed) to let it show. For a chronic gambler, he had one of the worst poker faces Stone had ever seen.

"You know, maybe we don't want to wait for the police."

Someone banged on the door in the floor. A harsh voice demanded entrance. More voices shouted loudly in frustration.

"Yikes!" The teen bolted from the basement. "This is not worth minimum wage!"

Stone and Dunphy raced up the stairs after him. The ground floor above had oodles more souvenirs on sale, but the men didn't give the merchandise a second glance as they dashed outdoors to find themselves right in the heart of Glitter Gulch, the neon-drenched birthplace of Sin City, where the very first casinos had gone up. Although long since eclipsed by the bigger, fancier resorts and hotels on the Strip, downtown Vegas was still home to several old and restored casinos, along with other tourist attractions. Night had fallen, so the men lost themselves in the crowds flocking to the Fremont Street Experience, a four-block-long pedestrian mall covered by an enormous vaulted canopy displaying a spectacular light show created by millions of brilliant LED lights. Throbbing music created a party atmosphere. Daring tourists soared below the lofty canopy on a zip line. Stone hoped the giddy festivities would hide them from Marjanah and her men, at least for the moment.

The warm Nevada air came as a drastic change from the air-conditioned restaurant. Stone looked up and down the busy thoroughfare, weighing their options. In the Gulch's glory days, a fleeing mob boss would have had a getaway car waiting with its engines running, but any such vehicles would be in a junkyard or antique auto show these days. He and Dunphy were going to have to hoof it to . . . where?

"I don't understand," Gus said, gasping for breath. This was probably the most physical exercise he'd gotten in years. "Who were those people?"

"Hell if I know." Stone noticed that Dunphy hadn't asked what they were after. He was dying to ask Gus about this whole Lamp business, but maybe after they had well and truly given their pursuers the slip. "We've got to find someplace safe to hole up while we figure this out."

Gus nodded. "My penthouse at Ali Baba's?"

"Nah. That's the first place they'll go looking for you."

Gus gulped at the thought. "What about the Flamingo? Or Caesar's Palace?"

"Forget the casinos," Stone said. "We need someplace where nobody would ever think to find you." He briefly considered whisking Dunphy off to the Annex, but taking a stranger touched by unknown magic into the Library was a huge security risk; there was no way Jenkins would stand for it. Racking his brains, Stone hit on another idea. "So, what do you think of Mondrian?"

"Who?"

"How about Chagall? Kandinsky?"

Dunphy's blank expression said it all.

"Never mind," Stone said, grinning. "I think I know just the right place."

13

"You sure we can trust this guy?" Flynn asked.

He and Shirin were crammed into a secret compartment beneath the bed of a pickup truck traveling northeast toward the mountainous border between Iraq and Iran. Their faces were only inches apart, making for an uncomfortably cozy trip. A load of heavy, handmade carpets was piled on top of the compartment, further concealing it from view. Tiny air holes, poked into the bottom of the compartment, kept them from suffocating. The only light came from their cell phones, which they used sparingly in order to preserve the batteries. Flynn was glad that he wasn't *too* claustrophobic.

"He's a smuggler." Shirin shrugged as much as she could, considering their cramped accommodations. "But he comes recommended, if you want to sneak across the border into Iran."

"Recommended by who again?"

"People who know people," she said vaguely. "These days most everybody knows someone who wants to get out of the country, and knows people who can make that happen . . . for the right price."

Flynn winced, remembering the price tag for this excursion. Charlene was not going be happy when she found out how much he had shelled out already, supposedly to cover all the necessary bribes and other expenses. *I'm guessing smugglers don't issue receipts.*

"I guess," he said uncertainly.

"We've gone over this already," she reminded him. "You wanted to know the best way to get into northern Iran, and that's through the border crossing at Penjwin, where there's a fair amount of trade and traffic going on most of the time. I suppose we could have gone through the appropriate channels and applied for the proper travel visas, but . . ."

"That would have taken too much time and possibly attracted too much attention," Flynn said. "Yeah, yeah, I know." She was right about one thing; it was too late to second-guess their strategy now. "Don't mind me. I'm just making conversation, since we've got kind of a long trip ahead of us."

They had already been driving for hours across the flatlands of central Iraq, over frequently bumpy roads and slowed by periodic checkpoints and traffic jams. Although they'd been provided with water, the stuffy compartment still felt like an oven. Flynn couldn't wait until they reached the cooler temperatures of the mountains bordering the northwest corner of Iran.

"Tell me about yourself," she suggested. "If we're going to be squeezed in here together all the way to Kurdistan, we might as well get to know each other a little better, especially since nobody is trying to kidnap or kill us at the moment."

"Knock on wood," he said. "Anyway, there's not much to tell. I grew up in New York—Queens, to be exact—and stayed in college for as long as I could, picking up twenty-plus degrees in everything from Egyptology to Botanical Studies before I was recruited to be the new Librarian."

"Which means what exactly?"

He answered carefully, not wanting to reveal too many of the Library's age-old secrets. "My job is pretty much the same as yours: unearthing the lost mysteries of the past and keeping them safe and out of the wrong hands. It's just that, in my case, that often involves a fair number of cultists, rival treasure hunters, and time-traveling ninjas."

"Time-traveling . . . ?"

He started to explain, but she placed a hand over his mouth.

"Never mind," she said. "I don't want to know. I'm still trying to keep one foot in reality, if you don't mind."

"Fair enough," he answered after she pulled her hand away. "Although I can't guarantee how long that's going to be possible as, with any luck, we get closer and closer to the Lamp." He shifted a leg to keep it from falling asleep, while trying not to encroach on Shirin's personal space more than was strictly necessary. "What about you? What's your story, aside from being the world's most glamorous museum curator?"

She arched an eyebrow. "Glamorous?"

"Did I say that?" he said, blushing. "I mean, aside from being the assiduous and intrepid archivist for the Baghdad Museum of Arts and Antiquities?"

She shrugged again, mercifully letting him off the hook for the moment. "What's there to say? Only child, middle-class roots, a lifelong fascination with the ancient writings and history, and parents who did not pressure me to get married instead of pursuing my career . . . well, at least, not too much. They moved out of city after the invasion, but I stuck it out in Baghdad and have been hiding out in the Archives for the last few years, while working to get the museum up and running again." A rueful look came over her face. "Until the other day, that is, when my life took an unfortunate turn toward the crazy."

"Sorry about that," Flynn said.

"Not your fault, really," she insisted. "You were right about the Forty coming after me, as hard as that it is to admit. And you've saved my life at least twice now." She smiled at him. "If I have to hide beneath carpets, like Cleopatra before Caesar, I could have worse company."

"Likewise," he said, "although, technically, Cleo was rolled up inside a carpet, not hiding beneath a heap of them. . . ."

"Don't be a pedant," she said. "Not that I'm comparing myself to Cleopatra, mind you."

"Why not?" Despite his best intentions, he found himself captivated by the dark eyes gazing back at him, which were only dimly visible in the faint light. Was it just his imagination, or was it getting even hotter inside the sweltering compartment? Acutely aware of just how tightly they were packed together, he tried to play it cool. "I can see it."

"Thanks," she said. "Just don't make an asp of yourself."

A pothole caused the truck to abruptly lurch to one side, throwing him up against her. Her soft curves cushioned the collision to an embarrassing degree.

"Oops!" he blurted. "Sorry about that."

"Stop apologizing." The truck righted itself, but she didn't pull away. "I'm fine. *We're* fine, and, honestly, I could use a hug after everything we've been through."

"Just a hug?" he couldn't resist asking. What was it about death-defying quests to save the world that always seemed to put him in the mood?

"Don't get ahead of yourself, Librarian," she teased. "Didn't anyone ever tell you it's not polite to skip ahead to the end of the book?"

———————

Hours passed as the truck gradually left the lowlands and began climbing toward the Zagros Mountains dividing Kurdish Iraq from Iran. At least it certainly felt as if they were driving uphill, which Flynn chose to take as a good sign. Exhaustion eventually caught up with them and they dozed off in each other's arms—until squealing brakes awoke Flynn rudely.

"Huh?"

Disoriented, he started to sit up, only to smack his head into the ceiling. *Right*, he remembered, *I'm hidden in the back of a truck.*

Shirin stirred beside him. "What is it? Why have we stopped?"

"I'm not sure." He settled back down against her and consulted the illuminated display on his wristwatch. "By my calculations, assuming a more or less consistent rate of speed, we've probably reached the border."

"And?" she asked.

"Now we see just how reliable a smuggler our driver is."

Border crossings tended to be time-consuming even if you had all your papers in order, which they most definitely did not, and this delay was more excruciating than most. Despite their driver's assurances that he had done this run many times before and had greased all the appropriate palms along the way, Flynn kept waiting for armed border guards to yank open the lid of the compartment and drag him and Shirin out into the harsh light of day. Keeping quiet, he listened tensely to the sounds of idling engines, pacing footsteps, and impatient voices arguing in Arabic.

Just the usual border hassles, he told himself. *Nothing to worry about.*

He hoped.

Although neither he nor Shirin dared speak to each other for fear of being overheard, he could feel the tension in her body as they snuggled together. In theory, the heavy carpets would muffle any noises coming from the hidden compartment, while also discouraging the border guards from searching the back of the truck too closely, but why take chances? There was nothing they could do now but keep mum and hope for the best.

Finally, just as Flynn was starting to think they were going to spend the rest of their lives entombed in the truck, to be discovered by future archaeologists millennia hence, the truck finally lurched forward and drove ahead for fifty yards or so— before coming to a halt again.

This time the arguing voices were in Persian.

Let me guess, he thought. *We've gone from the Iraqi checkpoint to the Iranian one.*

That's progress, I suppose.

Another interminable delay ensued, but eventually the truck rolled on again, driving uphill for several minutes before pulling off to the curb. Flynn sighed in relief as, accompanied by much strenuous grunting, the rolled-up carpets were shoved aside and the compartment's lid yanked open to let in fresh air and sunlight.

"End of the road," their driver announced. Ali was a stocky, affable fellow who nonetheless preferred to keep things on a first-name basis only. "For me, that is."

Flynn helped Shirin out of the compartment, even as his stiff limbs both rejoiced and protested at the activity. They found themselves alongside a winding mountain road, safely out of view of the border station. The rocky gray slopes of the Zagros Mountains loomed ahead, beneath a breathtaking blue sky. As arranged, a surplus army Jeep was waiting for them a few yards away. Both of them had already changed into proper hiking apparel back in Baghdad.

"This is as far as I go," Ali said. He held out his palm. "The rest of the payment, please."

Flynn reluctantly handed over a thick wad of dinarii from his money belt. "Um, I don't suppose I can get a receipt?"

Ali laughed out loud.

I was afraid of that, Flynn thought.

The smuggler did not stick around after getting paid. Following his example, Flynn and Shirin set off in the Jeep into the mountains, quickly diverging from the main routes onto twisty hillside byways that barely qualified as roads. Any semblance of blacktop was soon left behind as the Jeep bounced over crude dirt roads that almost had Flynn pining for their chauffeured trip in the back of the truck. A born New Yorker, accustomed to public transit, he let Shirin drive while he navigated, relying on both a secondhand GPS device they had picked up in a souk back in Baghdad and an old-fashioned paper map on which he had marked the supposed location of Scheherazade's tomb, at least according to Shirin's translation of her stolen copy of *The Arabian Nights*. The cooler climate at this elevation came as a blessed relief after the dry, arid heat of Baghdad and the sweaty confines of the smuggler's truck.

"Turn east up ahead," he instructed Shirin, "when the opportunity arises."

"Are we sure we're going the right way?" she asked dubiously. "Seems like we're heading deeper and deeper into nowhere."

"Which is a good sign, actually. In my experience, lost

tombs and such are generally found off the beaten track, far from major population centers—okay, except for the hidden crypt of Pope Joan underneath the Vatican, or that secret Masonic temple in the Paris catacombs. . . ."

"Forget I asked," she said. "I swear, I think you're just making most of this up, except when I'm scared that you're not."

"Scared, but curious, I hope."

"That, too," she admitted.

Flynn wondered how she was going to react if and when they finally stumbled onto an actual magic lamp or genie. He knew from personal experience that discovering the magical truth behind the myths could be a life-changing revelation. In his case, sheer excitement had won out over shock and disbelief, but who knew if that would apply to Shirin as well?

Thieves and assassins were one thing. A genuine Djinn was another.

He carefully tracked their progress on the map. Lacking a flying carpet or any other form of aircraft, they couldn't fly straight to where "X" marked the spot, forcing them to take frequent detours. Steep slopes tested the Jeep's four-wheel drive. Rocky cliffs rose on the left side of the road, while a sheer precipice dropped off sharply to the left. A notable lack of guardrails made the drive even more unnerving, as did weathered signs in Persian warning of possible rockslides and other hazards.

PROCEED AT OWN RISK read one sign, more or less.

Story of my life, Flynn thought. *Too bad it cost Leila hers.* . . .

That the bookseller's bravery—and sacrifice—had surely saved him and Shirin was not lost on Flynn. He figured that the best way he could honor Leila Hamza's memory was to make certain that she had not died in vain—by keeping the Lamp out of the hands of her murderers.

That's what she would have wanted, I'm guessing.

Shirin hit the brakes, tossing them both forward in their seats, as they rounded a corner to find a huge boulder blocking their path, along with additional rubble strewn upon the roadway. It was obvious at a glance that there was no way around the granite obstruction. From the looks of things, it was going to be a struggle squeezing past the boulder on foot.

"Now what?"

Flynn shrugged. "Now we get to stretch our legs some."

Abandoning the Jeep, they trekked up into the mountains on foot, pausing occasionally to rest and sip from their canteens. Roads turned into trails into rough, untracked climbs and crevices that felt more like an obstacle course than a route intended to be traversed by mortals. Scattered elms and walnut trees punctuated the rocky wilderness. Daylight retreated as the sun sank slowly toward the west. A hyena howled somewhere in the desolate hills.

"Should we stop for the night?" Shirin asked, sticking close to Flynn.

"You see a good camping spot?" Flynn consulted his GPS. "By my calculations, we should be almost there." He glanced around warily. "Given a choice, I think I'd rather spend the night in the shelter of an ancient tomb than out in the open."

"Seriously?" Shirin asked. "*Those* are our choices?"

"Beats being held prisoner by the Forty," he pointed out.

"That's a very low bar. When did sleeping peacefully in my own bed cease to be an option?"

When you found a certain long-lost book, he thought, *and let the wrong people hear about it.*

He was trying to craft a more comforting answer when the unmistakable whirr of an approaching helicopter disturbed the wilderness. He grabbed Shirin and pulled her beneath a lonely maple tree while looking around for a better hiding place amid the hills. Searchlights scoured the twilit landscape, probing the shadows, as though looking for two runaway scholars.

"Who is it?" Shirin whispered.

Flynn shrugged. "Maybe just a routine military patrol?"

"You really think so?" she asked.

"Not for a minute."

They flattened themselves against the tree trunk, hoping to evade the searchlights. Flynn regretted not trying to hide the Jeep earlier—not that there had really been a way to camouflage the abandoned vehicle, aside from maybe burying it under another rockslide. Long minutes passed, causing him to flash back to last night's tense vigil on the rooftop, while they waited for the helicopter to move on. Nightfall, along with the craggy terrain, helped to conceal them, although Flynn found himself wishing for the good old days of *The Arabian Nights*, when the Forty Thieves had not had access to aircraft. It was no doubt easier for fugitives to elude detection back then.

We could hide from a camel better than a helicopter.

None too soon, the chopper circled away from them, leading Flynn to assume that he and Shirin had gone undetected . . . for now.

"I think it's safe to move on," he said. "Thank heaven for small favors and rugged hills and canyons. Believe me, you don't want to try to keep out of sight of the bad guys while crossing a vast, empty desert in search of a forgotten oasis."

"I'll keep that in mind." She stared after the departing chopper. "You really think that was . . . our friends from before?"

"Probably," he admitted. "From what I hear, they've been

searching for the Lamp for more than seven hundred years now. Can't imagine they'll give up easily."

"But we left them behind in Baghdad," Shirin protested. "How could they trail us to these hills?"

"Who knows?" Flynn said. "Maybe Ali sold us out, or somebody else. A lone American civilian and a runaway Iraqi museum official looking to slip across the border into Iran? That's the kind of thing that gets people talking, even if only in hushed whispers, and I have to imagine that the Forty have their own connections to the smuggling trade." Thinking it over, another possibility occurred to him. "Or maybe the Forty managed to translate enough of your copy of the *Alf Layla* to point them in right general direction, northeast toward what used to be ancient Persia, where the story of Scheherazade began."

"That all sounds much too plausible." She leaned against the tree. "I suppose it was too much to hope that we had seen the last of them."

"Never underestimate the opposition," he said. "In my experience, the bad guys tend to be annoyingly persistent, and head starts seldom last for long. If I had a dinar for every time I thought I'd beaten the other team to the prize only to discover that—"

"I get the message," Shirin said. "All the more reason to move on, then."

"My thoughts exactly."

Twilight soon gave way to darkness, forcing them to rely on flashlights to make their way through the hills. Flynn kept his beam aimed down at the ground to avoid shining the light up into the sky. They stumbled awkwardly over the rough, uneven ground, passing through narrow defiles between steep, forbidding slopes. Flynn hoped the way down would be easier than the way up. His legs were already aching from the climb.

"Almost there," Flynn said, squinting at the GPS device. "Maybe fifty yards or so. . . ."

All at once, the trail dropped away in front of them. Flynn threw out an arm to block Shirin before she could step over the edge of the cliff.

"Careful," he warned. "Looks like a long way down."

They found themselves overlooking a deep ravine at least a hundred feet across. A rickety-looking rope bridge spanned the ravine to connect with a narrow ledge on the other side. Peering down over the edge of the precipice, Flynn glimpsed a desolate river valley maybe 150 feet below. White water surged over raging rapids, and massive boulders eliminated the possibility of any Butch-and-Sundance plunges into deep water. A chill mountain breeze caused the rope bridge to sway back and forth, reminding Flynn uncomfortably of crossing a similar bridge over the Amazon years ago. That bridge had literally disintegrated behind him as he'd run across it.

He wasn't looking forward to reliving that experience.

"*You have reached your destination,*" the GPS chirped.

"No," Shirin said. "That can't be right." She shined her own flashlight across the ravine. "Even if we cross that bridge, there's nothing on the other side but more rocks and hills." Bitterness crept into her voice. "I should have known better than to buy into all this nonsense. This is where the story ends, all right."

Flynn's ears perked up.

"That's right!" He consulted her notes by flashlight to refresh his memory. "The book said that Scheherazade was buried *where the story ends.*"

"So?" she asked, clearly puzzled by his reaction.

"So Scheherazade's stories never ended; that was the whole point of her tale. She practically invented the cliffhanger ending, so where better to bury her than in the face of a cliff?"

Overcome with curiosity and the always intoxicating thrill of possibly solving an age-old puzzle, he swept the beam of his flashlight over the opposite side of the ravine. At first he didn't see anything, but then the light of the beam was swallowed by a narrow black gap in the weathered stone face of the cliff, roughly twenty-five feet below the swinging rope bridge. Flecks of mica, embedded in the granite, sparkled in the beam, forming a constellation of tiny stars around the opening—as though marking the entrance to a hidden tomb carved into the very face of the cliff? Looking more closely, he saw that the flecks specifically mapped the constellation of Perseus, which was well known to medieval Arab astronomers, who actually named many of its stars, which still shone brightly in the . . . Arabian nights?

"Bingo," Flynn said. "That's it. It has to be."

"Maybe." Shirin stared at the enigmatic gap, sounding intrigued despite her earlier skepticism. "But even if that is an opening, it's at least seven meters beneath that ledge on the other side of the bridge. There's no way to get down to that gap unless you've brought along serious mountaineering gear . . . or a hang glider."

"Left the hang glider in my other jacket, I'm afraid, but give me a second to think."

Let's see, he thought, his mind racing. *If the bridge is approximately a hundred feet in length, and the entrance is roughly twenty-five feet below the top of the cliff . . .*

"I've got an idea," he said, "but you're probably going to think I'm crazy."

"Too late," she said.

14

※ *2006* ※

"I can't believe you talked me into this."

Shirin was lying face down on the decrepit rope bridge, clutching a wooden plank with both hands. Flynn was lying directly behind her, doing the same. Smoke rose from the red-hot flames licking at the nearer end of the bridge, eating way at the ropes.

"Just hold tight," he replied, "and brace for impact!"

Second thoughts assailed her. "But what if it can't support our weight—"

The ropes burned through, and the bridge tore loose from its moorings. Still connected to the opposite end of the ravine, at least for the moment, it swung toward the cliff face with alarming speed, smacking into the unyielding stone with bone-jarring force. The impact bruised Shirin's fingers and nearly caused her to lose her grip on the bridge, but she held on for dear life. Gravity tugged on her dangling legs until she managed to find a foothold on one of the planks below her.

"Flynn!" she shouted, once she caught her breath. "Did you make it?"

"Still hanging in there," he replied from below her. "Literally."

As hoped, the bridge had become a ladder, climbing up the side of the cliff. Risking a glance down, she spied Flynn holding onto the ladder right beneath her. Unfortunately, she also saw the flames at the bottom of the ladder climbing rapidly toward them, consuming the dry rope and wooden rungs. Smoke tickled her nostrils. A charred plank escaped the blazing ropes and plunged like a fallen angel toward the rapids far below, smoke and flames trailing behind it before it crashed into the foaming waters and disappeared from sight.

This is all my mother's fault, Shirin thought. *If she hadn't filled my head with wild stories about Scheherazade . . .*

Wasting no time, she and Flynn scrambled up the burning rope ladder until they reached the opening in the cliff face. Abandoning the ladder, she threw herself into the murky recess, then spun about to help pull Flynn into the cave entrance as well. To her relief, the gap was large enough to accommodate them both. He grinned at her in the dark.

"You see," he said. "It worked!"

The flames reached their level, and they backed away from the heat. Moments later, the flaming remains of the ladder fell away from the cliff and plummeted from sight. Shirin gulped.

"Wait a second," she said. "How are we supposed to get out of here now?"

Flynn shrugged. "One thing at a time, please. Let's find that tomb first."

His blasé attitude dumbfounded her, but she had no choice but to go along with it. "Just so you know, this is rather more peril than I'm accustomed to. I'm a scholar, not a daredevil."

"That's what I used to think, too," he said.

Turning away from the opening, they faced a dark tunnel leading deeper into the mountainside. "A natural cave?" she asked.

"I don't think so," he said. "Watch out for booby traps."

"Booby traps? Really?"

"There are *always* booby traps," he said. "Or guardians, or guardians *and* booby traps. . . ."

She stared at him, aghast. "How is it you're still alive?"

"Clean living and a well-rounded education?"

They advanced down the tunnel, which widened into a larger corridor that had obviously been shaped, at least in part, by human hands and artifice. Scenes from *The Arabian Nights* were carved into the walls on either side of them: Sinbad sailing the seas, an enchanted horse galloping above the clouds, Ali Baba discovering hidden treasure, Aladdin summoning the Genie from his Lamp. . . .

Shirin paused before the latter bas-relief carving. Was that really what this was all about? A quest for a magic lamp?

No, she scolded herself. *Don't be ridiculous. There's no such thing as magic.*

But a hidden tomb containing an original, handwritten copy of the *Alf Layla*? That was a discovery she could believe in, one that didn't require her to throw all her common sense and sanity off a cliff, as it were. That was archaeology, not fantasy.

No matter what Flynn seemed to think.

Something crunched beneath her feet, and she jumped in fright, almost dropping her flashlight. Flynn turned his own light toward her, exposing the shattered bones of some small animal. A rat, perhaps, or some other rodent.

She clutched her chest, feeling her heart racing. "Sorry. That gave me a start."

"No problem. Everybody gets spooked by their first hidden tomb." Flynn knelt to inspect the bones. "Nothing too exciting here, though. Most likely *Rattus norvegicus*, the common brown rat—which, as it happens, is found on every continent except Antarctica." He squinted at what was left of a broken skull. "Hmm. This appears to have been gnawed upon."

"By what?"

"Something with *very* sharp teeth," he surmised. "Possibly—"

A scuffling noise, coming from deeper within the mountain, interrupted him. Shirin spun toward the noise in time to glimpse a pair of luminous red eyes peering at them from the darkness. She raised her flashlight, hoping to expose the owner of the eyes, but the beam revealed only another stretch of corridor. The incarnadine eyes had vanished so quickly that she wondered if maybe her own eyes had deceived her.

"Did you see—?" she began.

"Two hellish red eyes spying on us?" Flynn said. "You bet."

The obvious apprehension in his voice did little to ease Shirin's nerves. She tightened her grip on her flashlight, in case she needed to use it as a club.

"Just another animal, perhaps, using this place as a lair?"

"We should be so lucky." Flynn crept forward cautiously, seemingly intent on continuing their investigation despite the unknown creature ahead. His flashlight's beam merged with hers. "Remember what I said about guardians before?"

Shirin stuck with him, partly for lack of any viable alternatives. "What kind of guardians, exactly?"

He paused at the end of the corridor, at what appeared to be the threshold to a larger chamber beyond. He swept his flashlight's beam over the scene before them.

"The hungry kind, I'm guessing."

Twin beams exposed a large, cavernous chamber littered with bones of varying shapes and sizes and species. The flesh-less remains were strewn about carelessly, creating a jumble of loose bones. The smaller ones presumably belonged to rats and birds and other fauna, but some of the others . . . Shirin's blood was chilled by the sight of a partial human skull and a ribcage, lying a few meters apart. A quick scan of the chamber suggested there were other human remains mixed in with the bones of animals. A broken femur was deeply scored, as though the flesh had been stripped from it by sharp fangs or claws. A rusty scimitar, broken in two, had apparently done its owner no good.

"Looks like we're not the first people to find this tomb." Flynn picked up the fallen sword hilt and examined it. A chipped metal blade lay a few feet away. "Approximately eleventh century, I estimate. Probably Turkish in origin. . . ."

Shirin's mind reeled at the grisly discovery, her excitement over locating the lost tomb warring with an almost superstitious dread of what might still be lurking in the shadows, waiting to pounce on them at any moment. She was tempted to flee, but there was no place to go.

"W-what do you think happened to them?"

A maniacal cackle came from behind them, and they darted further into the cavern, kicking aside the larger bones and crunching the smaller ones beneath their boots. Chalky white droppings reeked to high heaven.

"Cackling," Flynn muttered. "Have I mentioned how much I dislike cackling?"

A cord, strung low above the floor, snapped as the fleeing explorers ran through it. Bones rattled loudly as Flynn and Shirin were yanked off their feet by a net concealed beneath the gruesome debris. Before she knew it, Shirin found herself suspended high above the floor, trapped in the net with Flynn. They swung back and forth in the trap.

"A Guardian *and* a booby trap," he muttered. "Figures."

Torches, mounted in braziers upon the walls, flared to life simultaneously, lighting up the chamber—and revealing the inhuman being that had just captured them.

No, Shirin thought. *This can't be possible.*

The creature resembled a cross between a cadaver and a hyena. Leprous white flesh was stretched tight over a bony form whose ribcage was visible beneath the skin. Tufted ears, tapering to a point, and a canine snout eliminated any possibility that the figure was human. Feral jaws bared a mouthful of sharp white teeth well suited to gnawing on bones. Coarse gray fur sprouted beneath the monster's arms and across his shoulders. Elongated fingers and toes, each of which appeared to have one too many joints, ended in long yellow claws. A tattered loincloth protected the creature's modesty, much to Shirin's relief. Demonic red eyes gleefully inspected the hanging humans.

"Well," he cackled. "What have we here? More foolhardy grave robbers come to sate my appetite?"

Shirin's skepticism shattered into a million pieces. "Is that really—?"

"A ghoul," Flynn supplied. "Straight out of *The Arabian Nights.*"

Shirin was familiar with the legends, of course. A *ghul* was a demonic, shape-changing monster said to prey upon the bodies of the dead. According to the *Alf Layla*, they were known to haunt ruins, cemeteries, and tombs. But reading about them was one thing; actually laying eyes on one turned her entire world upside down—and suggested that Flynn had been right all along.

This is real. It's all real.
Even the ghoul.

———

"Of course," Flynn realized. "One of the brightest stars in the Perseus constellation is Algol, from the Arabic *al-Ghul*, meaning 'the ghoul.' That miniature constellation outside wasn't just a grave marker. It contained a warning as well." He slapped his forehead. "I really should have seen this coming."

The ghoul licked his lips and patted his sunken stomach.

"Dark meat and white," he chuckled, admiring his catch. His voice was as dry as the dusty bones beneath his feet. "A veritable feast."

"Hold on." Flynn clutched the metal sword hilt, even though it could be of little use against the ageless creature. "I thought ghouls only consumed the flesh of the dead. My companion and I are very much living."

"Oh, I'll kill you first," the ghoul replied, unconcerned by Flynn's objection, "then let you rot until you're good and tasty. It will be a pleasant change from rats and spiders. It's been ages since I've tasted man . . . or woman."

Shirin shuddered beside Flynn. "This is real," she murmured, more to herself than to him. "This is actually happening."

"I'm afraid so." He was impressed by how well she was coping, relatively speaking. Her entire worldview had just been altered irrevocably, yet she seemed to be holding it together, more or less. He resisted the temptation to tell her "I told you so."

That probably wouldn't be productive.

The ghoul crept toward them, drool dribbling from his muzzle. "Or perhaps I should keep one of you alive until I've finished consuming the other? No need to gorge on you both all at once." His head swung from side to side, admiring his catch. "But which to eat first? Decisions, decisions . . ."

Flynn had no interest in becoming either the first or second course. He hadn't spent all those years accumulating nearly two dozen degrees just to end up in a monster's belly. That would be a tragic waste of his advanced education, and a sad ending to Shirin's brilliant career as well.

"Any chance we can make a deal instead?" he asked.

"A deal, you say." The ghoul eyed him speculatively, sounding intrigued despite his ravenous appetite. "What do you have to offer in exchange for your lives?"

Flynn had no idea at first, then remembered where he was: the Tomb of Scheherazade.

"A story?"

The ghoul's eyes widened.

"A story," he said longingly. "I haven't heard a good story in even longer than it's been since I tasted human flesh, and I've read and reread all the Storyteller's famous tales for a thousand times a thousand nights."

Flynn could believe it. He doubted the ghoul got out much.

"By the Storyteller, you mean Scheherazade, correct?"

"Who else?" the ghoul replied. "The sultan tasked me to guard the Storyteller's resting place, compelling my obedience with a powerful enchantment cast by his grand vizier, but that was many centuries ago. How I crave a *new* story instead of an old one!"

New to you, Flynn thought. *I think I can manage that.*

"And if we tell you a story, one you've never heard before, will you let us go?"

"I make no promises, mortal." The ghoul squatted on the floor, settling in to be entertained. "You'll live as the long as the tale amuses me."

Just like Scheherazade, Flynn thought. *Well, if she could pull it off for a thousand and one nights, I should be able get us through tonight at least. . . .*

"Fair enough." Flynn cleared his throat and began. "Once upon a time there was an industrious young student who loved learning and wanted to stay in school forever. . . ."

He started strong, regaling the ghoul with his own early exploits as the Librarian, but keeping a story going for hours proved more arduous than he expected, both physically and mentally. After the first few hours, he found his energy flagging. He was tired and hungry, and his mouth felt as dry as the dusty bones littering the chamber. His tongue grew heavy and sticky and clumsy, so that just trying to string words together felt like laying bricks, and it didn't help that he was already worn out from their long hike into the mountains. He would have killed for a glass of water, but his canteen was empty. Glancing furtively at his watch, he saw that dawn was still hours away. They still had a long evening ahead of them, and the ghoul was showing no sign of wanting to call it a night.

"Um, any chance we can take a brief intermission?" he asked.

The ghoul's stomach rumbled. "Well, I suppose we could pause for a bite to eat. . . ."

"Never mind," Flynn said. "Forget I asked."

He tried to muster enough saliva to continue his story.

"And then the brave Librarian set out on another quest, for another legendary relic—"

The ghoul yawned. "Yes, yes, just like before and the time before that. I'm getting bored . . . and hungry."

Everyone's a critic, Flynn thought. "All right, let's skip ahead to something fresher." He tried to kick-start his brain, which was feeling more sluggish by the moment. Maybe he needed to venture beyond autobiography into something more fictional, some old story lurking at the back of his memory. "So then, after his quest, the hero set out on a fateful trip, departing from a tropic port on a three-hour cruise—"

"Let me guess," the ghoul interrupted. "There's a shipwreck, and he's marooned on a deserted island as Sinbad the Sailor so often was." He scowled impatiently. "I know this one."

Flynn gulped aridly. "Um, did I mention the millionaire and his wife?"

Snarling, the ghoul dropped to all fours and . . . changed. His contours blurred momentarily, like watercolors running in the rain, as he effortlessly transformed into a large, gray hyena. His hackles bristled and he bared his fangs. Flynn and Shirin gasped in unison, even as the startled Librarian realized that they probably should have seen this coming.

Ghouls were supposed to be shape-shifters, after all.

"Sit! Stay!" Flynn called out. "No need to do anything rash. I've still got plenty of stories left!"

The ghoul shifted back into his original form. "Such as?"

"Um, well, that is . . ."

Flynn knew that, in theory, he knew centuries of stories that were after the ghoul's time, but how many of them were truly new? It was often said, he recalled, that there were really only seven or so basic plots, and he guessed that the ghoul was more than familiar with all of them. More importantly, his brain had hit a brick wall when it came to thinking up yet another story; his mind went blank, like an actor forgetting his lines onstage in front of a hostile audience. Flop sweat dripped from his face as he felt a possibly fatal case of writer's block coming on.

It's not fair, he thought. *I'm a Librarian, not a storyteller.*

"I'm waiting," the ghoul said, "but not for much longer."

Flynn opened his mouth, but nothing came out. He figured he was about to go from entertainment to refreshments when Shirin spoke up instead.

"And also aboard that boat was a young maiden, who had always loved the old tales, but never truly believed in them . . . except in the deepest recesses of her heart. She grew up in a land ruled by a cruel tyrant, where women were not always accorded the respect they deserved, yet she dreamed of becoming a great scholar, although many in her family disapproved. *Shirin*, they told her night after night, day after day, *why can't you just marry a nice boy and start a family?* But she loved books more than anything else and wanted to protect them from the passage of time. . . ."

The ghoul settled back down onto the floor. "Go on," he said.

"I'm only just beginning," she promised him. "One day, the maiden left her home to pursue her dream, no matter what obstacles lay before her, and sought to prove herself to the most venerable scholars and teachers in the great city of Baghdad, that fabled center of learning. . . ."

Flynn sighed in relief as Shirin picked up the story and ran with it, giving him a literally life-saving break.

Seems like what I really needed was not inspiration but a collaborator.

As it turned out, Shirin had plenty of stories, unique to her own life and experiences. Stories poured out of her: her early years and studies, a failed romance that ended in heartbreak, and then the war and all the hardships and dangers she had endured over the last few years.

"The once-great city was divided by walls and strife. The people turned on one another, nursing grudges old and new, until it was not safe to pass from one neighborhood to another. One day, as the maiden was shopping in the market, a speeding carriage crashed deliberately into a building, causing a terrible explosion. And deafening noises hurt the maiden's ears, even as smoke and ash blotted out the sun, turning day to night. The maiden ran in terror from the destruction, afraid for her very life. . . ."

Her voice caught in her throat for a moment as she relived what had obviously been a harrowing ordeal. Flynn wondered if it helped or hurt her to get all of this out of her system. Granted, a flesh-eating ghoul was not the ideal therapist, but maybe there was something cathartic about it?

Flynn hoped as much, for her sake.

In any event, Shirin's story did what it was supposed to do: hold the ghoul's attention. The creature squatted mutely upon the floor, arguably more attentive than he had ever been during Flynn's stories. The Librarian felt a twinge of competitiveness.

Hey, that business with the Crystal Skull was pretty good, I thought.

Not that he could really complain about Shirin keeping the ghoul entertained. Hours passed, and the torches in the braziers began to sputter and die down. The ghoul yawned again, more sleepily this time, and his head began to droop. Flynn and Shirin exchanged hopeful looks. Maybe they were going to live to see the dawn after all?

"Then, one fateful night," Shirin continued, her voice growing hoarse, "thieves crept into the House of Wisdom, stealing a tome of ancient secrets that pointed the way toward a treasure beyond comprehension. The maiden, who had been entrusted with caring for the book, feared that it had been lost forever, but then a dashing stranger—the Librarian she had met on the sea voyage, remember?—came back into her life and revealed to her that magic truly existed in the world. . . ."

Her voice faltered, and Flynn could tell that she was running out of steam. The drowsy ghoul lifted his head, noting her silence. "Is that it? Are you done?"

"No, no," Flynn insisted. "We're just getting to the best part."

He whispered into Shirin's ear. "Keep it going . . . just for a little longer."

"I'm not sure I can," she said weakly. "I can barely think straight at this point."

Flynn remembered feeling the same way hours ago. "Don't worry about it. I've got this."

He picked up the tale where she left off, hoping his break had given him a second wind.

"Their reunion was a timely one, for the Librarian was also in search of the treasure and sought to find it before the wicked thieves did, but he needed the beautiful maiden's help—for she alone recalled the secrets recorded in the stolen book and grasped their meaning. Alas, she doubted him at first and kept her secrets to herself. . . ."

Shirin jabbed him with her elbow.

"Ouch!—he said, feeling the sting of her distrust, but he guessed that she too was in danger, so he followed her to a crowded marketplace, where a nameless woman of dubious virtue accosted the fair maiden and attempted to abduct her. . . ."

A snore interrupted Flynn's narration. Down on the floor, the ghoul's eyes had fallen shut, and he slumped over onto his side, making a nest for himself amid the scattered bones. Flynn felt mildly offended that the ghoul couldn't stay awake long enough to find out what happened next.

I was just getting to the part where I saved the day!

"You did it," Shirin whispered. "He's asleep."

"*We* did it," he corrected her.

Flynn glanced at his wristwatch. In theory, the sun had just risen outside.

"Seems ghouls are nocturnal," he said. "Good to know."

Using the jagged edge where the scimitar's blade had once been, Flynn began cutting a hole in the net until he had a gap big enough for them to pass through one at a time. "Try not to make too much noise," he advised Shirin as he helped her lower herself to the floor. Loose bones rattled quietly beneath her feet, causing the sleeping ghoul to stir worryingly, but he kept on slumbering while Flynn cautiously descended to the ground. He stretched his limbs to restore circulation to them.

"I think he's out like a light," Shirin said in a low voice.

"Lucky him." Flynn tiptoed away from the ghoul. "I could use a few winks myself."

She looked back the way they'd come. "Maybe we should try to find a way out of here?"

"Not without what we came for." He understood, however, that Shirin might not feel the same way after nearly becoming a ghoul's late-night snack. "But if you want to search for a way out and leave the rest up to me, that's okay, too. I signed up for this kind of craziness. You didn't."

She thought it over, but only for a moment.

"I've come this far. I might as well see it through." She contemplated the snoring ghoul. "Besides, if shape-shifting ghouls are real, I guess Aladdin's Lamp is not beyond the bounds of possibility either. Which means you were right all along: we can't let those killers find it first."

Flynn admired her resolve after all she'd been through. "Glad we're finally on the same page, so to speak. I wasn't kidding a few minutes ago when I said that I really needed your help."

"I remember," she said. "Something about a *beautiful maiden*, wasn't it?" She adopted a teasing tone. "Beautiful, you say?"

"I seem to recall something about a *dashing stranger*," he countered, raising an inquisitive eyebrow. "Dashing?"

"Poetic license," she said, blushing. "But never mind that now. Don't we have a tomb to explore?"

"Absolutely."

Flirting could wait. It was time to find Scheherazade . . . and the buried secrets of *The Arabian Nights*.

"After you, beautiful maiden."

15

Tiptoeing across the ghoul's lair, Flynn and Shirin entered the chamber beyond, where their eyes widened in amazement. Shirin gasped, but not in fright this time.

"This is it," she said in awe. "The tomb of Scheherazade . . . for real."

Flynn didn't immediately spot a marked vault or sarcophagus. "More like an antechamber, I suspect, but I know what you mean. This is . . . wow."

Unlike the gruesome, bone-filled lair, the subsequent cavern was a masterpiece of Arabian art and architecture. Instead of hanging stalactites, a domed ceiling gave the chamber a far more airy feel. Decorative tiles sporting endlessly repeating arabesques adorned every exposed surface, from the walls to the ceiling. Sunlight filtered into the ornate vault through tinted glass panes cunningly embedded in the high ceiling. An exquisitely crafted Persian carpet caught Flynn's eye before his attention was drawn to the rest of the chamber's decor. Carved stone shelves held an impressive collection of dusty books and scrolls, presumably from Scheherazade's personal library, as well as mementos from her stories, including a miniature sailing ship of classic Arabian design, a toy-sized mechanical stallion wrought of bronze and silver, and a shard of enormous egg shell.

But nothing resembling a lamp, magical or otherwise.

Because that would be too easy, Flynn thought.

Eyes wide, Shirin spun in a complete circle in the center of the chamber, taking it all in. "This is astounding," she said in a hushed tone. "But how on Earth did they manage to transport all these grave goods down the side of the cliff?"

"Magic?" Flynn speculated. "Or maybe the ghoul did most of the heavy lifting?"

As a librarian, Flynn could have spent days examining the priceless contents of just this antechamber, but as *the* Librarian, he knew they had to keep their eyes on the prize. A beaded curtain on the opposite side of the room veiled the portal to a further chamber, carved even deeper into the solid rock. Flynn sensed that they were nearing the end of their quest—or at least this stage of it.

He drew back the curtain and peeked ahead.

Eureka, he thought. "Shirin, you need to see this."

The next chamber was as elegantly appointed as the one before, with the same gleaming ceramic tiles and arabesques, but the elaborate ornamentation faded into background compared to the centerpiece of the burial chamber: a polished marble sarcophagus carved in the image of an exotically beautiful sultana, lying horizontally atop the tile floor. The sculpture's elegant stone eyes stared upward into eternity.

"It's her," Shirin whispered. "Scheherazade."

Flynn admired the sculpture's serene countenance.

"*She had perused the works of the poets and knew them by heart,*" he recited, "*she had studied philosophy and the sciences, arts and accomplishments, and she was pleasant and polite, wise and witty, well read and well bred."*

Shirin turned toward him, recognizing the quotation. "Sir Richard Burton, the 1885 translation."

"That's right." Flynn took a closer look at the carved face. "You know, she does kind of look like you."

"She does, doesn't she?" Shirin marveled at the resemblance. "You don't think my mother's stories were true, that I'm actually descended from her?"

"Could be," Flynn said. "You do seem two of a kind."

Shirin beamed at him, her rapt gaze briefly drawn away from the magnificent sarcophagus. "That just might be the most flattering thing anyone has ever said about me."

It required an effort to keep her smile from distracting him from the task at hand. Fortunately, there was no need to crack open the sarcophagus; a thick, leather-bound tome occupied a position of honor atop the stone coffin, clasped between the figure's slender marble hands. Inscribed in gold upon the front cover of the book was a title in Persian: *Hazar Afsan.*

"*A Thousand Tales,*" Shirin translated. "Plus or minus a story."

Flynn nodded at the ancient book. "Would you care to do the honors?"

"Try to stop me." Shirin approached the sarcophagus reverently and carefully extracted the book from the sculpture's grasp, holding her breath until it was safely liberated from the stone. "Damn. If only I'd thought to pack cotton gloves."

Flynn sympathized, but he had long ago realized that sometimes you had to make compromises in the field, especially when racing to beat the bad guys to a treasure. "You can't always do things by the book, no pun intended." He eyed the volume expectantly. "Is that it? The original version, as penned by Scheherazade?"

"I think so." Shirin laid the book down atop the sarcophagus and began to leaf delicately through its pages, which held line after line of fine calligraphy. She squinted at the delicate handwriting. "Although I can still hardly believe it. It doesn't seem possible."

"Believe it." Flynn used his flashlight to give her more light to read by. "I doubt our necrophagous friend out there would have spent centuries guarding a fake or facsimile."

"This is amazing," she enthused. "Just at a glance, I can tell that this copy is even older and more complete than the one I was translating before, more so than any other version known to exist." She kept flipping through the book, her gaze glued to the pages. "There are stories within stories within stories . . . I hardly know where to begin."

"Well, I don't want to rush you, but maybe you can skip ahead to the part about Aladdin, and what happened to his Lamp?"

"Yes, of course," she said. "I'm sorry. I'm still simply blown away by the fact that I'm actually handling the very first copy of the *Tales*, and in Scheherazade's own tomb no less!"

She began to peruse the pages more deliberately. Flynn stepped back to give her space, while still providing her with light from her flashlight. He glanced around the crypt, on the lookout for any further snares or booby traps. He noticed a conspicuous lack of cobwebs or vermin.

Guess the hungry ghoul keeps the pest problem under control, he thought. *Ick*.

He fought an urge to barge in and search the book himself. Shirin knew *The Arabian Nights* better than he did, backward and forward probably. He needed to sit back and let her do her thing, no matter how anxious he was to find another clue to the location of the Lamp. He caught himself tapping his foot impatiently against the tile floor and cut it out.

"Here it is," she said, excitement filling her voice. "A new section that I've never read before, in any of the myriad versions of the *Alf Layla*."

He came up behind her and peered over her shoulder. "What does it say?"

"The *Reader's Digest* version? It says here that Aladdin, in the twilight of his years, came to fear the dreadful power of the Djinn and what might become of the world should the willful spirit ever truly escape the Lamp and gain its freedom, so he entrusted the Lamp to his good friends and contemporaries, Sinbad and Ali Baba, who promised to hide it away on an enchanted island, in a cave guarded by a giant rock."

Her face fell as the meaning of what she'd just read sank in.

"A hidden cave on an unnamed island? None of that does us any good. How are we supposed to locate an enchanted island?"

Flynn observed that she wasn't questioning the existence of the island or the Lamp, just doubting their ability to find them. Apparently her encounter with the ghoul, and their discovery of the tomb, had wiped away the last traces of her skepticism. She was no longer playing Scully to his Mulder.

"Funny you should ask," he said. "I already have an idea about that."

But before he could elaborate, the rat-a-tat of machine-gun fire disturbed the sanctity of the ancient crypt. The alarming noise came from the ghoul's lair two chambers away. Flynn heard the surprised monster howl briefly in shock and distress before its keening was cut short by the gunfire. Apparently, the ageless ghoul was no match for modern weaponry.

"What is it?" Shirin snatched up the book and clutched it to her chest. "What's happening?"

Flynn remembered the helicopter that had been scouring the mountains before. "I think we're about to have company."

The words were barely out of his mouth when a small band of armed invaders barged into the crypt. Rifles targeted Flynn and Shirin. "Don't even think of trying something!" a scowling gunman warned. "And drop that sword . . . or whatever it is."

Flynn had forgotten the broken hilt in his hand. He let it fall to the floor.

"That's better," the gunman said. "Stay right where you are, Librarian."

Flynn thought he recognized the intruder from the attack on the bookshop. Anger flared inside the Librarian, warring with dismay, as he realized that he was most likely facing one of Leila Hamza's killers. Flynn was not a violent soul by nature, preferring to rely on his wits instead of weapons, but his fists clenched involuntarily at his sides. He stepped protectively in front of Shirin and the book.

"We found them!" the gunman called out. "You are cleared to enter."

The other intruders—at least a dozen in all—fanned out to take possession of the crypt. Moments later, more grave robbers entered the chamber, including the woman from the marketplace and the home invasion, now wearing a practical black sweater, trousers, and boots. She glared venomously at Flynn and Shirin, as though she was still holding a grudge over that turmeric he had blown in her face. Her fingers toyed with a vicious-looking dagger.

So much for letting bygones be bygones, Flynn thought.

She was accompanied by a tall, fit-looking man in rugged

outdoor gear. A dark indigo turban concealed both his scalp and the bottom half of his face, so that only a pair of icy blue eyes could be seen. He carried himself with authority as the rifle-toting gunmen stepped aside to admit him. A lone pistol was holstered at his hip. He spoke into a walkie-talkie.

"Chopper Alpha, we have acquired the targets. Stand by."

"*Roger that, First of Forty,*" a voice replied, over the sound of whirring rotors. "*Chopper out.*"

The man put his walkie-talkie away.

Pretty clear who's in charge here, Flynn thought. *Whoever he is.*

The man's eyes gleamed at the sight of the sarcophagus.

"At last," he said in English, albeit with an American accent slightly muffled by the fabric cloaking his face. "Well done, Mr. Carsen, Dr. Masri. You led us a merry chase, but, in the end, you brought us right to what we've been seeking for centuries."

Flynn mentally cursed the deceased ghoul for giving the Forty time to catch up with them. He briefly wondered how exactly the enemy had tracked them to this very location before realizing that it wouldn't have been too hard to retrace his and Shirin's path from the abandoned Jeep to the torched bridge dangling down the side of the ravine. Who knew, maybe they'd even figured out the "cliffhanger" business as well, then used their helicopter to gain access to the tomb entrance.

Just once, he thought, *I'd like to find a lost relic without the bad guys horning in on the action.*

"So you're the head of the Forty, I gather." Flynn tried to keep up a brave front. He wasn't sure what was scarier: a carrion-eating ghoul or professional criminals with automatic weapons. "You know our names, obviously, but I don't believe I caught yours."

"Call me Khoja," the man said, chuckling as though at a private joke.

"As in Khoja Hoseyn, the captain of the Forty Thieves in *The Arabian Nights*?" Flynn replied, seeing through the transparent alias. "I'm guessing that's not your real name, especially since you don't strike me as being of particularly Arab descent."

"Very good, Mr. Carsen. I see that the Library has not let its standards slip over the years, at least when it comes to the erudition of its Librarians. I did some digging on you, Carsen, and noted that you seemed manifestly overqualified for your official position at the New York Metropolitan Library—but, of course, that's not really who you work for."

Flynn didn't bother pretending that he didn't know what "Khoja" was referring to. According to Judson, the Library and the Forty were already well acquainted with each other.

"Everybody needs a day job," he said casually.

"Too true." Khoja gestured toward the lithe, unsmiling woman at his side. "I believe you've already met my second-in-command, Marjanah?"

Her dark eyes shot daggers at Flynn and Shirin, making him sweat nervously.

"Well, I can't say we were ever formally introduced. . . ."

"Trust me," she said acidly, "you made a lasting impression. Both of you."

That's what I was afraid of, Flynn thought. "So, about that business with the spice, you realize that was nothing personal. . . ."

She snickered cruelly. "We'll see about that."

"Enough pleasantries." Khoja peered past Flynn at Shirin. "The book, please, Dr. Masri."

She looked at Flynn. "Do we have any choice?"

"Not at the moment. You'd better do what he says."

"Listen to the Librarian." Marjanah shoved Flynn aside to reach Shirin, who reluctantly surrendered the volume to the other woman. "Smart girl."

She handed over the book to Khoja, who inspected it briefly. Flynn wondered how good his ancient Persian was. Khoja clapped the book shut and tucked it under his arm for safekeeping.

"I'm assuming you already perused the text," he said to Shirin. "What did it say about the location of the Lamp?"

"Nothing," Shirin fibbed. "Or at least nothing that a cursory examination could reveal. Translating a work such as this requires extensive study. We're talking hours, days, months, maybe even years."

"Don't lie to me, Doctor, or try to convince me that you're of no immediate use to us. Our own experts can decipher the book in time, if they have to, but your best chance of surviving the next few minutes lies in giving me the answers I need in a timely fashion." He drew his pistol and aimed it at Flynn. "Or perhaps we can simply do without Mr. Carsen from now on."

"No!" Shirin blurted. "You don't need to do that."

"So, you *do* have something to share with me? Some new clue gleaned from this book?"

Shirin faltered. "Maybe, but it's just a story, and not very informative."

"Let me be the judge of that." Khoja kept the gun pointed at Flynn. "Enlighten me."

Flynn cringed inwardly as Shirin divulged what she had read about the cave on the unknown island. "Guarded by an enormous rock," she concluded, "or so Scheherazade writes."

"I see," Khoja said. "And how exactly do we find this island?"

"I have no idea," Shirin said. "That's the truth, I swear!"

"Perhaps." Khoja swung the gun toward her. "What about you, Librarian? Surely you must have some thoughts as to our next move . . . that you might want to trade for Dr. Masri's life?"

Flynn stalled, hoping to find a way to save both Shirin and his secrets. "What makes you think that I'm not stumped, too?"

"Because you're the Librarian," Khoja said. "This is what you do." He cocked the weapon. "But if you're both truly of no more value to us. . . ."

Flynn was only a so-so poker player, but he didn't think Khoja was bluffing.

"The rug," he said, "in the antechamber."

"What about it?" Khoja asked impatiently. "Don't make me twist your arm, Carsen, figuratively or literally."

"I prefer pulling teeth," Marjanah added. "And, no, that's not just an expression."

Flynn gulped. These two meant business.

"The design of the rug, as per tradition, features geometric patterns extended mathematically from a single abstract figure, in this case a distinctive star formed of two interlaced triangles."

Shirin caught on immediately. "The Seal of Solomon."

"Precisely." Flynn had noted earlier how the carpet's design had been built around the Seal. "Which, according to legend, King Solomon used to command genies and all the powers of the Earth, both natural and supernatural." He couldn't resist pausing for dramatic effect. "Solomon is also said to have possessed a flying carpet that would carry him wherever he willed, to every corner of the globe."

Khoja nodded, understanding. "And you believe that carpet in the next room . . . ?"

"Is King Solomon's magic carpet, yes." Flynn was somewhat surprised that the gang leader was not more taken aback by the suggestion. "You're not at all skeptical?"

"We're searching for Aladdin's Lamp," Khoja reminded him.

"Good point." Flynn started toward the antechamber, only to be blocked by Khoja's henchmen. "If I may?"

"Let him through," Khoja said, "but keep your eyes on him. We wouldn't want him to give us the slip again."

Marjanah flinched at that last remark. Scowling, she shot Flynn another dirty look.

Okay, that didn't help matters any, he thought.

The gunmen parted to let him pass. Shirin started to follow him, but Khoja stopped her. "Why don't you stick close to us, Doctor, just in case the Librarian has something up his sleeve?"

"Nothing but my watch and a bad case of goose bumps," Flynn promised. "After me."

He led them all into the antechamber where the gorgeous carpet still rested on the floor. Golden tassels fringed the rug, which was composed of green silk with a golden weft, just as described in certain historical texts. He pointed out the intertwined triangles at the center of the carpet's design.

"There it is . . . the Seal of Solomon."

Shirin gaped at the seal. "I can't believe I missed that before!"

"Well, you were a little rattled from almost being eaten by a ghoul," he said. "Plus, I've probably had a bit more firsthand experience with Solomon's relics than you have."

Like throwing Solomon's personal spell book into a lava pit. . . .

"But do you truly think you can make this carpet fly?" Khoja asked. "All the way to this nameless island?"

"Seems like our best bet, in keeping with the spirit of *The Arabian Nights*." Flynn glanced at the various artifacts on display in the antechamber. "In fact, I'm betting that's how they managed to cart all this stuff up to the tomb in the first place: by means of the magic carpet."

He pictured the bygone spectacle: a flying carpet miraculously crossing the canyon outside, bearing priceless books and artifacts and, ultimately, the remains of a legendary storyteller. It was like a scene from one of Scheherazade's own tales. . . .

"Show me," Khoja said. "But don't even think of going far, if you want Dr. Masri to keep on breathing."

He and the others backed away from the carpet, taking Shirin with them. Flynn strode to the center of the carpet and swallowed hard.

"Arise! Ascend! Up, up, and away!"

Nothing happened. The carpet remained stretched out atop the floor like, well, a carpet.

Flynn started to sweat. He repeated the commands in both Arabic and Persian, but with equally unimpressive results. He started to wonder if maybe he was mistaken and this wasn't *the* carpet of Solomon, in which case he and Shirin might be in even worse trouble than they already were.

"You're disappointing me, Librarian," Khoja said. "What a shame . . . for both you."

Beside him, Marjanah grinned in cruel anticipation. "Let me kill just one of them, please?"

"Wait!" Shirin protested. "Let me take a closer look at that carpet. I might be able to help."

Khoja nodded and brought her closer to the rug, while holding on tightly to her arm. "Do it," he said, "but no tricks."

She examined the carpet, her smooth brow furrowing in concentration. Then her eyes lit up and Flynn could practically see the light bulb switch on over her head. This did not escape Khoja's notice.

"You found something. What is it?"

"Writing," she said. "Along with geometric patterns, calligraphy was often integrated into art and design back in the days of Solomon and Scheherazade. If you look closely, the decorative border around the edge of the carpet is actually a highly stylized inscription . . . possibly even an incantation."

Khoja eyed her with interest. "What makes you think that?"

"Traditionally, any writing used in this manner would be a quote from the Koran, but this is from the 'Song of Solomon': *Arise, my love, my beautiful one, and come away.*"

"That must be it!" Flynn enthused. Now that Shirin had called his attention to it, he could make out the woven incantation, too. "Stand back!"

He recited the words—and the carpet lifted off the floor.

"Whoa!" He struggled to keep his balance atop the levitating carpet as it hovered about a foot above the floor. The Seal of Solomon glowed briefly before fading back into the rug's complicated design. Its golden tassels dangled along the edge of the rug, and Flynn could feel a peculiar vibration beneath his feet. He somehow sensed that the carpet was eager to take flight.

"Bravo," Khoja said. "You two have just bought yourself a stay of execution."

"For now," Marjanah muttered.

"Let's not get ahead of ourselves," Khoja admonished his vindictive lieutenant. "Everyone aboard!"

Khoja and his gang, along with Shirin, climbed onto the carpet, which sagged beneath their collective weight, descending back onto the floor.

"What's the problem?" Khoja asked. "Talk to me."

"Looks like we're overloaded," Flynn guessed. "Sorry."

Khoja mulled that over. "How many people can the carpet lift?"

"Beats me." Flynn looked at Shirin. "You see anything in the book about the maximum carrying capacity of a magic carpet?"

"I'm afraid not," she replied. "It's not exactly a technical manual."

"I suppose not." Khoja nodded at his men. "Get off, one at a time."

"Yes, First of Forty," one gunman said, hopping off the carpet onto the tile floor beneath. More thieves joined him, but the rug remained weighed down to the ground.

"What about those two?" Marjanah asked, glaring at Flynn and Shirin. "Do we really need *both* of them now?"

"Possibly," Khoja said. "Who knows what new challenges or puzzles may await us where we're going? We may still have need of their combined scholarship down the road, at the end of the magic carpet ride."

Marjanah was visibly disappointed by her boss's decision. "If you say so."

The other henchmen disembarked from the carpet, which gradually lifted off from the floor again. In the end, only Khoja, Marjanah, Flynn, Shirin, and five additional gunmen were left aboard the floating rug. Flynn was disappointed that Marjanah was still along for the ride. He would have preferred leaving her behind.

But at least we thinned out some of the opposition, he thought. *Thank goodness this isn't the Boeing 747 of flying carpets.*

"I believe we are ready to depart," Khoja said. "Get on with it."

"All right." Flynn sat down on the carpet, not far from Shirin, and gestured for the other passengers to do the same. He gave Shirin the most reassuring look he could manage. "Everyone sit tight and prepare for takeoff."

His mouth dry, he recited the incantation again and specified their destination.

"In the name of King Solomon, master of all the spirits of the air and sky, convey us now to the secret hiding place of Aladdin's Lamp!"

The carpet took off like a shot.

16

The flying carpet went from zero to "Yikes!" in a heartbeat. For a split second, Flynn wondered belatedly how the carpet was going to make it through the various doorways and tunnels between the antechamber and the outdoors, but then the carpet rolled itself up tightly, cocooning its passengers before shooting out into the ravine, where it unfurled beneath the early morning sky. A helicopter hovering above the ravine had to dart out of the way of the carpet as it climbed sharply upward and took off into the sky at preternatural speed.

"Chopper Alpha!" Khoja barked into his walkie-talkie. "Pursue airborne carpet. Repeat: pursue airborne carpet!"

Flynn imagined that the chopper pilot had never received that particular order before and was probably still blinking in surprise at the carpet's miraculous exit from the tomb. Despite Khoja's order, however, the carpet swiftly left the helicopter behind.

"Slow this thing down!" Khoja shouted at Flynn.

Flynn threw up his hands. "Do you see a brake or gas pedal?"

The carpet was in charge now, accelerating much faster than your typical floor covering, while heading southeast away from the mountains. According to legend, Flynn recalled, Solomon's carpet flew so swiftly that the king could break-fast in Damascus and sup in far-off Media, all in the space of a day, so Flynn was not too surprised that the magical rug was eating up the miles at a voracious rate, while soaring high above the mountains. The edges of the carpet curled up to form a railing of sorts, which its passengers could hold onto for safety's sake—although Flynn would have preferred seat belts and a pressurized hull, not to mention a parachute or two.

Flying carpets are perfectly safe, he thought. *At least in the movies. . . .*

The vertiginous flight was too much for one of the name-less henchmen, who panicked in a big way.

"Take us down!" The man aimed his rifle at Flynn. Terri-fied eyes bulged from their sockets. "Take us down right this minute, or—"

Marjanah shoved him off the carpet. She snorted in dis-gust as the man plummeted to his doom, his dying scream trailing behind him.

"Coward."

Khoja arched an eyebrow. "That was a bit drastic."

"I never liked him anyway," she said with a shrug. "Shame about the gun, though."

Khoja didn't appear overly concerned about the loss of the gun or his henchman. "I think we can afford to trade a foot soldier for a genie."

Flynn remembered Judson's dire warnings about the Djinn. "About that genie," he began, "you might want to rethink your plans for the Lamp."

"And why is that?" Khoja asked suspiciously.

"He's not a nice genie. There's a reason he's confined to that Lamp, and every time he's summoned, he gets stronger and the Lamp gets weaker, so one of these days he's going to break free . . . and nobody wants that, or so I'm told."

"By who?" Khoja asked. "The Library? An institution so terrified of magic that for thousands of years it's done nothing but lock it away and let it gather dust on a shelf? You'll forgive me if I take your cautionary advice with a grain of a salt." He sneered at Flynn. "When has the Library *ever* not considered some great source of mystic power to be too dangerous to be employed out in the world?"

"Well, there's always . . . or maybe . . ." Flynn faltered as nothing came readily to mind. "Look, magic *is* dangerous. Trust me on this. I know what I'm talking about."

"But the Djinn *does* grant unlimited wishes to any who hold the Lamp, bringing them incalculable wealth and power?"

"Well, yes," Flynn conceded, "according to the stories, but—"

"But nothing." Khoja looked away from Flynn, turning his attention to whatever glorious future he envisioned. "Soon the Lamp will be mine, and with it the ability to turn my most impossible wishes into reality."

"*Our* wishes," Marjanah corrected him. "For generations, the Forty have sought the Lamp, ever since the *Alf Layla* eluded our grasp during the sack of Baghdad more than seven hundred and fifty years ago. But now our patience will finally be rewarded . . . and the Forty shall at last reign supreme."

Flynn considered his adversaries. Khoja struck him as driven by personal ambition, but Marjanah seemed to be more about the "glorious" legacy of the Forty.

"Wow, you're a true believer, aren't you?"

"She should be," Khoja said. "Marjanah's family claims direct descent from the original Forty Thieves. Her father, in fact, was the First before me—until she helped me overthrow him."

"He was weak and stuck in the past," she said unapologetically. "He lacked the strength and vision to guide the Forty into the twenty-first century . . . and claim the Lamp at long last."

The carpet zoomed across Iran's airspace, flying low enough to allow them to breathe comfortably while hopefully evading radar detection. Shirin, who had been tossed toward Flynn during the carpet's headlong escape from the tomb, scooted close enough to grab hold of his hand as the rug carried them over the Persian Gulf to the Arabian Sea, hundreds of miles from the Zagros Mountains. Despite their perilous situation, Flynn found the magic carpet ride more than a little exhilarating. Glancing at Shirin, he saw a look of utter wonder on her face as well.

Might as well enjoy it, he thought. *How often do you get to glide above the world on a flying carpet?*

Too bad the company left something to be desired.

"So where the devil is this mythical island?" Marjanah said, squirming restlessly upon the carpet. Her dark hair blew in the wind.

"Patience," Khoja chided her. "We seem to be making excellent time toward . . . wherever."

In no time at all, the carpet began to descend from the sky into a thick patch of cloud and fog somewhere in the middle of the sea. A clammy mist briefly chilled Flynn before the mystery island came into view. A barren gray mountain, overlooking a small cove guarded by jagged rocks, rose from a fringe of woods and brush circling its base. At first glance, the vaguely *U*-shaped isle appeared to be uninhabited and untouched since the days of Sinbad. Flynn wondered if there actually was some enchantment shielding the isle from discovery, as with Brigadoon or Shangri-La.

I wouldn't be at all surprised.

The carpet slowed as it descended, much to Flynn's relief and concern. They were getting closer to the Lamp, which meant, unfortunately, that the Forty was getting closer to liberating the Djinn, possibly for good. He and Shirin needed to get away from their captors and find the Lamp before it was too late. What had Scheherazade written next about its location? Something about a hidden cave guarded by an enormous rock?

"Attention, all passengers," he announced. "Prepare for landing."

A loud cawing noise came from above. Peering upward, Flynn dimly glimpsed a large shape soaring through the dense clouds overhead. He suddenly remembered the immense piece of eggshell on display in the tomb. . . .

"Er, Shirin? Did the book say the cave was guarded by a huge rock—or a *roc*?"

Her face fell as she grasped what he was asking. "You mean—?"

The answer came in the feathered form of a colossal bird, which came swooping down from the clouds toward the carpet, its grasping talons extended, as though straight out of "The Second Voyage of Sinbad." The roc was just as described in the classic tales: a monstrous bird of prey whose wingspan was at least fifty feet long, with ominous gray plumage that turned bloodred at the tips. Its pointed beak was that of a raptor, and large enough to swallow a grown man or woman in one gulp. Its prodigious shadow fell over the carpet and its stunned passengers.

"Sorry," Shirin said. "I might have misread that line."

"You think?" Flynn replied. "Granted, it *was* a rush job. . . ."

Gasps and shouts greeted the roc's attack. Dive-bombing the carpet, the monster grabbed a henchman with its talons and carried him, shrieking, back up into the clouds, while everyone else ducked low to avoid the speeding roc. The wind from its giant wings rippled the surface of the carpet.

Caught by surprise, Khoja took a moment to respond to the threat. "Open fire!" he shouted, lifting his head. "Bring that bird down!"

"But, First of Forty," another gunman said, "what about Ahmed?"

"Never mind Ahmed! Open fire, I said!"

The thieves shot at the sky, the sharp report of the gunfire hurting Flynn's ears, but all they succeeded in accomplishing was making the roc drop its human cargo. Still screaming, Ahmed hurtled past the carpet, barely missing it, before plunging toward the rocky peaks below. The remaining thieves, including Marjanah, continued firing at the roc, which only seemed to make the monster angrier. Apparently, hitting a swiftly moving target from a wobbly flying carpet was even trickier than you might think.

Flynn took another tack.

"In the name of Solomon . . . evasive action!"

The carpet responded immediately, careening wildly through the sky in a desperate attempt to elude the roc, which flapped after them in pursuit, squawking furiously. The aerodynamic rug banked sharply to the right, then to the left, while zigzagging up and down and from side to side. Flynn held onto the raised edge of the rug for dear life, while regretting that flying carpets did not come with airsick bags. Khoja and his gang kept firing at the roc, but the carpet's barnstorming maneuvers tossed them all about, making it all but impossible for anyone to get a bead on the monster, which continued chasing after the carpet with surprising speed. Flynn recalled that Sinbad had once escaped a deserted island by strapping himself to a roc's leg and letting the gargantuan bird carry him away.

Talk about brave, he thought, *or desperate*.

The roc took another run at them, as though engaging in an old-fashioned aerial dogfight, and the carpet flipped over to shield its passengers from the winged monster's talons, which tore ragged gashes in the fabric, only inches from where Flynn and Shirin and the others had been crouching right before they were unceremoniously dumped into the empty air below the carpet. Gravity tore Shirin's hand from Flynn's as they found themselves in freefall, plummeting toward the rocky hills far below.

Seatbelts, he thought. *I knew that rug* needed *seatbelts*.

The wind howled in his ears, almost drowning out the screams of Shirin and the rest as they accelerated toward the ground at 9.8 meters-per-second-squared—which did not, he lamented, give him much time to formulate a clever strategy, no matter how many degrees he'd earned. His favorite books passed before his eyes, along with other indelible memories, some more recent than others.

I'm so sorry, Shirin. Your story deserved a happier ending.

Then, just when it seemed as though the Library were about to have an opening for a new Librarian, the carpet looped beneath the falling men and women to catch them before they hit terminal velocity. Flynn and the others smacked back onto the carpet, which absorbed the impact like a safety net. He found Shirin's hand and pulled her close. He could feel her trembling, almost as much as he was.

"Let's not do that again," she suggested.

"Don't talk to me. Talk to the rug."

Deep tears in the carpet, where the roc had slashed it, impaired the rug's lifting capacity, causing it to sink ever farther toward the island, fleeing the upper reaches of the mountain to glide over the scraggly woods below. For a moment, Flynn dared to hope that the roc would be content with chasing them away from the hills, but apparently the cave's guardian was as stubborn as, well, that other kind of rock.

"Here it comes again!" Marjanah shouted, having been caught by the carpet along with her cohorts. Typically, she looked more angry than scared. "Send it back to Hades!"

The wind from the roc's mighty wings buffeted the carpet and its besieged passengers, causing it to toss back and forth as though adrift atop choppy waters and tearing wider the gaping rents in the fabric. Marjanah and her fellow thieves fired ineffectively from the unstable carpet, which was dipping ever faster toward the earth. Tearing his gaze away from the hostile roc, Flynn looked ahead and saw that the carpet's headlong retreat was bringing them back toward the small cove cutting into the island. Pristine blue waters reflected the cloudy sky. He also noted that, preoccupied with the roc, none of the Forty were paying the least bit of attention to their captives at the moment.

"Can you swim?" he asked Shirin.

"Yes. Why do you ask?"

There was no time explain. The cove was coming up quickly. It was now or never.

"Take a deep breath!"

He shoved her off the carpet without another word of warning, then dived after her. Gravity seized them again as they fell toward the cove dozens of feet below. Inhaling deeply, he hoped the carpet was too busy evading the roc to dive after them again, and that the Forty were also otherwise engaged, *and* that the inlet was deep enough that he and Shirin could survive this plunge.

On second thought, that's a heck of a lot of question marks. . . .

Gunfire blared overhead, competing with the raucous cawing of the roc, as the pair hit the water at high speed and sank beneath the surface. The cool water came as a shock, but at least they didn't encounter any hidden reefs or boulders. Holding his breath, Flynn kicked his way back to the surface and poked his head above the salty water. Sputtering, he searched frantically for Shirin.

"Shirin?" he called out. "Shirin!"

"Flynn! Over here!"

She was bobbing in the brine not far away. To his relief, she appeared soaked but unharmed. They kicked toward each other.

"Warn me next time!"

"Don't worry," he said. "I'm not planning a repeat performance anytime soon."

Now that he knew they had both survived, he peered up at the sky, but he caught no sight of either the carpet or the roc. He wondered what had become of Khoja and his minions. Had they fallen victim to the roc or perhaps made a crash landing elsewhere on the island?

"You see what happened to the others?" he asked Shirin. "Or the roc?"

"Sorry, I was too busy falling from a flying carpet." A distraught look came over her face. "The book! Scheherazade's book . . . we've lost it!"

He understood her distress. She was a scholar and historian, after all; losing the priceless tome had to be a huge blow to her, no matter what other challenges faced them.

"It couldn't be helped," he offered by way of consolation. "But at least we're not bird food, and we still have a chance to find the Lamp before anyone else does."

A faint smile lightened her expression. "Anyone ever tell you that you're an incorrigible optimist? Even for an American?"

"Comes with the job," he replied. "You kind of need to think of the grail as always being half full."

"Grail? As in the *Holy* Grail?"

"Remind me to tell you about how I broke it on my very first day on the job." He winced at the memory before turning his attention to a sandy shore, studded with boulders, some fifty feet away. "Maybe after we're back on dry land again."

A strenuous swim later, they dragged themselves up onto the beach and collapsed, soggy and exhausted. They were soaked to the skin and weighed down by their sodden garments. Flynn couldn't remember the last time they'd really been able to rest and recuperate—and, no, those hours they'd spent stowed in the back of the pickup truck didn't count. His stomach grumbled, and he wondered what kind of foodstuffs might be found on an enchanted isle in the Arabian Sea. Shellfish, maybe, or a stray seagull?

Roc eggs were probably off the menu.

Shirin slumped against him. "I've never felt so exhausted."

"You and me both," he said. "But we can't rest too long. For all we know, some of the Forty might have survived—"

A gun cocked behind them.

Flynn groaned. Turning his head, he saw Khoja, Marjanah, and two of their henchmen emerge from the woods and brush fringing the beach. They looked a bit beaten up and disheveled, but Khoja had managed to hang on to the turban hiding his face—and his pistol.

"Have a nice swim?" he asked.

17

small decorative illustration of an owl sitting on a book

※ *2006* ※

Flynn's spirits sank deeper than the bottom of the cove. Just when he'd thought they'd gotten away from the Forty, they were right back where they started, just a good deal wetter than before. He took off his boot and dumped out a canteen's worth of water. He was too exhausted and out of breath to even think about trying to flee from the armed criminals.

"If you don't mind my asking," he said, "did you manage to bring down the roc?"

"I wish!" Marjanah snarled. "That filthy, feathered monstrosity nearly killed us all. I'd like to see it roasting on a spit!"

Flynn was starting to think the Second of the Forty had anger-management issues.

"Then how . . . ?" he started.

"Did we survive?" Khoja said. "After you deserted us? We were in dire straits, I admit, with the carpet ripping apart beneath us even as that blasted bird kept on coming. In desperation, we sliced the rug into fragments, one for each of us, and used them to parachute down to the ground, while dividing the roc's attention so that *most* of us made it to safety in one piece." He shrugged. "A shame about poor Harufa, but let's hope his tough hide gives the beast indigestion—or at least a full belly for the time being."

Flynn cast a nervous gaze upward, but he didn't see the roc. He made a mental note to keep watching the skies.

"What about the book?" Shirin asked anxiously. "Did you manage to save the book?"

"Spoken like a museum curator," Khoja observed. "But I'm afraid the book was lost during the tumult. It could have landed anywhere on the island."

Shirin's face fell. "Oh."

"We managed to salvage the bulk of the carpet, however." Khoja gestured toward one of the surviving henchmen, who had apparently been drafted into toting the shredded fragments on his back. "Who knows? Maybe the carpet can be stitched back together at some point, perhaps with the Genie's help. Indeed, maybe he can even help us find your precious book."

Flynn saw another opportunity to try to reason with Khoja. "You know, releasing that Djinn is a seriously bad idea. From what I hear, he's much too dangerous to let loose from his Lamp, especially if you empower him by rubbing it too often."

"You Librarians," Khoja said scornfully. "You have access to some of the most powerful magical relics on the planet, yet you're too timid to wield that power."

"That's because we know how easy it is for such powers to end up using you," Flynn said. "And just think what could happen if you lost control of the Djinn, which is a very real possibility."

Khoja didn't want to hear it.

"You're wasting your breath and my time," he said. "You're

not going to scare me away from our prize, not when we're finally this close." He waved his pistol at Flynn and Shirin. "Let's get a move on, before that bird gets hungry and comes hunting for us."

Flynn *was* feeling a tad exposed on the beach, beneath the open sky. The beckoning woods, meager as they were, did offer slightly more cover. He grudgingly stood up and helped Shirin to her feet. Gritty sand clung to their soaked clothing despite their best attempts to brush it off. Shirin swept her wet hair away from her face.

"That's more like it." Khoja turned to Marjanah. "Any luck contacting our people?"

She shook her head while scowling at her satellite phone. "I'm not getting anything: voice communication or GPS. Something is jamming us."

"Magic," Flynn guessed. "This whole island is probably cut off from the modern world, like on *Lost*." He frowned for a moment. "You know, I never could figure that show out."

"Let's hope that you're better at locating hidden caves," Khoja said. "I trust I don't need to repeat the usual threats?"

Flynn didn't need to be a Librarian to grasp that he and Shirin were still outnumbered and outgunned by their enemies, despite the roc reducing the bad guys' numbers by one more henchman.

"I think we can skip that part," he agreed.

Khoja lowered his gun, although Marjanah kept fondling her knife in a way that Flynn could have done without.

"So where to next?" the First of the Forty asked.

Flynn contemplated the desolate gray mountain looming above them. It was small compared to the towering peaks of the Zagros back in Iran, but it was large enough to hide any number of hidden caves. He wished Scheherazade had been a little more specific in her directions.

A map would have been nice.

He looked to Shirin for assistance. "Do you remember anything else from the book?"

"Not really. An island, a cave, a rock . . . sorry, a *roc*."

Flynn considered his options. He could insist he was stumped, probably at the cost of his and Shirin's lives, but that would still leave Khoja and his minions free to search the island on their own, with no guarantee that the determined criminals wouldn't find the cave eventually. Flynn decided he wasn't willing to sacrifice Shirin just to slow the Forty down.

"Let me have one of those carpet fragments," he said.

"Why?" Khoja asked. "They're no good for flying in their present state. At best, they just slowed our descent like parachutes. If you're entertaining some desperate fantasy of making a speedy getaway with Dr. Masri on a scrap of rug, you can forget about that right away. You're grounded like the rest of us."

"The thought never crossed my mind," Flynn fibbed. "But I may have another use for that magic fabric."

Khoja's eyes narrowed suspiciously, but he assented after a moment's consideration. "Fine. Let's see what you have in mind." He glanced at the henchman serving as a porter. "Rahan, give Mr. Carsen a piece of the carpet. A *small* one."

"As you wish, First of Forty." The man handed Flynn a remnant of the carpet about the size of a welcome mat and threw in a surly look as a bonus. "I'm watching you, Librarian."

"We all are," Khoja added. "You're on, Carsen. Show us what you're up to."

Flynn gulped, not at all positive this trick was going to work. Holding onto the remnant with both hands, he held it out in front of him so that it dangled above the sand. He recited the incantation once again and repeated his earlier command.

"In the name of Solomon, take us to the Cave of the Lamp."

Golden light shimmered briefly along the sliced edges of the fragment, which came alive in Flynn's grasp, rising up so that it was horizontal with the ground. His fingers tingled as the piece of the carpet tugged, pulling him toward the looming mountain.

"It wants to go this way," he said. "I think."

Khoja caught on immediately. "A homing device. You're using it as a homing device."

"More like a dowsing rod," Flynn said, "but that's the basic idea, yes."

"Ingenious," Khoja said. "You continue to impress me, Carsen. I don't suppose you'd be interested in switching sides and joining our organization?"

Flynn didn't even think about it. He'd dealt with a turncoat Librarian before. It was not a path he ever intended to go down.

"Not interested, sorry."

Khoja shrugged. "Worth a try. Perhaps you'll change your mind once we have the Lamp in hand, and the world is ours for the taking."

"Again, not a good idea. Releasing the Djinn, I mean."

"I beg to differ." Khoja nodded at the mountain. "Lead the way, Librarian."

The floating remnant tugged insistently. Flynn sighed and let it guide them forward.

He hoped he wasn't making a big mistake.

18

"Watch your step," Flynn warned.

"I think that goes without saying," Shirin said, "but thanks."

Guided by the eager carpet remnant, they hiked up a narrow ledge along the side of the mountain. It had been a long and arduous climb already. The party, which was now comprised of Flynn, Shirin, Khoja, Marjanah, and the two bonus cutthroats, had quickly left any trace of vegetation behind, so that nothing lay before them but lifeless rock, dirt, and debris, along with the daunting prospect of yet more uphill hiking. A sharp drop-off on the left threatened to make a careless step one's last. Loose dirt and pebbles rolled beneath Flynn's feet, adding to the danger. Sinbad and Ali Baba had clearly gone out of their way to make certain that the route to the hidden cave—and the Lamp—was as difficult as possible.

Thanks a lot, guys, Flynn thought.

His legs ached from the climb. His damp clothes were cold and clammy, and his boots still sloshed with every step as he trudged wearily at the head of the procession. He was breathing hard, as was Shirin, who was right behind him. Khoja and his crew took up the rear, almost as though they didn't want to turn their backs on their captives while navigating the precarious ledge.

Flynn couldn't imagine why.

"How much further?" Khoja asked.

"Only the carpet knows," Flynn replied, "and it's not talk-ing." The levitating scrap continued to tug at him, like a blood-hound straining at its leash. "But it feels like we're getting warmer."

"You'd best hope so, Librarian," the chief thief said omi-nously. "If it turns out that you've been leading us on a wild goose chase . . ."

A goose is not the bird we need to worry about, Flynn thought. He kept one eye on the sky and the other on the challenging path ahead, which left him wishing he had borrowed a Third Eye from the Library's Optical Sciences gallery. Even with-out an extra eye, he doubted that they had seen the last of the roc, especially as they climbed higher toward its moun-tain aerie and the forbidden cave. *Chances are, it will be show-ing up any minute now.*

"Incoming!" Marjanah shouted. "Big bird at eleven o'clock!"

Called it, Flynn thought. *Lucky us.*

He couldn't fault the keen-eyed kidnapper's vigilance. Looking up, he spotted the roc swooping toward them with renewed ferocity. Its harsh caw echoed off the stony hills. The wind from its wings gusted against the hikers, blowing them backward into the granite slope on the right side of the ledge and churning up a cloud of dust and grit. Flynn threw up an arm to protect himself from the swirling debris. Shirin coughed hoarsely.

We're dead ducks, Flynn thought, before swearing off avian idioms forever. *On the bright side, I guess the Forty's not claim-ing that Lamp today.*

"Get it!" Khoja hollered. "Before it gets us!"

"I have a better idea." Marjanah turned and shot the hench-man behind her, who tumbled off the ledge toward the rocks below. The load of carpet fragments strapped to his back caused him to drift slowly downward like a leaf on the wind, presenting a tempting target for the hungry roc, which veered away from Flynn and the others to dive after the screaming morsel. Marjanah tucked her pistol back into her holster. "That should keep it busy for a few minutes at least. We shouldn't waste them."

If the cold-blooded tactic shocked Khoja, he didn't let it show.

"You heard the Second," he ordered. "Move it!"

Although shaken by the brutal murder, Flynn didn't want to stick around, either. With nowhere to go but forward, the surviving members of the party scrambled up the trail faster than would have been prudent under less frantic circum-stances. Flynn's foot hit a loose patch of gravel and, losing his balance, he tottered on the brink of the precipice before Shirin grabbed his arm and pulled him to safety.

"Forget it," she said. "You're not leaving me alone with this bunch."

Flynn's heart was beating harder than the roc's wings. "I wouldn't think of it."

Racing up the trail, they turned a corner to find themselves at a dead end. The curving path widened to form a large rocky ledge, the size of a backyard patio, which faced a looming wall of solid granite that blocked their path entirely. The ledge of-fered a great view of the island, including the cove a good ways off, but no protection from the winged monster pursuing them.

"Great," Flynn said. "We're stuck between a roc and a hard place."

Shirin stared at him in disbelief. "Really? You had to go there?"

"How could I not? I mean, *somebody* had to say it."

"That's highly debatable."

Khoja ignored their banter. "What's this?" he demanded, glaring at the rock wall before them. "You've led us to our doom!"

"Not necessarily." Flynn let the magical remnant pull him toward the seemingly impassable barrier. "Scheherazade did write that it was a *hidden* cave."

"Then unhide it, Carsen," Khoja barked. "Before we're the next items on that monster's menu."

No pressure there, Flynn thought. He hastily examined the rock face, searching for a secret passage or lever, but came up empty. There weren't even the usual enigmatic hieroglyphics to decipher. *Where's a puzzling pictograph when you need one?*

"Get on with it, Librarian," Marjanah said, "or I'll feed you and your girlfriend to the bird myself!"

Flynn noted that the remaining henchman was backing away from her nervously, no doubt remembering how she had distracted the roc only minutes ago. "I'm not sure *girlfriend* is quite the right label. We're still just getting to know each other. . . ."

"*So* not the point right now," Marjanah said icily. "Show us the way, you babbling idiot!"

The flapping of mighty wings heralded the return of the roc, which soared up from below to reclaim the sky above the exposed ledge. A human leg dangled from its beak as it circled around to come at the party again.

"Point taken." Flynn ran his hands over the rough stone, finding no telltale cracks or seams. His desperate mind turned to *The Arabian Nights* for inspiration. *What would Sinbad do?*

"No," he realized, "not Sinbad."

Hidden caves were more Ali Baba's thing.

"Open sesame!" he commanded, and stepped back in anticipation.

Nothing happened. The dead end stayed dead.

"Open sesame!" he tried again, more in panic this time. "Open rye . . . barley . . . poppy seed . . ."

"Not in English!" Shirin shouted. "Old Persian!"

Shirin rushed forward and addressed the wall in flawless ancient Persian.

All at once, the solid rock shimmered like a mirage, fading away to reveal the mouth of a cave. Darkness waited beyond the entrance, but there was no time to wonder what lay within the cave, not when the roc was swooping down for the kill.

"Inside!" Khoja shouted unnecessarily. "Hurry!"

The party stampeded into the cave, shoving past each other in order to get away from the voracious roc. It would have been an ideal opportunity for him and Shirin to try to slip away from their captors, Flynn observed, if not for the giant bird out to eat them. He would have to look for another chance to turn the tables on the Forty, and the sooner the better.

Maybe the cave had a back door?

The roc cawed in frustration as the tiny humans vanished into the cave, whose entrance was not nearly wide enough for the giant bird to pass through. It squeezed its head into the cave and snapped its beak at the tasty morsels just beyond its reach. Its strident cries echoed through the cave, accompanied by the sound of angrily flapping wings outside on the ledge. Flynn and the others backed away from the angry roc's head, putting more distance between them and that beak.

"Thanks for the emergency translation, by the way," Flynn

said to Shirin. "You probably couldn't tell, but I was getting a little rattled out there."

"Is that so?" she said diplomatically. "I had no idea."

Khoja intruded on their moment. "Well done, you two. I take back some of the vile things I was just wishing on you."

"Only some?"

"Don't press your luck, Librarian," Khoja said. Turning away from the entrance, he peered into the waiting shadows. "Now then, what have we here?"

Flashlights clicked on, illuminating a wide tunnel leading deeper into the mountain. *Here we go again*, thought Flynn, who was starting to feel more like a spelunker than a scholar. Unlike the cliffside burial chambers back in Iran, however, this looked and felt more like an actual cave than a crypt. No artwork adorned the rough stone walls. The floor was bumpy and uneven. This was not a royal tomb decked out to honor the memory of a beloved sultana; this was a hole for hiding loot, magical or otherwise.

"Step carefully, everyone." Flynn felt obliged to warn the others before anyone went rushing off to search for the Lamp. "There could be booby traps ahead."

"An excellent point," Khoja said. "You go first."

"Somehow I knew you were going to say that."

Borrowing a flashlight from the last of the henchmen, Flynn advanced cautiously into the cave, with Shirin sticking close to him. "Not another ghoul, please," she whispered. "I'm all storied out."

The tunnel led to a natural stone bridge across a seemingly bottomless chasm. Barely two feet in width, the bridge triggered Flynn's natural fear of heights, which had already gotten a workout on the narrow ledge they'd climbed to reach the hidden cavern, not to mention that burning rope ladder earlier. Taking a deep breath to steady his nerves, he led Shirin out onto the bridge while wondering, not for the first time, why the nameless builders of lost tombs, temples, and treasure troves never seemed to take reasonable safety precautions into account.

Would it have killed them to have installed a guard rail or two?

The chasm was a gaping wound in the solid rock, dropping steeply into Stygian darkness. A loose pebble, dislodged by Flynn's boot, rolled off the bridge into the abyss. Flynn listened, but never heard it hit bottom. Finding it all too easy to imagine pointy stalagmites waiting to impale him if he slipped, he was tempted to crawl across the bridge on his hands and knees just to be safe, but he couldn't quite bring himself to do so in front of Shirin and the others. As the Librarian, he did have a certain dignity to maintain . . . sort of.

The bridge was less than twenty yards long and, in reality, took only a few minutes to cross, but Flynn let out a huge sigh of relief as he and Shirin reached the other side, followed closely by their captors. Continuing on, they discovered a large, roomy grotto that appeared to be yet another dead end. Not a single lamp was in view, only rows of large ceramic jars lining the perimeter of the chamber. Each jar was roughly waist high and identical to the others, lacking any distinguishing labels or markings. Jagged stalactites hung from the ceiling like the fangs of some giant petrified carnivore.

"If and when we get out of this," Shirin said with a shudder, "I'm going to want plenty of sun and wide-open spaces. A beach, maybe, far from caves and cliffs."

"It's a date," he said.

"A *date*-date?" she asked. "Just to be clear."

"That's what I'm thinking."

Khoja and his crew entered the grotto after them, clearly unwilling to let their reluctant "guides" out of their sight. "I wouldn't be making any long-term plans just yet," Khoja cautioned them. "There's a fine but crucial line between optimism and false hope."

The First of the Forty surveyed the grotto with interest, but prudently refrained from rushing to root through the jars in search of the Lamp. For better or for worse, he had evidently taken Flynn's warning about booby traps to heart.

"So . . . jars," he observed. "A good many jars."

"Thirty-eight," Flynn guessed. He quickly counted them to confirm his theory. "As in the story of 'Ali Baba and the Forty Thieves.' As you recall, your illustrious predecessor, the original captain of the thieves, hid thirty-seven of his men in oil jars just like these as part of a diabolical plan to get revenge on Ali Baba for stealing their ill-gotten booty. He had only thirty-seven men left," Flynn felt obliged to explain, "because he'd already beheaded two of his own men for failing to lead him to Ali Baba earlier."

The surviving minion glanced furtively at Marjanah. Although nearly twice her size, and built like a bouncer, he had to be feeling a bit expendable himself by this point, or so Flynn assumed.

"I'm familiar with the story," Khoja said dryly.

"Then you remember that the thirty-eighth jar was actually filled with sesame oil, which a clever servant girl—named Marjanah, as it happens—used to drown the lurking thieves by pouring the oil into the other jars, thereby saving Ali Baba and his household from being slaughtered in their sleep."

"Not one of our finer hours," Khoja conceded. "If the tales are to be believed, that is."

"Scheherazade hasn't led us astray yet." Flynn worked his way around the circumference of the grotto, rapping his knuckles against each jar and listening for echoes. When he was done, he couldn't resist grinning in vindication. "Just as I expected: all the jars but the first one are empty."

Khoja approached the jar in question. "Perhaps the Lamp is hidden in this jar, then, submerged beneath the oil?"

"No way," Flynn scoffed. "That would be too easy."

Khoja glowered at Flynn. "Then what do you suggest, Carsen?"

"My best guess? We take our cues from the original story and divide the oil equally between all thirty-eight jars."

"Which would accomplish what, precisely?" Khoja asked.

"Beats me," Flynn said, "but, in my experience, these kind of quests almost always involve tests and puzzles as well as traps, as though they were devised by the world's first and most devious game designers." He cast a disparaging look at the modern-day remnants of the Forty. "The problem with relying on guns and knives and threats all the time is that it takes the place of thinking and learning."

"Do tell," Marjanah said, scowling.

Flynn tapped his skull—which, unlike the thirty-seven jars, was far from empty. "This is how you solve problems, not through brute force or intimidation."

"I don't know." Marjanah drew her knife. "I can think of a few problems I could easily solve with this blade."

For a second, Flynn feared he'd gone too far, but Khoja reached out and placed a restraining hand on her arm, which she grudgingly lowered. Her baleful expression remained in place, however.

"Very well, Carsen," the First of the Forty said. "Demonstrate just how good your brain is."

Good enough to outsmart you, Flynn hoped. *Eventually, in theory . . .*

An empty canteen was drafted into service to transfer the oil from the full jar to the others. Flynn offered the container to Marjanah. "Would you care to do the honors, like your namesake?"

She sneered at the suggestion. "Do I look like a servant girl to you?"

"Just a thought," he said, backing off. "No offense intended."

"Let me help," Shirin volunteered. "And, by the way, that resourceful servant girl is the true hero of the story if you actually pay attention. It's an honor to emulate her."

Working together, the two scholars uncapped the first jar. Still worried about booby traps, Flynn braced himself for an unpleasant surprise, but all they encountered was the distinctive aroma of perfectly preserved sesame oil wafting up from the jar, which was filled almost to the brim. He swept his gaze over the thirty-seven empty jars waiting to be filled and silently groaned in expectation. This was going to be a long and tedious chore.

"What are you waiting for?" Khoja demanded. "Get going."

Carefully, methodically, Flynn and Shirin went about the task, slowly doling out equal measures of the oil to each jar, one after another, round after round. The job was just as time-consuming and monotonous as Flynn had anticipated, so he was actually getting a bit bored by the time the oil was *almost* at the same level in all three-dozen-plus jars. He figured one more canteen of oil into the final jar would do the trick—if there was actually a trick to be done.

"Here goes nothing," he whispered to Shirin. "Hope this wasn't a huge waste of time."

"You're the Librarian," she said. "You know what you're doing."

He appreciated the vote of confidence as he poured one more measure of oil into the final jar, bringing its contents up to same level as in all the other jars, plus or minus a drop or two. He held his breath.

But not for long.

A rumbling noise, as of ancient gears creaking back to life, emanated from beneath the floor of the grotto, as the redistributed weight of the oil tripped some concealed mechanism. Flynn glanced up nervously at the overhanging stalactites, worried he might have been tricked into setting off a long-slumbering deathtrap, but then Shirin shouted and pointed at the first row of jars.

"It's working! Something's happening!"

The first jar sank into the floor of the grotto, revealing a hidden staircase leading down into the interior of the mountain. Flynn, who loved uncovering secret passages almost as much as he loved reading about them, felt a familiar thrill of excitement before remembering that he had probably just brought the Forty one step closer to obtaining the Lamp.

A nicely effective deathtrap might have been better for the world, he thought. *If not for us personally.*

"Bravo, Carsen." Khoja applauded Flynn's efforts. "I should never have doubted you. Perhaps we of the Forty *have* come to rely on blades and bullets too much. I'll have to exercise my brain and think carefully about my wishes once we have a genie at our command."

"*Our* wishes," Marjanah corrected him.

"Naturally," he said, "although rank does have its privileges, as does the chain of command. Remember that, Second of Forty."

"Always," she said. "How could I forget?"

Flynn didn't want to imagine what Khoja, let alone his bloodthirsty Second, might wish for should they acquire the Lamp. Even putting aside the highly alarming possibility that the reputedly fearsome Djinn might gain his freedom and run amuck, the Forty were not the kind of people who were likely to wish for puppies, sunshine, or world peace.

"Let's find out where these stairs lead." Khoja gestured at Flynn and Shirin. "After you, of course."

A flickering golden light radiated from somewhere beyond the foot of the stairs. Flynn was grateful for the extra illumination as the party descended the slablike stone steps toward whatever lay below. Dust and cobwebs indicated that nobody had come this way in a long time, while the fact that the steps were far from well worn suggested that the hidden staircase had never seen a lot of foot traffic, even back in the days of Aladdin and his Lamp. Despite the ever-increasing peril, Flynn had to marvel at this amazing discovery.

"Just think," he said. "We're literally walking in the footsteps of Sinbad and Ali Baba."

Shirin looked equally awed. "How many people today can say they've done that?" She squeezed his hand. "Thank you, Flynn. I mean it."

Iron braziers, mounted on the walls of the cavern, flared to life one after another, guiding them onward. Flynn speculated that the torches had been ignited by the same mechanism he had just triggered upstairs in the grotto. It was even possible that the flames were being fueled by oil tapped from the jars, via some newly activated system of gravity-powered pumps.

"Clever," he murmured. "Very clever."

"Talking to yourself, Librarian?" Marjanah mocked him. "Don't get too cocky. Your usefulness is coming to an end."

Don't remind me, he thought. *One way or another, we're nearing the endgame here.*

Reaching the end of the long stairway, they passed through a short tunnel into another grotto, where they froze in place, transfixed by the startling sight before them, which left Flynn torn between dismay and laughter.

"So, was somebody looking for a lamp?"

19

They'd hit the motherlode. Lamps galore, of all shapes and sizes, filled the torchlit cavern. They crowded roughhewn stone shelves by the dozens, spilling over onto the floor, so that the grotto resembled a lost subterranean lamp market, displaying antique oil lamps from every corner of the ancient world. Just at a glance, Flynn identified a prehistoric rock lamp, possibly of Neolithic origin; a ceremonial temple lamp from third-dynasty Egypt; a simple terra-cotta lamp from classical Greece; a red slip lamp from fourth-century Africa; and even a striking jade lamp from Zhou-Dynasty China. There were simple lamps made of shell or stone, and more ornate lamps exquisitely fashioned from bronze, silver, ivory, horn, alabaster, and other materials. It was a veritable treasury of lamps, albeit thrown together in a rather haphazard fashion. The Librarian in Flynn would have gone for a more organized collection, perhaps arranged chronologically and/or geographically . . . ?

"You've got to hand it to them," Flynn said with grudging admiration. "Where better to hide a lamp than in a hoard of lamps?"

Khoja was less amused by the ploy. "I've had enough of puzzles." He shoved Flynn toward the daunting cornucopia of lamps. "Pick out *the* Lamp, Carsen, and don't try to tell me you can't. You've more than proven that you're up for the job."

Possibly a mistake on my part, Flynn thought. "Thanks, I guess."

This was it. His last chance to deprive the Forty of the Lamp, if his agile brain could make one more leap—and stick the landing.

Taking his time, while sweating profusely beneath his soggy attire, he paced back and forth before the lamps, looking them all over. Polished metal and ceramic glazes gleamed beneath the flickering light of the torches. He started to reach for a simple bowl-shaped lamp to examine it more closely, but guns cocked in protest. Marjanah flashed her knife once more.

"Hands off, Librarian," she warned. "You even try to rub a lamp and you lose a hand, got it?" She watched him suspiciously. "You can look but not touch."

"Heard that before," Flynn muttered, withdrawing his hand. Acutely aware of Marjanah's scrutiny, not to mention her simmering lust for revenge, he contented himself with simply inspecting the lamps visually for the time being. His gaze lingered on a burnished brass lamp of Arabic design that looked just like the magic lamp in the storybooks. Feigning disinterest, he quickly averted his eyes from the lamp and stepped past it, only to spin around abruptly and grab for it.

"Not so fast, Librarian!"

Springing forward like a panther, Marjanah slashed at Flynn's outstretched hands with her knife. He yanked them back barely in time to avoid being nicknamed Stumpy.

"Okay, okay! I got the message!" Flynn retreated from the lamp. "It's all yours."

"At last!" Khoja shoved past Flynn to claim the brass lamp for himself. He held it up to the light, admiring it, while his minions looked on expectantly. "After centuries of striving, Aladdin's Lamp is in our possession, and with it, the power to reshape the world!"

"One more time," Flynn attempted. "I wouldn't rub that if I were you."

"Save your scare tactics for more timid souls." Khoja gazed greedily at the lamp. His muffled voice rang with triumph. "From this moment on, the Genie—and destiny itself—are ours to command!"

Flynn shrugged. "Don't say I didn't warn you."

Heedless of the Librarian's advice, Khoja cradled the lamp against his chest and caressed it with his bare right hand. The brass relic responded at once; a preternatural golden glow seemed to light up the lamp from the inside even as thick green smoke billowed from the lamp's upturned nozzle. The smoke had a harsh, unpleasant odor, but Khoja didn't seem to care.

"Yes!" he exulted. "It's working!" He held the smoking lamp out before him. "Arise, Genie, to greet your master!"

"Master*s*," Marjanah added, gazing raptly at the spectacle. "Plural, you mean."

For the first time in what felt like hours, all eyes were on the lamp instead of Flynn and Shirin. He sidled up to her and whispered in her ear.

"Wait for it."

Dark green smoke gushed from the lamp, which grew brighter and brighter by the moment, its golden radiance shifting to a fiery red. Whimpers of pain and discomfort supplanted Khoja's victory speeches. Sweat beaded on his brow. His face contorted behind the scarves concealing his mouth.

"Something's wrong," he gasped. "It's becoming too hot to handle."

"Let go of it." Marjanah held out her hands. "Pass it to me."

"Never! Not after all I've—"

A scream tore itself from his lungs, cutting off his refusal, as the glow of the lamp escalated from a hellish red to a blinding, white-hot incandescence that blazed like a beacon even through the stifling green smoke fogging the grotto. He shook his arm wildly, trying to fling the blazing lamp away from him, but it was seared to his flesh. His hand started sizzling, and a stomach-turning odor competed with the acrid aroma of the smoke from the lamp.

"It burns!" he shrieked. "It's burning me!"

Marjanah backed away from him, visibly freaked out and uncertain what to do. She held out her knife like a talisman to ward off evil. "Don't just stand there, Badar!" she barked at her final henchman. "Do something!"

"Like what?" The man was equally at a loss, as he stared with a horrified expression on his face. "What do you want me to do, Second of Forty?"

"I don't know, you idiot! Something!"

The disarray among their captors was not lost on Shirin. "This is our chance," she whispered to Flynn before grabbing a random bronze lamp off a shelf and braining Badar with it. The walloped thief staggered and fell to his knees, clutching his head, as Shirin grabbed Flynn by his arm and started to drag him toward the exit. "Come on, Flynn! Let's get out of here!"

"Just a second," he said.

Pulling away from her, much to her consternation, he plunged back into the smoke, letting the unearthly glow of the lamp guide him back to the ornate jade lamp, of Chinese extraction, that he had spotted earlier. He snatched the lamp from its shelf and sprinted back to an understandably confused and frantic Shirin. "Flynn!"

"Okay," he informed her. "*Now* we can go."

Chaos, along with smoke, continued to fill the cave of lamps. Khoja flailed about wildly, screaming in pain and knocking scores of lamps onto the floor, while Marjanah appeared paralyzed with shock and confusion. A seemingly infinite amount of smoke kept spewing from the lamp, but nothing resembling a genie manifested. Tremors began to shake the grotto, spilling more lamps onto the floor. Metal lamps clattered loudly. Glass and ceramic lamps shattered.

"Help!" Khoja shrieked above the tumult. "Somebody help me!"

He lunged toward Marjanah, who panicked and kicked his legs out from under him, so that he tumbled onto the floor along with the other lamps. Seeing Flynn and Shirin make a break for it, she hesitated momentarily, visibly torn between staying with her leader and pursuing the escapees. Still reeling from the blow to his head, Badar looked to her for guidance.

"Second?"

Marjanah made up her mind. "After them! Don't let them get away!"

So much for honor among thieves, Flynn thought. *Figures*.

He and Shirin dashed out of the grotto into the tunnel beyond them, pursued by Marjanah and Badar as well as by the spreading green smoke. He clutched the jade lamp to his chest as they raced back up the stairs toward the cave of jars. No way was he leaving that behind. Tremors rocked the stone steps.

"I don't understand," Shirin said. "What's happening?"

"It's a funny thing," he explained on the run. "The earliest known versions of the Aladdin story have him finding the magic lamp in the exotic, far-off land of *China*. Modern re-tellings tend to overlook that part since one naturally expects an Arabian Nights story to take place in, well, Arabia, not the Far East, but if you go by the original story, Aladdin's Lamp should be Chinese in appearance. As it happens, the Zhou Dynasty, to which this lamp dates back, was roughly contem-poraneous with the reign of King Solomon, who is said to have confined the Djinn in the first place."

"Right! I should have thought of that." Shirin stumbled on the shaking steps, almost losing her balance. "And that other lamp, the one Khoja grabbed . . . ?"

"Another booby trap, apparently, which I may have delib-erately led Khoja to believe was the genuine article." He re-called faking a grab for the brass lamp, then flinched at the memory of Khoja's flesh sizzling before their eyes. "To be fair, I warned him not to rub it."

He held on tightly to the *real* Lamp as the tremors increased in intensity. Dust and debris began to rain down on them, raising the dire possibility of a cave-in, as they scrambled up the steps into the cave of jars. Flynn heard Marjanah and her accomplice chasing after them, shouting in anger as they abandoned Khoja to his fate.

"Run all you want, Librarian!" she shouted. "You're not get-ting away from me!"

Flynn wasn't sure if she was after the jade lamp or just revenge, but he had no intention of granting her either. Or letting her getting anywhere near Shirin.

Stalactites fell from the ceiling, barely missing Flynn and Shirin. They smashed into the ceramic jars, spilling sesame oil onto the quaking floor. Slipping on the unsteady surface,

Shirin tumbled and cried out. Flynn hastily helped her to her feet, only to see her wincing in pain.

"Are you okay?" he asked.

"My ankle," she explained. "I think I twisted it."

"Can you walk?"

"I think so . . . maybe."

Holding onto the Lamp, he threw his other arm around her to help support her weight as they limped awkwardly out of the cave and onto the perilous stone bridge beyond. Shirin's injury slowed them down, decreasing their odds of making it across the bridge before it collapsed—or before Marjanah and Badar caught up with them.

"Forget about me," she urged him. "Take the Lamp and go."

"Not going to happen. Librarians always return what they've borrowed."

They were only halfway across the bridge when Marjanah and Badar emerged from the smoke behind them. She hesitated at the start of the bridge, as though understandably reluctant to venture out onto the narrow span during an earthquake.

"You've gone far enough, Librarian. Bring back that Lamp!"

So she *had* seen him grab the jade lamp on his way out. All the more reason, Flynn reasoned, to get away from her and her hulking henchman if they still could.

"How about we discuss this outside," he shouted, "before this whole place caves in?"

A huge stalactite fell past the bridge, plummeting into the chasm. Bits and pieces of the bridge began to break away, following the stalactite into the bottomless dark. Marjanah stared at the crumbling structure before nodding.

"Point taken, Librarian."

Along with Badar, she hurried onto the bridge as quickly

as she could under the circumstances. Before she could reach
Flynn and Shirin, however, an anguished wail froze her in her
tracks.

"Marjanah!"

Incredibly, Khoja staggered out of the cave of jars, the
decoy lamp still welded to his palm. His facecloth had come
loose, but the swirling green smoke obscured his features
nonetheless. Flynn was amazed that the man was still on
his feet, let alone that he had managed to come this far on
his own. Khoja dropped to his knees in the entrance to the
grotto.

"Help me, Marjanah! Don't leave me!"

Her gaze swung back and forth between Khoja and Flynn.
Cracks snaked across the pathway ahead of her. Another chunk
of bridge plunged into the abyss.

"Second?" Badar asked anxiously.

Her face hardened as she turned her back on her former
leader.

"Call me the First."

The bridge gave way between them and Flynn, creating a
four-foot gap between the Forty and their prey. The whole
structure tottered on the brink of collapse.

"Jump!" she shouted at Badar. "Jump for your life!"

"NOOO!" Khoja shouted. "Don't you dare leave—!"

Flynn didn't wait to see if the remaining thieves made the
leap. Half dragging, half supporting Shirin, he stumbled across
what was left of the bridge and down the tunnel onto the
ledge outside, where he feared the hungry roc would still be
waiting.

Out of the frying pan . . . into a bird's gullet?

It was still light outside. Compared to the smoky, torchlit
gloom of the caverns, the afternoon sun was almost as bright

as the infernal glow of the brass lamp. Blinking at the glare, Flynn dared to hope that the roc had been scared away by the tremors shaking the mountain, but then an ominous shadow fell over the ledge, blotting out the sun, and Flynn looked up to see the roc circling high overhead. Earthquake or not, he doubted the winged monster would let him and Shirin make it back down the side of the mountain without being attacked.

And neither would their human foes.

Any hope that Marjanah and her henchman had been left behind at the bridge was dashed when the last two thieves scurried out of the mountain onto the ledge, only seconds before the tunnel entrance collapsed behind them in a rumble of falling rock. Dusty, disheveled, and out of breath, Marjanah was looking less than her best, but Flynn saw with alarm that she'd managed to hang onto her knife through all her travails, and that her murderous gaze looked just as scary as ever.

Badar didn't look too happy, either. Meaty fingers massaged his skull where Shirin had clobbered him. His other hand gripped a gun.

"Hand over the Lamp," Marjanah ordered, brandishing her favorite weapon. "And maybe I'll only feed one of you to the bird."

As the roc swooped down from the heights, Flynn swiftly assessed the situation, which struck him as the worst story problem ever. Between the roc, the bloodthirsty thieves, and Shirin's twisted ankle, making a successful run for it was about as unlikely as Charlene forgetting to inquire about his receipts, which meant that the only option left to him was the one thing he had been emphatically warned *never* to do.

"Sorry, Judson."

Despite his mentor's warning, Flynn rubbed the Lamp.

"No!" Marjanah cried out. "Don't!"

The roc squawked in alarm as well.

Too late, Flynn thought. *I'm letting this genie out of the bottle.*

A plume of luminous azure smoke, which literally shimmered with its own coruscating radiance, erupted from the Lamp's spout, climbing high above their heads. Cawing in fright, the roc aborted its deadly swoop and flapped away from the rising column of smoke as fast as its enormous wings would carry it.

Flynn was afraid the roc knew what it was doing.

Unlike the harsh green smoke from the decoy lamp, the sparkling blue vapors smelled of exotic spices and incense, as though from a Middle Eastern bazaar, and instead of dispersing they formed a huge pillar of smoke that rapidly solidified into . . .

"The Genie," Shirin gasped. "The Genie from the Lamp."

The giant Djinn towered above them. His dark blue skin had an iridescent sheen that hinted at his supernatural nature. Pointed ears, adorned with golden rings the size of hula hoops, along with a neatly trimmed red beard and mustache, gave him a disturbingly Satanic mien. A gold silk vest and purple harem pants clothed his immense frame, which looked remarkably fit and muscular considering that the Djinn had presumably not gotten any exercise for centuries, leading Flynn to wonder if the Lamp had a fully equipped gym stuffed inside it as well. He worried briefly that the ledge might not be able to support the giant's weight before recalling that, despite appearances, genies were basically creatures of smoke and fire. . . .

"FREE!" the Djinn thundered in a deep, booming voice that made Darth Vader sound like a soprano. His mammoth legs spread wide, he threw out his equally humongous arms, obviously relishing his liberation from the Lamp. Fierce golden eyes flashed like lightning. "FREE TO STRIDE THE WORLD ONCE MORE!"

The Genie's terrifying appearance was enough to convince Marjanah and her cohort that the roc had had the right idea.

"Run!" she shouted at Badar. "Before the Librarian sics that demon on us!"

Fearful of the Genie's wrath, or Flynn's, or some dreadful combination thereof, the surviving bandits bolted from the scene, fleeing in panic down the precarious trail leading to the woods below. Flynn was glad to see them go for more than one reason. Gazing up at the colossal Djinn, he figured he had enough on his plate at the moment without having to deal with a pair of vengeful thieves as well.

"Um, excuse me." Flynn cleared his throat to get the giant's attention. "Paging the former occupant of the Lamp?"

The Djinn deigned to peer down at him. "WHO ART THOU, INSIGNIFICANT MORTAL, WHO NOW HOLDS MY LAMP?"

"I'm the Librarian."

"INDEED?" The Genie sounded slightly more impressed. "VERY WELL, LIBRARIAN, I AM AT THY COMMAND. WHAT WISHES SHALL I GRANT THEE, O SCHOLAR OF THE AGES?"

Plenty of possibilities popped into Flynn's mind, up to and including a trip for two back to the Library, as well as justice for the murder of Leila Hamza back in Baghdad, but he had not entirely forgotten Judson's dire warnings about the Lamp. Inspecting the jade artifact more closely, he noted with dismay that a number of hairline fractures could already be seen in the Lamp's exquisite jade housing. Just as Judson had predicted, years of rubbing the Lamp for wishes had empowered the Genie and compromised the structural integrity of his prison, so that it appeared to be on the verge of breaking into pieces. Who knew how many more wishes it might take to free the Djinn once and for all?

Which, according to Judson, would be a very bad thing.

"SPEAK!" the Genie exhorted Flynn. "WHAT IS THY DESIRE, O LEARNED ONE?"

After all he and Shirin had been through, Flynn *was* sorely tempted to use the Djinn's power to make all their problems go away, but that was a slippery slope that might just put the entire world at the mercy of the vindictive genie. At best, Flynn decided, he could risk only a single wish.

"May you and the Lamp be lost forever!"

"NOOOOO!" the Genie raged, dissolving back into smoke from the bottom up. "MY CURSE UPON THEE, LIBRAR-IAN, AND ALL WHO FOLLOW IN THY FOOTSTEPS, FROM NOW UNTIL THE END OF DAYS!"

The Lamp sucked the vaporizing Djinn in like a shiny jade vacuum cleaner. He clawed frantically at the air, vainly seeking purchase, until his head and shoulders and upper extremities also dissolved and disappeared into the Lamp. Spinning to face the brink of the ledge, Flynn hurled the Lamp (and its furious resident) toward the distant bay. Ordinarily, he could never have thrown it that far, but the power of his wish caused it to arc above the wooded slopes and sandy beaches below before splashing down into the bay, where it disappeared beneath the waves, never to be found again.

Or so Flynn had wished.

"Well, that's that." He washed his hands of the Lamp, which was apparently not going to be added to the Library's collection. "Aladdin's Lamp is lost forever."

"Probably just as well," Shirin said. "All things considered, I think I prefer reading about genies to actually meeting them. Ditto for ghouls, rocs, and the Forty Thieves."

Flynn knew how she felt, even if he would have liked to have claimed the Lamp for the Library. Still, he had kept the Lamp from falling into the wrong hands, which was what really mattered, as Judson would surely agree.

I'm going to call this a win, he thought.

Shirin leaned against him, favoring her injured ankle. She gazed over the enchanted island and the vast sea beyond. "Just one thing," she said. "How exactly are we going to get home?"

Flynn already had an idea about that, lifted straight from the pages of *One Thousand and One Nights*. They just needed to ask themselves what Sinbad would do.

"How do you feel about trying to hitch a ride on a roc?"

20

A vintage candlestick phone from the 1900s, complete with a rotary dial, rang in the Annex. Jenkins picked up the receiver and held it to his ear.

"Mr. Stone?" he said into the transmitter, knowing already who was calling. "How may I help you?"

"We've got this all wrong," Stone replied. *"It's not about the penny at all."*

"Yes, we've already determined that. I'm afraid you're behind the times there. Do you have any new information to impart?"

"You bet I do. Dunphy and I just had a run-in with some seriously brutal competition. They are looking for some kind of lamp."

"A lamp?" A chill ran down Jenkins's spine. Surely it couldn't be. Not after all this time.

Although he was a fine one to talk like that. Some might say the same of him.

"Tell me everything," he said gravely. "Omitting no detail."

Baird was relieved to find both Cassandra *and* Ezekiel waiting for her in the hotel lobby. Approaching them, she caught the tail end of a whispered conversation.

"You 'borrowed' what?" Cassandra said, in a low voice, visibly appalled.

"The world's largest gold nugget," Ezekiel bragged. "All 875 ounces, on display at a local casino." He shrugged off Cassandra's shocked reaction. "Come on. Like I seriously wasn't going to take a run at that?"

"But you are going to put it back where it belongs at some point, aren't you?" Cassandra asked hopefully. "This was just all about the challenge, right?"

He hedged. "Well . . ."

Baird looked to the heavens for strength, but saw only the lobby's opulent trompe l'oeil ceiling, which simulated a bright Arabian sky. This was absolutely the last thing she needed at the moment. She wondered briefly where Ezekiel had stowed the stolen nugget before deciding that she didn't want to know.

"Drop it, both of you," she said. "We can sort this out later, *after* we figure out what we're actually supposed to be looking for here." She looked at Ezekiel. "Cassandra told you about the penny?"

"Yes." A frown replaced his cocky expression. "I can't believe I wasted my time and talent on an ordinary copper penny."

"Actually, it's 97.5 percent zinc," Cassandra volunteered. "Just to be accurate."

"Not really the point now," Baird said, trying to keep the discussion on track. "The Clipping Book sent us here for a reason, and we need to find out what that is."

Cassandra pondered the issue. "You said Stone was hanging out with Dunphy. Maybe he's learned something that might steer us in the right direction?"

"Couldn't hurt to ask." Baird took out her phone, but before she could contact Stone, she received a call from the Library, which she chose to pick up instead. She couldn't help hoping that Jenkins was calling to say that he'd missed something before and that the penny really was magical after all. "Baird here. What's up?"

"I'm afraid I have some rather disturbing news to impart," he said dolefully. *"Is the remainder of the team with you?"*

"All but Stone." Baird switched to speakerphone and beckoned Cassandra and Ezekiel to draw nearer. Passing tourists, intent on their own diversions, ignored the huddled conclave. "He's with Dunphy, enjoying a nice steak dinner, last I heard."

"Would that were the case," Jenkins said, *"but I just heard from Mr. Stone, whose dinner expedition proved to be much more eventful than anticipated . . . in a way that raises a profoundly troubling possibility."*

Baird could tell from his voice that this was serious. "Tell us."

She shared a worried look with the others as Jenkins proceeded to inform them of Stone and Dunphy's narrow escape from unknown assailants intent on a certain lamp.

"A lamp?" Baird asked. "What sort of lamp?"

"Aladdin's Lamp," Jenkins said. *"If my suspicions are correct, and I very much fear they are, we are in pursuit of the fabled magic lamp . . . and the Djinn bound to it."*

"But you told us once that it was never the Genie's Lamp," Cassandra protested. "When we were investigating all that fairy-tale weirdness last year."

"So I did," he admitted, *"because I had every reason to believe that the Lamp had been lost forever, thanks to the ingenuity of Mr. Carsen some years ago."*

"Flynn?" Baird asked. "What's he got to do with this?"

"A good deal, as it happens, although that was before your time, back when he was the sole Librarian."

Going into briefing mode, as was his wont, Jenkins informed them of an old adventure of Flynn's involving Aladdin's Lamp, a fearsome genie, and . . . the Forty Thieves?

"A flying carpet?" Cassandra was unable to control her excitement. "I'm *sooo* jealous!"

"Sounds like he could've used me back then," Ezekiel said. "A bunch of so-called thieves from the olden days would have been no match for the likes of Ezekiel Jones. I would have stolen that Lamp so fast their turbans would have spun."

"Do not underestimate the Forty," Jenkins said. *"We're talking a ruthless criminal organization that has endured for nearly thirteen centuries . . . and it will stop at nothing to obtain the Lamp at long last."*

Baird struggled to process all this new intel. "I've never heard of any of this before. Flynn never said a word to me about it."

"With all due respect, Colonel, Mr. Carsen was flying solo as it were long before you were recruited by the Library. Indeed, he has survived as a Librarian longer than any individual on record. I imagine there are quite a few incidents that he has not had occasion to mention to you."

"Possibly because he never sticks around long enough to do so," Baird said a bit testily. Despite the severity of the present situation, she couldn't help wondering what became of this Shirin Masri woman and how close she and Flynn might have been back in the day. There was still a lot she didn't know about his past exploits, romantic or otherwise—although, to be fair, it was not as though she had told him all her old war stories, either. "But . . . point taken."

She forced herself to stay on mission.

"I don't understand," she said. "If Flynn wished for the Lamp to never again be found, how has it turned up in Vegas ten years later? Hypothetically, that is."

"An excellent question, Colonel," Jenkins replied, *"worthy of further investigation. For now, I can only speculate that the release of wild magic back into the world somehow caused the Lamp to surface again after all these years . . . with potentially dire consequences."*

Baird contemplated the lobby's exotic decor. "Aladdin's Lamp? A casino with an Arabian Nights theme? Could there be a connection there, or is it just a coincidence?"

"In our line of work," Jenkins said, *"coincidence is often merely a failure to recognize invisible forces at work. I suspect we can attribute Mr. Dunphy's current accommodations to the Djinn. Genies are not by nature very imaginative, so where else would he whisk his new master but to a lavish Middle Eastern palace straight out of the* Thousand and One Nights *. . . or a nearby facsimile thereof."*

"Makes sense," Baird said. "This place would be smack in a genie's comfort zone."

"Hey!" Cassandra blurted, struck by an idea. "Along those lines, you don't suppose Morgan le Fay has booked herself into the Excalibur, for old time's sake?"

"Do not even jest about that, Miss Cillian," Jenkins said sternly. Arthurian matters struck far too close to home for him, for reasons Baird well understood. *"We face grievous enough hazards without invoking that duplicitous enchantress."*

"Really?" Ezekiel said skeptically. "Some sad-sack loser is

using a magic lamp to turn his luck around. How bad can things get?"

"Were you not listening before?" Jenkins said. *"Beyond the obvious necessity of keeping the Lamp away from the latest incarnation of the Forty, there is the even more dreadful threat posed by the Djinn himself."*

Ezekiel still looked dubious. "So not a friendly genie, then?"

"Make no mistake, all of you," Jenkins said, so gravely that you could practically hear him frowning over the phone. *"This Djinn is no cheerful cartoon character who sings show tunes while showering you with undeserved riches. He's a malevolent magical menace who has been stuck in solitary confinement inside a lamp for untold ages. Don't expect him to be in a good mood. He's been waiting a long time to get his revenge on the world . . . and the Library, in particular."*

"Thanks for the pep talk," Baird said.

"You're welcome," he replied. *"Anytime."*

21

The crystal scrying bowl had once belonged to the god-kings of ancient Persepolis. Seven rings of archaic cuneiform were inscribed along the outer surface of the bowl, which Jenkins had retrieved from the Divination wing of the Library. Now it rested on the conference table in the Annex, where he filled it with ordinary tap water, before proceeding with a streamlined version of a traditional Bronze Age summoning spell. There was a certain personage he needed to consult at once, and he had neither the time nor the patience to stand on ceremony.

"In the name of Enlil and Astarte and the Eternal Flame, yadda yadda yadda, so on and so forth, et cetera, I summon he who speaks for the Court of Smoke." He waved a perfectly preserved green feather, plucked from the Bird of Paradise, over the bowl in a desultory fashion and blew upon the still, clear water. "Paging the Envoy, ASAP."

To his annoyance, nothing happened at first. Sighing impatiently, he ran his index finger along the rim of the bowl, producing a high-pitched ringing tone that grated on his ears.

"I can keep this up for as long as I have to," he warned the bowl. "Rely on it."

That did the trick. A luminous aura traced the markings on the bowl. The water rippled and Jenkins's reflection was replaced by the visage of another, whose bristling black beard and mustache compensated for a hairless cranium. A single golden earring made the reflection look like that of a stereotypical pirate or, more accurately, a genie. The face on the water bore a distinctly aggrieved expression, just as Jenkins had anticipated.

"Galeas?" the water spoke, addressing Jenkins by a name he had not employed since the fall of Camelot. "How dare you disturb the repose of Dobra of the City of Bronze? Were I not in a merciful mood, I would drown the world in blood for such presumption!"

"Spare me the usual histrionics," Jenkins replied, unimpressed. He knew from experience that this genie's bluster was usually just that. "I require information on a matter of some urgency."

Dobra currently represented the Djinn when it came to dealing with the Library and other mystical realms and factions. Jenkins had last encountered him at a recent high-level Conclave regarding an incipient war between two rival clans of dragons. Dobra had been just as difficult and full of himself then.

"Am I a dog to speak at your command? You overstep yourself, mortal."

"I am anything but mortal, as you well know. And I would not call upon you unless I had good reason to do so."

"Easy for you to say, you monkish relic. I have seven wives to attend to, not to mention assorted concubines."

"All of whom can certainly survive without your attentions for the time it takes to provide me with the answers I seek."

Dobra scoffed. "And why should I comply with your request?"

"The Electrum Covenant. Article twelve, clause b-thirty-two, subsection five-hundred and sixty-seven." Jenkins paused in his citation. "Need I go on?"

The reflection rippled in irritation, but was bound by the terms of the treaty.

"Very well. Make your inquiry, but be swift about it."

Jenkins got straight to the point. "The Lamp of Aladdin. Is it in play again?"

"Oh, that." Dobra suddenly looked more uncomfortable than irritated. He tugged nervously on his beard. "I'm afraid I can neither confirm nor deny anything regarding that topic."

Jenkins was vexed by the evasion. "Come now, Dobra. If the Lamp is back, this is no time for diplomatic persiflage. We can't afford to waste time on games."

Dobra winced at that inconvenient truth. Looking about cautiously, he lowered his voice and appeared to lean forward, so that his reflection in the water acquired a fisheye effect.

"Well, strictly off the record, even if, hypothetically, a certain lamp *were* once more abroad in your world, we of the Djinn would not readily acknowledge such a fact."

"And why is that?" Jenkins asked. "One would think this would fall squarely under your jurisdiction, or have you no interest in policing your own?"

"It is not that simple. The Genie of the Lamp, whose very name none dare utter, has never bowed to the authority of the Court of Smoke. He is a rogue, an outlaw, and a most formidable one at that. We lack the power to constrain him . . . and can take no responsibility for his deeds."

"I see," Jenkins said, as a clearer picture emerged. "In other words, you're all scared to death of this particular black sheep and don't have the nerve to challenge him." He didn't bother to keep the scorn out of his voice. "Have I got that right?"

Dobra got all defensive. "You don't grasp the delicacy of our position."

"Oh, I think I grasp it just fine. I take it then that the Court is wiping its hands of the situation and that we can expect no assistance from you or your fellow Djinn when it comes to coping with your wayward kinsman?"

"Sadly not . . . hypothetically." Dobra raised his voice in a pathetically transparent attempt to save face. "Let it be known, however, that were my hands not tied in this affair, the Nameless One would most assuredly feel the full force of my wrath. A thousand mighty blows would I rain down upon him, so that he would rue the day he crossed Dobra of the City of Bronze. He would plead for mercy, lest I snuff out his divine fire and cast his substance to the four winds. Greatly would he be punished for his transgressions, and well would he tremble before—"

"Oh, yes, I'm sure that's exactly how it would go down," Jenkins said sarcastically. "Anyway, this has been *very* helpful, but I'm afraid that some of us have actual business to attend to."

He poked the feather in the water and stirred Dobra's image away, brusquely dismissing the useless genie without any of the customary formalities. Carefully picking up the bowl, so as to avoid slopping the water onto the table, Jenkins carried it across the Library to the actual Black Hole of Calcutta, where he dumped the water into the abyss with a degree of satisfaction.

Still, he reflected, his aggravating tête-à-tête with Dobra had not been entirely a waste of time. He had managed to confirm two things: that the Genie's Lamp was no longer lost forever, and that the Librarians and their Guardian were on their own where the Forty—and the rogue Djinn—were concerned.

Same old, same old, he thought.

———————

The Pissaro Gallery of Art was one of the few attractions in Las Vegas that didn't come complete with slot machines. Too few tourists knew that the city was home to many fine art galleries and museums and not just to casinos, a regrettable fact that Stone nevertheless hoped to take advantage of. He and Dunphy practically had the gallery to themselves, not that Gus seemed to appreciate the outstanding collection of Neo-Impressionist paintings and drawings currently on display.

"I didn't even get to finish my steak," Dunphy whined, oblivious to the stunning Matisse right in front of him. He squatted on a bench, wallowing in self-pity. "What did I do to deserve this? Ever since I lost my lucky penny, I can't get a break."

"Yeah, about that." Stone tore himself away from admiring an early charcoal study by Seurat to sit down beside Dunphy. "I may know something about that, but we both know that penny isn't really what this is all about. The Lamp is what matters. Aladdin's Lamp."

"Aladdin . . ." Dunphy's jaw dropped "How do you know about . . . I mean, you're joking, right?"

"Not by a long shot," Stone said. Jenkins had briefed him on his suspicions while he and Dunphy were en route to the art gallery. "Don't try to con me, Gus. You're in over your head here, with some seriously dangerous customers hot on your trail. I can't help you unless we level with each other."

"Who are you anyway?" Dunphy stared at Stone in bewilderment. "That woman at the restaurant, she called you a librarian?"

"And she wasn't wrong," Stone said. "I'm a Librarian all right, but not the kind you're thinking of. My colleagues and I track down dangerous magical items . . . like the Lamp."

Gus started sweating, despite the air conditioning. "I swear to God, I have no idea what you're talking about."

"Give me a break, Gus. That didn't work back at the steakhouse, and it's not going to work now. The cat is out of the bag, man. You're not fooling anyone."

Dunphy opened his mouth to issue another denial, but his heart wasn't in it. "You really know about all that?"

"Yep, and so does our new friend Marjanah and her friends. Seems they belong to a secret society that calls itself the Forty. By all accounts, they're a pretty cutthroat bunch, and they have been after the Lamp for a long, long time."

Gus twitched nervously. "How long?"

"A thousand-plus years, give or take a few centuries, so they're not about to give up just because we got away from them once. You need our help, Gus, which means you need to tell us where you stowed the Lamp."

He obviously didn't have the Lamp on him, so Stone had to assume that Dunphy had tucked it away somewhere, far from the trailer that the Forty had already ransacked. *At least we know now what they were looking for,* he thought.

"That's what that woman said, too, aside from the whole slicing me to ribbons thing. How do I know I can trust you?"

" 'Cause I've already saved your butt twice now?" Stone backed off a little, not wanting to press Dunphy too hard just as he was trying to win his trust. "Look, forget about letting me in on where the Lamp is for the moment. Can you at least tell me how exactly you came into possession of it in the first place? To be honest, I'm still a little fuzzy on that point."

"Pure dumb luck," Gus said. "I was hiding out—I mean, vacationing—in Santa Barbara last week when it washed up on the beach, covered in seaweed. I wiped it off, thinking it might be worth something . . . and, poof, this king-sized genie appeared in a puff of smoke, like a magic act on the Strip but ten times bigger and more awesome." He threw out his arms to try to convey how enormous the Djinn was. "I gotta tell you, Jake, I was positively petrified at first. Part of me was afraid I had gone loco, and another part was afraid I hadn't."

"I hear you, man," Stone said. "I've seen some pretty freaky stuff as a Librarian, let me tell you."

"You have no idea." Dunphy shuddered at the memory. "That genie dude is scary as all get-out, and big as a house to boot. I'm not ashamed to admit that I nearly dropped that Lamp right then and there and ran for the hills."

Stone could believe it. "But you didn't."

"Well, genies are all about granting wishes. Everyone knows that, right, so how could I pass up a chance like that? I was down to my last penny anyway, so what did I have to lose? I figured maybe I had finally hit the jackpot at last. A big, scary jackpot, but still . . ."

Stone understood where Gus was coming from. His dad had often lived from paycheck to paycheck, while squandering the family finances on booze and bad bets. Growing up, Stone had seen firsthand how reckless that could make a man—and how hungry for that one big break that would turn everything around.

"So what did you wish for?" he asked.

"For luck, naturally. What else?" Gus seemed genuinely surprised by the question. "Not enough to win every time, 'cause where would be the fun in that, but enough to beat the house and make me a real high roller at last." He smiled wanly at the memory. "It's not like I was actually cheating or anything. I just wanted a bit of an edge, you know?"

"I get it," Stone said. "But here's the thing, Gus. Magic like that is never free, not really. It always comes with a price, and usually a steep one. That's why my friends and I try to keep objects like that Lamp filed away where they can't do any harm . . . to you or anyone else."

Dunphy didn't want to hear it. "But I wasn't hurting anyone."

"Maybe," Stone said, "but what about what the Forty might do if they get control of that Lamp? Do you really think that somebody like Marjanah cares about what her wishes might do to innocent people? And what if the Genie himself ever escapes from the Lamp and runs amok? You said yourself that he's scary as hell and nothing we can risk setting loose on the world. From what I hear, there's a reason he was bound to the Lamp centuries ago. He's not on your side, Gus. In the long run, he's not on anybody's side but his own."

"I don't know," Gus said, waffling. "He's done all right by me so far."

"For now, maybe, but look at all the trouble he's already gotten you in. You really want to live like this, always looking over your shoulder, waiting for the other shoe to drop?" Stone reached out to Dunphy, man to man. "You strike me as a good guy at heart, Gus. Let us take the Lamp off your hands and put it somewhere safe."

"Forget it." Dunphy shook his head emphatically. "That Lamp changed everything for me. No way am I going back to being a loser again."

"Even if it gets you killed?"

22

A private elevator led from the lobby to the penthouse suites on the top floor of Ali Baba's Palace. As she and Ezekiel stepped into the empty elevator, Cassandra fretted that she wasn't dressed expensively enough to pull this off. She kept expecting someone to call her out as a trespasser.

"Remind me why we're doing this again?"

Ezekiel waited for the elevator doors to close before replying. "It only figures that Dunphy would want to keep the Lamp close at hand, so his sweet new digs are the obvious place to look, especially since Stone says that Dunphy isn't about to turn it over to us willingly." He grinned impishly. "I can live with that. Stealing things is always more fun than asking for them."

Unlike Cassandra, he looked perfectly relaxed, as though breaking into a luxury hotel suite was no big deal. If anything, he seemed to be enjoying himself a little too much.

Stands to reason, she thought. "So I guess casino heists are your happy place?"

"That and priceless museum exhibits," he replied. "Those are a treat, too."

Cassandra envied his confidence. "I suppose this *is* kind of exciting," she said, trying to borrow some of his dashing, devil-may-care attitude. "It's like we're in one of those Ocean's Eleven movies."

"Please!" Ezekiel rolled his eyes. "That's the Hollywood version of a heist. If they really wanted to get it right, they should have consulted an actual master thief, such as yours truly." He gave her a devilish wink. "You want to see a true professional at work, get a load of this."

The button panel inside the express elevator featured only two destinations: the lobby and the top floor. Ezekiel produced a blank key card that he slid into a slot in the panel before pushing the upper button, which lit up at his touch. The elevator immediately commenced a smooth ascent.

"See," he bragged, "real thieving requires research and technical expertise, not to mention a huge amount of sheer natural talent." He retrieved the key card and returned it to his pocket. "I spoofed my first electronic skeleton key before I was old enough to boost a car for a joy ride."

Cassandra had to admit that Ezekiel knew what he was doing when it came to hacking into locks and security systems. She made a mental note to thoroughly erase her web history as soon as they got back to the Annex, even as the elevator shot straight to the top of the hotel. A bell chimed to announce their arrival. The elevator doors slid open.

"Voilà!" Ezekiel crowed. "Do I know my way around a security system or not?"

"I never doubted it," she said.

They stepped out of the elevator into a circular waiting area directly beneath the Palace's gilded dome. Radiating from the circle were the penthouse suites themselves, four in all.

Ornate Arabic numerals marked the doors to each suite. Cassandra automatically calculated the dimensions of the accommodations, deducting the space occupied by the elevator shaft, and concluded that each suite was approximately 15.3 percent larger than her modest apartment back in Portland. She could only imagine what the nightly room rate was, including taxes.

"This way," Ezekiel said. "Trust me, I'm just getting warmed up."

He headed straight to the door of Dunphy's suite. A "Do Not Disturb" sign hung from the doorknob, despite the fact that Stone was currently keeping Gus under wraps in the Fine Arts district across town, where the Forty would (hopefully) never think to look for him. Cassandra wondered if maybe Dunphy had hung the sign to keep the housekeeping staff from poking around in the suite when he wasn't around—or had the Forty hung the sign to keep from being interrupted while they searched the place?

"Careful," she warned Ezekiel. "Remember, we're not the only ones looking for the Lamp."

"Yeah, but they're not Ezekiel Jones." He rapped on the door. "Hello? Room service."

No one answered, which eased Cassandra's concerns somewhat. Still, she remained on guard as Ezekiel tried the knob and chuckled in amusement.

"Got to love these state-of-the-art electronic locks. The older, mechanical ones were a bit trickier to pick. Not impossible, mind you, just trickier."

He slid his counterfeit key card into the lock, which clicked from red to green.

"Open sesame," he said with a smirk.

"A literary reference?" Cassandra remarked. "From you?"

Despite being a Librarian, Ezekiel wasn't much of a reader, aside from take-out menus and technical manuals.

"Hey, I've seen the movies, too." He shrugged. "Well, at least the ones that weren't made before I was born."

Moving quickly, so as not to be observed, they slipped quietly into the suite and shut the door behind them.

"Oh, dear," Cassandra said. "Are we too late?"

At first glance, it appeared that the luxurious suite, which, like the rest of Ali Baba's Palace, was decked out in ersatz Arabian Nights splendor, had already been looted. The place was a mess, with discarded clothes strewn across the carpeted floor, closet doors hanging open, empty champagne bottles cluttering coffee tables and counters, dirty glasses piled high in the sink of a built-in bar, rumpled bathroom towels draped over the back of a plush divan, and other evidence of disorder. Something squished beneath Cassandra's feet, and she looked down to see that she had stepped on a cold, greasy pizza crust.

Ick.

"Nah," Ezekiel said, looking around. "I think Dunphy's just a slob." He made a face as he delicately picked a rumpled sock from the floor and gave it a sniff before dropping it in disgust. "I swear, some blokes have no class at all."

Looking closer, Cassandra realized Ezekiel was probably right. Aside from the dirty laundry and other refuse scattered everywhere, the suite had not actually been trashed the way Dunphy's trailer had been. Nobody had sliced open any cushions or emptied the drawers and closets onto the floor, which Cassandra chose to take as a sign that they were one step ahead of the Forty for once.

Taking out her phone, she rang Baird, who was maintaining a lookout downstairs in the lobby. "We're in," she reported. "Are we still clear?"

"So far," Baird replied. *"Nobody matching Stone's description of his assailants has gone anywhere near the penthouse elevator, so you shouldn't be interrupted. I'll let you know if it ever looks like you're expecting company. Any sign of the Lamp yet?"*

Cassandra swept her gaze over the messy suite. "I'll have to get back to you on that."

Wrapping up the call, she saw that Ezekiel was already casing the scene. A loose pile of chips, in high denominations, was gathering dust on an end table. He casually pocketed them on his way to a Persian carpet hanging like a tapestry on a wall.

"They're making this way too bloody easy," he sighed. "I'm almost insulted."

He swept aside the tapestry to expose a concealed wall safe, no doubt provided as a convenience for the big-time gamblers and A-list guests who usually occupied the penthouse. Of course, they probably just stowed cash and jewelry for safe-keeping, not a magic lamp.

"Can you open it?" Cassandra asked.

He shot her an incredulous look. "Okay, now I *am* insulted."

"Sorry." She was starting to wonder why she had even bothered joining Ezekiel on this operation. "Never mind. Do your thing."

"Don't get too comfortable," he said, confidently working the keypad on the safe. "The day I can't crack a Model Nine Glen Reader commercial wall safe is the day I go straight for good . . . so, in other words, never."

The safe chirped cooperatively.

"I rest my case." He tugged open the safe, then blinked in surprise. "Okay, that I was not expecting."

Instead of Aladdin's Lamp, as described by Jenkins, they found only a cheap resin trophy cup of the sort awarded at high school assemblies. Ezekiel squinted at the inscription on the base, reading it aloud.

"*Augustus Dunphy. Voted Mostly Likely to Hit the Jackpot. Class of 1998.*" Ezekiel stared at the trophy in disbelief. "You've got to be kidding me!"

Cassandra groped for an explanation. "Maybe it has . . . sentimental value?"

"But this doesn't make any sense," Ezekiel griped. "Who doesn't store their valuables in a safe if there's one available?"

"Someone who is worried about people like you?" Cassandra suggested. "Or who maybe doesn't trust the casino they're taking to the cleaners?"

"Good point," Ezekiel said. "I know I'd be worried about me, if I wasn't me." He shuddered. "There's a scary thought, *not* being Ezekiel Jones."

Funny, Cassandra thought. *Up until recently, I would have given anything to be someone else.*

But that was before she became a Librarian.

"You might as well tell Baird that we struck out." Ezekiel closed the safe with a little more force than was strictly necessary. He trudged toward the door. "Talk about a waste of time."

"Hang on," she said. "Give me a chance here."

Throwing open her hands to unlock her synesthetic senses, so that hallucinatory diagrams and formulae floated before her eyes, she made a sweep of the suite, going from room to room, calculating the volume of every object that might contain an antique Chinese lamp: vases, cushions, cabinets, ice buckets, and overflowing waste baskets. Spatial geometries spun luminously, accompanied by the taste of raspberry jam

and a melodic ringing in her ears, as she worked her way
through the living room, dining area, and bar, before entering
a mock Arabian bedchamber, complete with an elaborate
canopy bed that looked as though it hadn't been made for
days. Something about the bed captured her attention, although she couldn't quite place it right away. She paused to
examine it more closely.

"What is it?" Ezekiel tagged along behind her. "Are you
onto something?"

"Shh," she hushed him. "Let me concentrate."

She paced the room, computing its angles and comparing
the height of the room to the height of the bed. By her esti-
mation, there was at least an eight-inch gap between the top
of the canopy and the ceiling, which might be large enough
to hide the Lamp.

"Up there," she said, pointing. "There's a space above the
bed that could hold the Lamp, at least if the canopy isn't
stretched too taut." Collapsing her private blackboard, she
hopped onto the messy bed, cringing at the sloppy sheets, and
laid down on her back, peering up at the stretched fabric overhead. Was it just her imagination, or was the canopy sagging
in the middle more than it ought?

No, she decided, *something's up there, weighing it down.*

Her heart racing in excitement, she rolled out of the bed
onto her feet and stood on tippy-toes to try to peer into the
gap, only to find that she was still too short to see over the
top of the canopy without a boost.

"Find me something to stand on!"

A brass tea table rested on the carpet a few feet away from
the bed. As Ezekiel shoved it toward her, pushing aside scattered items of clothing, Cassandra spotted another clue: four
deep indentations in the carpet, as though a heavyish piece

of furniture had once resided there—before Dunphy moved it to use as a stepstool and then tried to put it back where it belonged? The indentations perfectly matched the feet of the tray table.

"This is it!" she exclaimed. "We've found it! Almost."

"You've got to be kidding me," Ezekiel said, sounding positively offended. "He hid a priceless magical relic on top of the bed? Who does that?"

"Got by you, didn't it?" Cassandra couldn't resist puncturing his supercharged ego just a bit. "And I'll bet not even the maids look up there very often."

Scrambling atop the table so that she could just reach the gap, she groped for the Lamp, straining and stretching until she was rewarded by the feel of something hard and polished atop the canopy. Her extended fingertips grazed the surface of the object, which felt oddly warm to the touch.

"I knew it!" she exclaimed. "There's something here, but I can't quite get hold of it."

"Don't worry about that." Ezekiel clambered onto the bed and sliced the canopy open with an icepick, so that the unseen object tumbled into his grasp. "Sorry, mate, looks like you're not getting your damage deposit back."

"Is that it?" Cassandra hopped down onto the floor. "The Lamp?"

"None other." He handed it over to her. "Take a gander."

Eagerly accepting the artifact, she saw at once that the jade lamp fit the description of the Lamp that Flynn had discovered a decade ago. Standing less than foot tall, it resembled a traditional Chinese lantern, but was made of polished jade rather than paper. Stone could surely pin the lamp to a specific dynasty or era, but Cassandra didn't care about that.

"Oh my goodness," she said in awe. "This is really it. Aladdin's Lamp."

"And we're the ones who found it." Ezekiel seemed more enthused about outsmarting Dunphy than recovering a legendary relic from the pages of *The Arabian Nights*. "Who needs magic luck when you can make your own?"

By contrast, Cassandra gazed at the Lamp in wonder, thunderstruck to realize that she was actually holding a genuine piece of history, or mythology, or some combination thereof. On closer inspection, however, she was alarmed to see that the Lamp had seen better days. Hairline cracks and fractures threatened the Lamp's structural integrity, so that even one more wish might allow the Djinn to shatter his prison completely. She noted again, more anxiously than before, how warm the jade lamp felt, as though the caged Djinn was seething impatiently, ready for the day he was finally set loose upon the world. . . .

"This is not good." She cradled the Lamp against her chest, terrified of breaking it. "Not good at all."

"Not to worry," Ezekiel said. "Everything's aces now . . . unless you feel like treating yourself to a wish or two?"

"Don't tempt me!"

Despite her apprehensions regarding the time-worn Lamp, she'd be lying if she didn't admit that she was indeed tempted to command the Djinn to magic away her brain tumor, so that she could live a long and productive life, free of the grapesized time bomb ticking away in her head. But, no, she had learned the hard way that being a Librarian was not about using magic for personal gain. She had no intention of ever making that mistake again, even though she suspected this was going to be an ongoing struggle for her—until her inevitable rendezvous with the Grim Reaper.

"Sorry," Ezekiel said. "Didn't mean to hit a nerve."

"It's fine." She placed the Lamp carefully down on the tea table and took out her phone. "I'm going to let Baird know we've acquired the Lamp."

To her surprise, though, Baird didn't pick up.

"That's funny," Cassandra said. "Why isn't she answering?"

23

"Hello again," Krieger said. "This must be my lucky day."

Baird was staked out in the lobby, keeping watch over the entrance to the penthouse elevator, when Mark Krieger surprised her once more. He strolled across the lobby to greet her, his bandaged arm still in a sling. Obviously glad to see her, he grinned as he approached.

"Hi." She faked a smile even though his timing left something to be desired. "Fancy running into you again."

"I know," he said cheerfully. "What are the odds?"

Cassandra could probably tell you, Baird thought, *if we didn't have more important tasks requiring her talents.*

"This is Vegas," she quipped. "Never count on the odds."

"Good point." He moved in closer. "So, at the risk of pushing my luck, have you had dinner yet?"

I wish, she thought. Ordinarily, she'd have welcomed the invitation, but she had too many other balls in the air at the moment. "Can I take a rain check? I'm afraid I have other plans."

Krieger's smile froze as the warmth drained from his eyes, replaced by a cold, calculating look she recalled from his interrogations of suspected insurgents overseas.

"I'm afraid I'm going to have to insist, Eve."

His gaze shifted to her chest, where an ominous red dot suddenly appeared above her heart. Baird froze, realizing that she was in the sights of a sniper. She glanced around quickly, trying to identify the location of the shooter—or a possible escape route. Her own gun was hidden beneath her jacket, tucked into the waistband of her slacks. As a Guardian, she made it a point to be armed, but the sniper already had the drop on her.

She didn't need to be Cassandra to calculate the sniper's possible positions. Lifting her eyes, she spotted the casino's costumed "camel" mascot up on the mezzanine overlooking the lobby. A ruby-red light, all but unnoticeable unless you were looking for it, came from inside the "camel's" mouth. Unknown eyes were presumably hidden behind the mascot's flaring nostrils. Baird suddenly had the sneaking suspicion that the performer who was usually inside the costume had been replaced by one of the Forty.

Great, she thought, *a seven-foot-tall plush camel has the drop on me.*

"Don't even think of making a break for it," Krieger warned, "or using the crowd for cover. I'm sure you wouldn't want any happy-go-lucky vacationers to end up as collateral damage."

Oh, hell, she thought. "What's this all about, Mark?"

"The Lamp, course. What else?"

———

"I don't understand." Cassandra scanned the crowded lobby for Baird. "Where is she?"

Ezekiel shrugged as he looked around as well. He hung onto the Lamp, which was tucked inside a large Ali Baba shopping bag they'd discovered in Dunphy's suite. "Beats me. Maybe she just skipped out for a few minutes?"

That's what I might do, he thought, *if I got bored enough.*

"No." Cassandra shook her head. "That's not like her." She tried again to call Baird, but without success. "It's no good. It keeps going straight to voice mail." Her brow crinkled in concern. "Something is wrong."

Ezekiel was getting worried, too, although he tried to maintain a breezy attitude just to keep up appearances. "Possibly, but you know Baird. If anybody can handle herself in a tight spot, it's her." That sounded uncharacteristically sappy for him, so he hurried to amend it. "Well, aside from yours truly, of course."

This didn't seem to reassure her. "Can you track her phone by GPS or something?"

"Probably, in a pinch. But maybe Jenkins knows something? Or Stone?"

"I can check," Cassandra said, "but I can't believe that Eve would just ditch us like that, without even alerting us first."

"Yeah," he admitted. "Neither can I."

The bag holding the Lamp suddenly seemed to feel a whole lot heavier. Had they obtained the Lamp, only to lose Baird in the process?

That was not how this heist was supposed to go!

———

"Smile," Krieger said softly to Baird, "while I ensure that everything stays friendly between us."

Baird clenched her fists at her side. "You know, I don't really see that happening."

"Try to keep an open mind, Eve."

He circled around behind her, so as not to block the sight line of the disguised sniper, and discreetly relieved her of her gun and phone, depositing the pistol in the pocket of his jacket. Baird cringed at his touch. Being disarmed at gunpoint was bad enough, but by an old comrade-in-arms, no less? The betrayal stung . . . badly.

"Got to say I'm disappointed in you, Mark. I always thought we were on the same side." She spoke more in sorrow than in anger. "I would have never expected this of you."

"Perhaps that's because you were too focused on the enemy you knew to keep a close enough eye on those around you," he suggested. "Although, to be fair, I'm assuming you hadn't been recruited as a Guardian yet, so you had no idea what the true shape of the world was, or who the real players were."

"But you did?"

"I saw enough overseas to catch on—unexplainable phenomena that convinced me power and treasures beyond imagining awaited those who had the guts to go after them." A scary gleam came into his eyes. "But we should continue this discussion somewhere more comfortable, away from all this nonstop frivolity." He quietly nudged her with his bandaged hand, which easily slipped free of its sling. "To the stairs, please, over there past the elevators."

Baird saw no choice but to comply for the present. The ominous red dot followed her across the lobby. Acting casual, Krieger guided her to a stairwell leading to the upper floors of the hotel. His good hand was tucked in his pocket, gripping the concealed handgun as he fell back behind Baird and paused at the base of the stairs.

"You first," he instructed. "Believe it or not, Eve, I'd just as soon not shoot you, if only for old time's sake, so let's just make this easy for both of us."

Fat chance, she thought, waiting for an opportunity to turn the tables on Krieger. So what if he had her gun? She was no slouch when it came to hand-to-hand combat. *All I need is an opening.*

Too bad Krieger was no amateur, either. He took care to stay a few steps below her as they climbed the stairs, safely out of a range of any sudden strikes on her part. Baird stewed in frustration as he marched her up the stairs, where they were met by a party of giggling young women on their way down to the lobby.

"I don't get it," one of them said. "Why didn't we just wait for the elevator?"

"For the exercise, of course. We've got to burn off all those drinks we still haven't gotten to yet!"

"Oh my god, who knew bachelorette parties were so aerobic?"

Baird briefly considered trying to join the women, or maybe signal that she was in trouble, but then she remembered what Krieger had said earlier about "collateral damage" and decided she couldn't risk it. Biting her tongue, she stepped aside to let the oblivious partyers pass.

Sometimes being the good guy really gets in your way.

"Good call," Krieger said softly, as though reading her mind. He waited for the women to leave them and their laughter to fade away before marching her up three more floors and down a carpeted hallway to the door of an unremarkable hotel room far below the penthouse where Dunphy was staying.

"Here we are," he said, keeping the pocketed gun aimed at her. "Would you mind knocking? My hands are otherwise occupied."

She rapped on the door, wishing it was Krieger's duplicitous face instead. She heard a chain being drawn on the opposite side of the door, which opened just a crack. A sliver of a face peered out warily.

"It's all right, Omar," Krieger stated. "Let us in."

The sentry nodded and admitted them to the room, where Baird found four more hostiles waiting, including a striking Middle Eastern woman who had to be the same individual who was stalking Dunphy and the Lamp, and very possibly the same woman Flynn had clashed with a decade ago.

"Marjanah, I presume?"

The other woman smirked at Baird. "My reputation precedes me, I see. How gratifying."

All the pieces came together to form an ugly picture. Baird turned to face Krieger.

"You're with the Forty."

"The First of the Forty," he clarified, "as I was when I first crossed paths with your friend Flynn Carsen many years ago. Although he knew me as Khoja Hoseyn."

That was a lot for Baird to process. "Major Mark Krieger of the US Army is also the First of the Forty? How does that even happen?"

He made himself comfortable on a Moroccan-style couch, while shrugging off his sling, which appeared to serve no purpose aside from camouflage. He poured himself a glass of water from a pitcher on the coffee table in front of him.

"It was back in Baghdad, after the shock and awe. I was investigating black-market trafficking in looted art and antiquities when I stumbled onto the existence of the Forty. They were in a sorry state, merely a shadow of their former glory and lacking proper leadership, but I saw an opportunity to build them back into something great and finally achieve their ultimate goal: obtaining the Lamp and all the riches and power that entails." A scary gleam came into his eyes. "It was as though destiny had brought me to that dry, dusty hellhole for a reason."

Baird chose to stay standing. This was a side of Krieger that she had never seen before. She couldn't say she cared for it.

"And I came so close," he said bitterly, "only to be tricked by that Librarian just as I was on the verge of obtaining the fabled magic lamp." He clenched his bandaged left hand. "A shame he's AWOL this time around. I still have a score to settle with him."

"As do we all," Marjanah added.

Baird recalled Jenkins's concise recap of Flynn's long-ago Arabian adventure. "Hang on," she said. "Weren't you lost in that cave-in way back when?"

"Buried alive, yes, but alive nonetheless." His expression darkened at the memory. "But I eventually managed to dig myself out of that treacherous cavern, with some assistance from my other right hand, Marjanah, who atoned somewhat for her earlier desertion by returning to look for me . . . eventually."

Marjanah scowled. "That was ten years ago. When are you going to let it go?"

"When I have the Lamp, perhaps." He resumed speaking to Baird. "At the risk of boring you, we eventually made our way off that accursed island, but not without a souvenir or two."

He slowly unwrapped his bandaged hand to reveal a palm that had been badly burned at some point.

From when Flynn tricked him into rubbing the decoy lamp? Baird winced at the sight of the scarred flesh. *But that was at least a decade ago?* She kicked herself for not making the connection earlier, but, really, how could she have suspected that her friend Mark had anything to do with Flynn's encounter with the Forty back in 2006? *If only Flynn wasn't flitting around the world and could have joined us on this case. He might have recognized Krieger even after all these years.*

Krieger displayed his seared hand. "Not very pretty, I know.

Skin grafts repaired the damage years ago, but the scars returned and began throbbing again a little over a week ago." He rescued a bottle of pain pills from his pocket and washed a couple down with a gulp of water. "That's when I began to suspect that the Lamp had resurfaced at last and felt myself drawn to Vegas, where the throbbing only increased in intensity the nearer we drew to this fabricated desert oasis."

How exactly does that work? Baird wondered. No doubt Cassandra would have some theory involving mystical entanglement or some such technobabble, but Baird decided to just chalk it up to the usual magical weirdness. "And that led you to Dunphy?"

"More or less," Krieger said. "You can't expect me to divulge all my tricks at this juncture. Suffice it to say that we were closing in on Dunphy when you and your Librarian friends stuck your noses into our business." He began to rewrap his hand. "Imagine my surprise to discover that you'd enlisted with the competition."

"You think you're surprised?" Baird said. "You don't want to know what I'm thinking right now."

"Oh, I think I can hazard a guess. But it doesn't have to be that way. We made a good team, back in the day. Why not come over to our side? Why waste your talents playing den mother to a pack of loose-cannon Librarians?"

"Because some of us care more about duty and protecting innocents than riches and power," she replied. "I'm a Guardian. You're just a thief with delusions of grandeur."

"An exceptional thief," he corrected her, "and we'll see how delusional I am when the Lamp is ours." He scrutinized her features. "Have you found it yet? Your side has always excelled at that, I'll give you that."

"No idea," she said honestly. "You kidnapped me before I could find out."

"Good point." He took out her phone and inspected it. "Hmm. You have several recent voice mails." He handed the phone to her. "Access them."

"Or?" she asked.

"Consider the threat implied." He bestowed an icy smile upon her. "You've seen me in combat, Eve. You know what I'm capable of if necessary."

"Ditto," she pointed out, but she recognized that Krieger had the upper hand at present. Reluctantly, she keyed in her password and switched the device to speakerphone. *Please*, she thought, *let there not be any vital intel in those messages*.

Any such hopes were dashed as Cassandra's anxious voice emerged from the phone.

"Baird? Eve? We've found the Lamp, but where are you? Why aren't you taking our calls?"

Marjanah plucked the phone from Baird's hand and laid it down on the coffee table so that they could all listen to Cassandra's messages, which were basically more of the same. Krieger grinned triumphantly.

"Congratulations, Eve," he said mockingly. "Clearly, the moral here is to never send a thief to do a Librarian's job." He shot a disparaging glance at Marjanah, who bristled in response. "The trick is making sure they don't get to keep it."

"That's where we come in," Marjanah said. "Taking what we want, when we want it, has always been the way of the Forty, whether by theft . . . or ransom."

Uh-oh, Baird thought. *I don't like where this is going.*

"So it is," Krieger agreed. Reclaiming the phone, he called Cassandra back.

"Hello?" she answered immediately. *"Where have you been, Eve?"*

"I'm afraid Colonel Baird is presently in our custody," Krieger said. "But you can get her back . . . in exchange for the Lamp."

A stunned silence greeted his proposal, before Cassandra finally spoke up again.

"Who is this?"

"An old friend of Eve's who has a vested interest in obtaining the Lamp. I trust we can work out an equitable transaction: your Guardian for the Lamp."

"Let us talk to her," Ezekiel's voice broke into the debate. *"We need proof of life."*

"Fair enough," Krieger said, handing the phone to Baird with a warning. "Watch what you say. Marjanah is not in a good mood."

"You can say that again," the woman said.

Baird recalled that Stone had foiled her earlier. "Cassandra, it's me. Whatever you do, you can't let them get the Lamp. Remember what Jenkins said—"

"That's enough!"

Marjanah snatched the phone from Baird's grip and gave it back to Krieger, who resumed his negotiations.

"There you have it," he said. "Eve is still in good condition, but I can't guarantee that she will stay that way if you don't cooperate. I'll give you an hour to think it over. Expect my call . . . and don't disappoint me."

He hung up on Cassandra and Ezekiel. Baird wanted to think they would listen to her and not surrender the Lamp on her behalf, but she couldn't really imagine any of her Librarians could do that. They weren't soldiers. They didn't understand about acceptable losses.

Which meant it was up to Jenkins to talk sense to them.

24

"Absolutely not," Jenkins said. "We cannot under any circumstances turn over the Lamp to the Forty, no matter the cost."

Stone and the others had returned to the Annex to figure out what to do next. The newly acquired Lamp rested atop the conference table, alongside Cassandra's phone. Attempts to track the Forty's call to its source had not panned out; apparently the thieves had upgraded their technical prowess since the days of Aladdin. Stone had been tempted to bring Dunphy with him for safekeeping, but, as Jenkins had quickly reminded him, the Library did not have visiting hours, nor was it to be used as a safe house for wayward civilians. He would have to hope that Gus would be safe enough now that he was no longer in possession of the Lamp.

"But what about Baird?" Cassandra asked. "We can't just leave her in the hands of the Forty."

"Do not think I say this lightly," Jenkins said, his face grave, "but Colonel Baird would hardly be the first Guardian to put the safety of others before her own. She is a soldier. She willingly chose the risks that arduous duty entails."

"Easy for you to say," Stone protested. "I get that you've

buried generations of Guardians and Librarians, but I'm not about to write off Baird as expendable, not while there's still a chance to save her."

"You misjudge me, Mr. Stone, if you think that this comes at all easily to me, but we must remain cognizant of the larger picture. Do we truly desire the Forty to gain the power of the Lamp? And need I remind you that the Djinn once vowed eternal vengeance on this very Library?"

"The Lamp *is* in pretty bad shape," Cassandra conceded.

"That is putting it mildly." Jenkins called their attention to the hairline cracks riddling its polished jade surface. He had even put down a coaster to protect the table's finish from the unnatural heat of the Lamp. "I would venture to say that it is on the verge of imminent collapse, making it all the more imperative that we keep it away from the reckless hands of the Forty. By all logic, I should be filing the Lamp away in a secure vault at this very moment, preferably with an abundance of bubble wrap and packing peanuts."

"But we're the Librarians," Stone said, "which makes it our call, right?"

They seldom pulled rank on Jenkins, whose exact duties at the Annex were, well, undefined, but Stone was not above doing so where a friend's life was concerned.

"If you insist, sir." Jenkins sighed philosophically. "But I would urge you all to consider the possible consequences of whatever course you choose." He consulted his wristwatch. "In the three minutes, fourteen seconds that remain, that is."

Time was running out as the Forty's deadline approached.

"Maybe we ought to give Baird the benefit to the doubt," Cassandra said, grasping at straws. "This is Eve we're talking about. She probably already has a plan to get away from those thieves."

"Don't call them that," Ezekiel said with surprising heat. "They're not thieves. Kidnappers, robbers, extortionists, maybe, but not thieves. Real thieves don't need to take hostages. . . ."

"*Bandits* is perhaps the better term," Jenkins agreed, "but who am I to second-guess Scheherazade? Regardless, they are a genuine threat to both Colonel Baird and the world at large. We can certainly hope that she will indeed extricate herself from their clutches, but we cannot rely on that. She is indisputably in jeopardy."

Stone scowled at Jenkins, not appreciating his pessimistic attitude. "I thought you didn't want us trading the Lamp for her, so why rub in how much danger she's in?"

"As you noted before, Mr. Stone, the final decision is yours. I merely wish to be certain that you all understand what is truly at stake, whichever course you choose. Wishful thinking is no substitute for an accurate appraisal of one's situation." A hint of melancholy infiltrated his voice. "Trust me when I say I learned that the hard way."

"Doesn't mean we have to give up on Baird, though." Stone directed his words at Cassandra and Ezekiel as well. "Baird has put herself on the line for every one of us more times than I can count. I say we don't write her off without taking a few risks of our own."

"And the Forty?" Jenkins asked. "And the Djinn?"

"We'll roll with the punches as they come," Stone said, "and deal with the Forty *after* we get Baird back. As my pop used to say, sometimes you have to take a few hits before you win the fight."

"That's what Napoleon said, too," Jenkins said. "And Custer."

Stone ignored the mordant remark. This was no time to assume the worst.

"I say saving our friend is job one. What about the rest of you?"

Cassandra wrung her hands, obviously conflicted. "Baird wouldn't want us to lose the Lamp for her sake, but . . ." A look of determination came over her face. "No, I'm not ready to lose her, no matter what she said. We need to do right thing, even if it's not necessarily the smart thing."

Jenkins looked like he wanted to respond to that, but he reconsidered and kept mum.

"Count me in," Ezekiel said. "I don't bargain with kidnappers who call themselves thieves. And I suppose I owe Baird a favor or two. She's a good egg, even if she doesn't always appreciate just how much I bring to this outfit."

"Good enough for me," Stone said. "Sounds like we're all on the same—"

Cassandra's phone rang. Stone picked it up.

"You have a deal," he said grimly. "When and where?"

25

"So this is how you got off that island?"

Baird crouched upon the flying carpet as it carried her and her captors southeast toward Arizona, soaring through the night sky at an altitude of approximately five hundred feet. Krieger and Marjanah sat to her left and right, having left their henchmen behind in Vegas. Apparently, the carpet's carrying capacity was not what it had once been, before that roc had torn it to shreds a decade ago.

"It wasn't as easy as you make it sound." Krieger, whom Baird could no longer think of as *Mark*, watched over her closely despite the fact that the carpet's extreme altitude forestalled any possibility of escape. "Marjanah and I scoured that blasted island for weeks, forever watching out for the roc, before we managed to salvage all the scattered pieces of the carpet and stitch it back together. Those were trying times, especially after we lost the last of our bodyguards to that damn bird." He paused reflectively. "What was his name again?"

Marjanah shrugged. "Does it matter?"

"I suppose not." He patted the intricate pattern of the

carpet, which was now marred by several crude stitches. "Sadly, despite our attempts to mend it, the carpet is still somewhat the worse for wear. It could not guide us directly to the Lamp, as it did before, but was only able to trace it to the right general vicinity, more or less."

Baird could connect the rest of the dots. *We had the Clipping Book,* she thought. *They had the crippled carpet. Both of which pointed us toward Vegas.*

A cool dry wind blew against her face as the carpet cruised over seemingly endless vistas of grass and sagebrush. Even after all she had experienced as a Guardian, Baird found it hard to believe that she was actually riding a flying carpet across the sky. Cassandra was going to be sorry she missed this, aside from the whole taken-hostage-by-ruthless-criminals thing.

"One thing I still don't get," Baird said. "How come you didn't search Dunphy's penthouse like you did his trailer?"

Cassandra had not mentioned anything about the penthouse being ransacked when she and Ezekiel apparently found the Lamp there.

"Oh, we did," Krieger assured her, "just a good deal more discreetly. Tossing a run-down trailer in some miserable dump of a trailer park is one thing. Breaking into a luxury suite on the richest part of the Strip is something else altogether. That requires a more subtle touch in order to avoid attracting unwelcome attention."

"The Forty has always operated in the shadows," Marjanah added. "We came and went without notice, leaving no trace of our presence behind."

"But you didn't find the Lamp," Baird said. "Did you?"

Marjanah shot Baird a dirty look. "No," she confessed.

Because you didn't have Cassandra or Ezekiel, Baird thought, proud of her Librarians. She enjoyed the other woman's sullen expression. *Take that, Second of the Forty. Sucks to come up short all the time.*

"Not that it matters," Krieger said. "Soon the Lamp will be ours again."

Not if my team has anything to say about it, Baird thought. "I don't suppose there's any point in trying to convince you that summoning the Djinn is a truly terrible idea?"

"Like Carsen did years ago?" Krieger contemplated his injured hand, which, along with his other hand, was now protected by a thick leather glove. "I've waited too long, endured too much, to give up now."

"We both have," Marjanah said, "and the Forty has waited even longer. But now at last we will achieve the honor and glory we have been denied for centuries."

"I think we have very different definitions of *honor.*" Baird looked at Krieger, still stung by his treachery. "Dare I ask what exactly you have in mind if and when you get your double-crossing hands on the Lamp?"

"Not if, *when,*" he declared. "And to begin with, a preemptive strike against the Library to prevent you and yours from ever interfering with our enterprises again." He smiled mirthlessly. "Considering how Carsen foiled him before, I can only imagine that the Djinn will be happy to oblige."

That was all too likely, Baird feared, given what Jenkins had said about how angry and vindictive the Djinn was known to be. Her body tensed as the carpet, traveling at hundreds of miles an hour, carried them past the sagebrush to the woods and forests beyond, skimming above the tops of towering ponderosa pines as the time and place of the exchange grew nearer. The sun was just beginning to rise as the ground below dropped away sharply. A vast, red-walled chasm, many miles across, stretched before her, cutting deeply into the earth. Sunlight lit up vast cliffs, pillars, and plateaus. Bands of colored rock, pressed together like the pages of a book, testified to millions of years of geological history.

Dawn had come to the Grand Canyon.

———

White light, accompanied by the crackle of eldritch lightning, spilled from the doorway of a shuttered park rangers' station as Stone and his fellow Librarians burst through the door onto a remote lookout point at the North Rim of the Grand Canyon, accessible only by a challenging dirt trail. Sunrise was approaching fast, but Stone took a moment to survey his new surroundings. It was the off-season, and this stretch of the Canyon had been abandoned by the tourists who routinely flocked to the more popular South Rim several miles away. The Forty had clearly put some thought into picking the site for the exchange. They were unlikely to be interrupted here, although Stone wondered how the kidnappers intended to reach the out-of-the way site without the aid of a magical Back Door.

"No sign of the bad guys," Ezekiel said, looking around. "Looks like we're the first ones here." He walked to the edge of the rim and peered over the precipice. "Whoa. That's a long way down."

"Roughly a mile." Stone joined him at the edge. He'd visited the Grand Canyon with his family years ago and later studied the art and history of the various Native American tribes populating the region. He cradled the Lamp against his chest, troubled by its warmth. "See what looks like a tiny little stream way down there at the bottom of the canyon? That's actually the Colorado River viewed from a mile up."

He hoped the Forty weren't going to be arriving by boat. It would be a long hike down to reach them.

No, he reminded himself, *they told us to meet them at this lookout point at sunrise, and they're going to be out to make the exchange as swiftly as possible. They want the Lamp almost as much as we want we want Baird back.*

"Are we absolutely sure we're doing the right thing?" Cassandra asked, hugging herself to combat the early-morning chill. "You heard what Jenkins said. . . ."

Jenkins remained back at the Annex, battening down the hatches (mystically and otherwise) just in case everything went pear-shaped and the Djinn got loose. *Probably a reasonable precaution*, Stone thought. *This could all go wrong very easily.*

"Not that I don't want to save Baird," Cassandra said. "It's just that there's a lot at stake."

"Too late to second-guess ourselves now," Stone said. "We've just got to roll the dice and hope we don't crap out when it matters."

Cassandra smiled wanly. "Good thing I've still got Dunphy's lucky penny on me then."

"Couldn't hurt," Stone said. "We can use all the luck we can get."

Ezekiel snorted. "I keep telling you, mates. I make my own luck."

"I'm going to hold you to that," Stone said, "for everybody's sake."

Turning their backs to the canyon, they gazed expectantly at the rugged trail leading up to the North Rim by way of a thick pine forest. Stone listened in vain for the sound of anyone drawing near.

"Where are they?" Cassandra asked anxiously. "What are they waiting for?"

Stone tried not to get too worried yet. "*Sunrise* is not an exact meeting time."

"Sure it is." Cassandra sounded perplexed by his statement. She waved her hands before her eyes, peering up at some invisible orrery generated by her own remarkable brain. "This time of year, at this segment of the equator, allowing for the axial tilt of the Earth and our relative distance from the sun, sunrise should be at exactly . . . 6:19 a.m." She collapsed her imaginary calculator. "Mountain Standard Time, naturally."

Stone cracked a smile, despite the tense situation. "I'm just saying that the Forty may not be quite as precise as you are."

Few people were.

He peeked at his wristwatch. It was 6:22.

Keep cool, he thought. *But those scumbags had better not be making us sweat on purpose.*

Ezekiel turned away from the fruitless vigil to check out the view of the canyon once more. He froze and pointed out over the chasm. "Um, look sharp, mates. We have incoming . . . arriving by air."

A helicopter?

Puzzled because he didn't hear any whirring rotors, Stone spun around to behold an actual *flying carpet* descending toward them, as though straight from *The Arabian Nights*.

"Okay," he muttered, "I should've seen this coming."

Cassandra was agog with excitement. "Oh my God, do you see that?"

"Eyes on the prize, Cassie," Stone reminded her. "Remember why we're here."

She nodded, coming back down to Earth. "Right. Sorry."

"No problem. It's pretty amazing, I've got to admit."

The carpet slowed as it approached, bearing Eve, Marjanah, and . . . Baird's old army buddy?

"What the hell?" Stone realized that he had missed a twist or two. He could only guess at the full story, but he'd bet the farm that Baird had been double-crossed somehow—and that her "accidental" meeting with her friend had been anything but. *Explains how the Forty managed to get the drop on her*, he thought. *Baird probably never saw it coming.*

The carpet leveled off above the canyon, hovering parallel to the edge of the cliff, so that only a twelve-foot gap separated the Librarians from Baird and the bad guys. Marjanah gave Stone the evil eye; apparently she had not gotten over that incident with the black pepper.

"All right," Stone called out. "We're here, just like you asked. Let's get on with this."

"I commend your punctuality, Mr. Stone," the man on the carpet said. "And I'm just as eager to conclude this transaction."

"And you are?" Ezekiel asked.

"Major Mark Krieger," Baird said quickly, before anyone could stop her. "AKA the First of the Forty."

"Silence!" Marjanah snapped. "Hold your tongue, witch, or I'll cut it out!"

"Curb your temper," Krieger addressed his bloodthirsty lieutenant. "I'm sure the Librarians don't wish to pay for damaged merchandise. And as for divulging my identity . . . well, no harm done. Once we obtain the Lamp, we can become whoever we want to be."

Rising to his feet atop the floating carpet, he yanked Baird upright as well.

"Toss me the Lamp," he ordered, "or Eve makes a one-way trip to the bottom of the canyon."

"Don't do it, Stone!" Baird shouted. "You can't let them win!"

"I know," Stone said, "but we're not about to lose you."

Scowling, he lobbed the Lamp over to Krieger, who caught it easily. The treacherous major barked in Arabic at the carpet, which glided up and away from the cliff, widening the gap between the Librarians and Baird to about twenty feet or so.

"Hey!" Stone yelled. "We had a deal."

"Which I fully intend to honor," Krieger called back, "*after* I ascertain that this is the genuine article and not another trick."

Stone noted belatedly that thick leather gloves protected the man's hands, while the canyon itself offered a convenient way to dispose of a booby-trapped lamp should the need arise. He suspected that such considerations had factored into the selection of the meeting site, along with the way the canyon lent itself to a speedy escape by magic carpet. Even now, there was no way for Stone and the others to reach Baird or come to her aid, nor could they readily pursue the carpet if it flew away with her.

"Make it quick," Stone snarled.

"That was always my intention."

Krieger examined the jade artifact carefully before holding it up for Marjanah's inspection. "What do you think? Is this the Lamp you remember?"

"That was ten years ago," she said, squinting at the Lamp, "and there was a mountain coming down on us, and a hungry roc, but . . . yes, I believe that's it." An avaricious glint shone in her eyes. "If you'd like, I could try rubbing it first."

Krieger scoffed at the offer. "I think I'll reserve that privilege for myself. It's not that I don't trust you, of course, but . . ."

"One more time, Krieger," Baird said. "Don't do this."

"You're wasting your breath, Eve." He took a deep breath, betraying only the slightest trace of trepidation, before rubbing the Lamp, just as Flynn had done a decade ago. "Arise, O Genie of the Lamp!"

The effect was instantaneous, as though the imprisoned Djinn couldn't wait to escape the confines of the ancient Lamp. Rising upon a billowing plume of luminous azure smoke, the Djinn towered above the carpet, his immense feet resting solidly upon empty air. Stone's jaw dropped at the sight of the Djinn in all his terrible majesty; the blue-skinned giant made even a minotaur or the Big Bad Wolf seem like pipsqueaks by comparison.

"FREE!" the Djinn boomed. "FREE TO SEEK VENGANCE UPON THE WORLD!"

"All in good time." Krieger raised his voice to address the looming genie. "I hold your Lamp now!"

The Djinn peered down at him. A morning breeze rippled the surface of the genie's iridescent blue substance. Blazing golden eyes gazed upon the awestruck mortals.

"SO I SEE. AND WHO ART THOU, WHO IS CARRIED ALOFT BY THE VERY CARPET OF SOLOMON?"

"The First of the Forty," Krieger declared, "and your new master!"

The Djinn scowled, as though vexed by the reminder of his bondage, but offered a grudging salaam to Krieger, dipping his massive head in respect and placing a log-sized finger against his brow.

"VERY WELL, O CHIEF OF THIEVES. WHAT IS THY FIRST COMMAND?"

Krieger beamed in triumph. "To begin with—"

With all eyes on the Djinn, Baird drove her elbow into

Krieger's throat, cutting him off midsentence. He staggered backward, clutching his throat. His mouth opened, but no words emerged, only a strangled croak.

His larynx, Stone realized. *She crushed his larynx so he can't make a wish.*

Marjanah raced to aid him, but not before Baird kicked his legs out from beneath him. Still croaking, he toppled onto the carpet, and the Lamp slipped from his grasp. Marjanah abruptly changed course and dived for the Lamp instead.

"No one touch it! It's mine!"

Looming above, the Djinn laughed scornfully at the tussle on the carpet, declining to intervene in the absence of an expressed wish. His thundering laughter roiled the air and caused rocks and pebbles to tumble down the side of the cliff.

"WHAT SPLENDID SPORT! SCURRY, LITTLE MORTALS, WHILE YOU CAN!"

The commotion rocked the carpet, causing the Lamp to bounce randomly across the bucking rug. Eluding Marjanah, it came dangerously close to the fraying edge of the carpet. Stone grimaced at the thought of the Lamp tumbling down into the canyon where anyone could find it, maybe even Krieger and Marjanah once they regained control of the situation and the carpet.

"Baird!" he shouted. "Over here!"

"No!" Marjanah shrieked, drawing her blade. "It belongs to the Forty."

She pounced, about to claim the Lamp for her own, when Baird rushed forward and kicked it off the carpet toward the Librarians.

"Catch!" she shouted.

26

The Lamp arced across the gap between the carpet and the rim of the canyon, descending toward the lookout point. Angry winds, stirred up by the Djinn, buffeted the Lamp as Marjanah shouted frantically at the carpet in Arabic, causing it to dive after the Lamp. Clearly, she was not letting the magical artifact get away from her so easily.

"Spread out!" Stone shouted. "Somebody catch that Lamp!"

I'll try, Cassandra thought, although hand-eye coordination had never been her forte. She couldn't remember the last time she'd managed to catch a book or scroll tossed to her from the Library's mezzanine, let alone a tumbling magic lamp.

But perhaps it had never truly mattered as much before. . . .

As Stone and Ezekiel darted back and forth atop the Rim, trying to eyeball where exactly the Lamp would fall, Cassandra resorted to her brain instead. Her hands spread out before her eyes as she murmured to herself.

"Given the weight of the Lamp and the angle of descent, allowing for variations in wind velocity and direction, as well as the estimated force of the kick, and any potential obstacles . . ." Her head turned toward the ranger's station a few yards away. "There!"

She sprinted toward the log cabin, arriving at the base of the south wall just as the Lamp struck the slanted roof of the station and ricocheted off it. Cassandra threw out her hands to catch it.

Please, she thought, *don't let me mess this up*.

The Lamp landed squarely in her open palms.

"Yes!" she squealed. "I got it!"

Her momentary triumph was quickly dampened, however, when she saw the sorry shape the Lamp was in, now that the Djinn had been released once more. Krieger's summons had been the last straw as far as the moribund Lamp was concerned; it was literally falling apart in her hands. Golden light, as bright as the harsh Arabian sun, escaped the widening cracks zigzagging across the disintegrating surface of the Lamp, which was growing ever hotter to the touch. Wafer-thin shards of jade flaked off the Lamp to land at her feet at a rapidly accelerating rate, like a landslide gaining speed and momentum. The legendary Lamp would soon be history.

Returning the Djinn to the Lamp was no longer an option, Cassandra realized. At best, there was only time enough to make one last wish before the Djinn was finally free to lash out at the entire world, up to and including the Library.

"YES! YES!" the terrifying blue giant exulted. "MY PRISON WALLS CRUMBLE AT LAST! AFTER UNTOLD AGES OF BITTER CAPTIVITY AND BONDAGE, MY FREEDOM IS AT HAND! NOW WILL THE WORLD TREMBLE BEFORE MY WRATH, NOW WILL ALL MANKIND SUFFER AS I HAVE SUFFERED . . . UNTIL THE VERY END OF ETERNITY!"

"Not yet." Cassandra struggled to hold the splintering Lamp together for just a few more moments. "You're not free yet."

One more wish.

For a fraction of a heartbeat, she was tempted once more to wish her tumor away, but, as ever, the greater good took precedent.

"Genie!" she shouted above the increasingly violent winds. "I wish you . . . an unlimited imagination!"

"WHAT?" He peered down at Cassandra in surprise. "WHAT DIDST THOU SAY?"

His incandescent eyes blazed brighter than before as her wish took effect.

"BY THE ETERNAL FLAME, I CAN SEE IT NOW! MY MIND IS AFIRE WITH POSSIBILITY! A THOU-SAND AND ONE POTENTIALS IGNITE MY IMAGI-NATION . . . NAY, A MILLION . . . A HUNDRED MILLION . . . A HUNDRED HUNDRED MILLION. . . ."

He clutched his skull, as though trying to hold in all the new ideas flooding his mind. The very atmosphere reflected his turmoil, growing wilder and more turbulent by the second. Storm clouds gathered overhead. Hot desert winds blew in every direction, so that Cassandra and the other Librari-ans were driven backward atop the North Rim, shielding their faces against the wind and grit. Dust devils swirled around the Djinn like random ideas bursting from his being. He tot-tered alarmingly above the canyon and the carpet as though drunk on his own feverish imaginings.

"MY THOUGHTS RACE EVER FASTER AND FASTER, LIKE A HERD OF WILD STALLIONS STAMPEDING BEYOND MY CONTROL!"

Cassandra knew the feeling. This was like one of her melt-downs, taken to the *n*th degree.

Not so easy to handle, is it?

Dismay contorted his face as he struggled to rein in his newly unbridled imagination, which was already coupled with nearly limitless power. "NO! IT IS TOO MUCH! I CANNOT CHOOSE. I CAN DO ANYTHING, BE ANYTHING, GO ANYWHERE. . . ."

His iridescent flesh began to boil and steam away as he was literally torn in a billion directions at once. Expanding infinitely, the Djinn simultaneously grew ever thinner and less substantial until nothing remained but a few faint wisps of smoke that swiftly dispersed upon the raging winds, even as the Lamp crumbled to pieces in Cassandra's grasp, leaving nothing but fragile shards and splinters behind.

And that's why genies don't have much in the way of imaginations, Cassandra realized. *They can't handle them.*

She wiped her hands of the last bits and pieces of the Lamp.

———

The Djinn's stormy evaporation whipped up the winds accosting the carpet, whose edges curled upward to try to hold onto its imperiled passengers. Baird appreciated the effort, but would have preferred seatbelts or a proper aerial extraction. She dropped facedown onto the pitching carpet to keep from being thrown from the rug.

Smart girl, Cassandra, Baird thought. *Hope I live to congratulate you.*

Marjanah, who had dived unsuccessfully for the Lamp only moments before, stayed down as well, but Krieger did the opposite. Scrambling to his feet, despite the choppy weather, he snatched desperately at the dissipating wisps of genie, which literally slipped between his fingers, leaving him empty-handed. Crazed eyes bulged from their sockets. An anguished croak escaped his lips.

"Get down, you fool!" Marjanah snapped at Krieger. "Have you gone mad?"

Possibly, Baird thought. *Not that he was apparently all that sane to begin with.*

Paying no heed to his cohort's furious exhortations, or the violent atmospheric conditions, the First of the Forty ranted silently while shaking his gloved fist at the vanished Djinn. An angry gust of wind nearly capsized the carpet, and he went tumbling over the edge, unable to scream even as he plummeted to his doom more than a mile below. Despite everything, Baird winced at the thought of her onetime friend and comrade crashing onto the rocks and rapids at the bottom of the Canyon.

Damn you, Krieger. You didn't have to check out like this.

If the tragic loss of her leader affected Marjanah, it was impossible to tell. Intent on her own survival, she stabbed her dagger into the carpet to anchor herself to it, holding onto the hilt with both hands as she lay prone atop the storm-tossed rug.

Not a bad idea, actually.

Wriggling forward on her stomach, Baird grabbed onto the knife as well, clasping her hands over Marjanah's and hanging on for dear life. She had no intention of joining Krieger at the bottom of the canyon, not if she could help it.

"Let go, Guardian!" Marjanah spat. "You ruined everything, you and your friends!"

"Ruined . . . saved. Depends on your perspective."

The weather was only slowly settling down in the wake of the Djinn's departure, causing the carpet to waft about without direction. Calling upon her basic Arabic, which she'd picked up on various tours of duty in the Middle East, Baird shouted at the carpet.

"Take us down to my friends! Gently!"

"No! Don't listen to her!" Marjanah commanded, her accent slightly better than Baird's. "Take me away from my enemies!"

"Belay that last order! Take us down!"

"No, carry me away from these wretched Librarians!"

The carpet jerked back and forth beneath them as the women fought verbally for control, shouting over each other. Its tassels vibrated in confusion.

"Stop fighting me," Baird yelled. "You're going to get us both killed!"

"And place my fate in your hands? Never!"

A loud ripping sound hushed them both.

Oh, crap, Baird thought.

To her horror, the conflicted carpet tore in half across its width, yanking the women away from each other. Baird tried to hang onto Marjanah's hand, just to hold the two halves of the carpet together, but the severed fragments were straining too hard to go their own ways. Baird lost her grip on the other woman's hand as the bisected carpet dived toward opposite sides of the canyon.

Not the safest way to fly, she concluded. *Give me a plain old chopper any day.*

Forgetting about Marjanah for the moment, due to her own heart-pounding predicament, Baird held on tightly to the ragged edge of the carpet fragment as it descended at a roughly forty-five degree angle toward the lookout point where her friends were beckoning and calling out to her.

"Baird!" Stone shouted. "Hurry! You're losing altitude!"

Tell me something I don't know, she thought. Lacking Cassandra's computer brain, Baird figured it was even money as to whether she made it to the North Rim—or crashed into the rocky red walls of the canyon.

"Come on," she urged the faltering carpet. "You can do it. Just a few yards more."

It was like landing a fighter jet on the deck of an aircraft carrier, except that ejecting was not an option. Coming in fast, and at far too steep an angle, the carpet looked as though it was going to slam into the cliff instead, but, with a final burst of power, it pulled up just enough to be able to clear the canyon wall after all. Gasping in relief, Baird still worried about how rough a landing she was in for.

"Watch out!" Stone shouted to Cassandra and Ezekiel. "Here she comes!"

The Librarians scrambled out of the way, clearing a path for the incoming carpet. Bracing herself for impact, Baird was startled when the half-sized fragment suddenly wrapped itself around her like a cocoon. Rolled up tightly inside the rug, like Cleopatra before Caesar, she hit the top of the North Rim and skidded across several yards of dirt and gravel before finally coming to a stop. Her heart racing, she gasped out loud, then conducted a quick bodily inventory. She was going to be bruised all over, but nothing felt broken, while the overlapping layers of carpet had apparently spared her from the mother of all skid burns.

Bottom line: she was alive.

How about that? Guess wonders never do cease.

The exhausted carpet turned into dead weight. Footsteps stampeded toward her, and she heard the Librarians shouting words of encouragement. "Hang on!" Stone hollered. "We'll get you out of there!"

Within moments, they had unrolled her from the carpet and helped her to her feet. Sore and out of breath, she remained focused on the mission.

"Marjanah?" she asked.

"See for yourself," Ezekiel said, nodding toward the canyon. "It's not looking good for her."

Baird saw what he meant. Trying to make for the far side of the canyon, at least ten miles away, Marjanah and her half of the carpet had lost too much altitude already. Veering away from the cliff face at the last minute, the carpet spiraled down toward the Colorado River, dropping out of sight. Baird and the others rushed to the edge of the cliff just in time to see the carpet and its bloodthirsty rider splash down into the river and be washed away almost instantly.

"You think she made it?" Cassandra asked.

"Hard to tell from this height," Stone said. "Not without binoculars."

"Doesn't matter." Baird stepped away from the ledge. "No way is she—or the rest of the Forty—ever getting their hands on the Lamp or the Genie now. You guys took care of that."

"And without losing you," Cassandra said. "Thank goodness!"

"Works for me," Baird decided. "Good job, team."

"Was there ever any doubt?" Ezekiel said. "You had Ezekiel Jones on your side."

"Don't remind me." Stone started toward the ranger's station. "So, back to the Library now?"

"Maybe a quick detour first," Cassandra said. "We still have one last errand to run."

27

"So the Lamp is gone for good?"

They'd found Dunphy at an all-night diner on Carson Avenue, feeding five-dollar bills into one of the ubiquitous slot machines. Given the rate he was going through them, as well as the size of the tip he had left for a *very* attractive waitress, Stone imagined that Gus would blow through what remained of his winnings in no time at all.

"I'm afraid so," Stone said. They had tried to scoop up the broken shards, just to be safe, but the fragile pieces had pretty much crumbled to powder at the slightest touch. "On the bright side, you're not going to have as many sore losers and secret societies chasing you anymore."

"You got a point there," Gus admitted. "I'm not going to miss that part, for sure."

With any luck, the Forty would cash in their chips and hightail it back to Baghdad now that their centuries-long quest for the Lamp had finally ended in failure. Certainly, they no longer had any reason to go after Dunphy, who was taking the loss of the Lamp much better than Stone had expected.

"You okay with this?" he asked.

Gus shrugged philosophically. "No winning streak lasts forever, but at least I got to be a real high roller for a while." He smiled at the memory. "Although, to be honest, gambling wasn't quite as exciting when you knew you were always going to come out ahead. Where's the thrill in that?"

"You learn anything else from this experience?" Baird asked. "About relying on luck perhaps?"

"Oh, sure! Lady Luck is fickle, but when you crap out you just gotta keep on gambling until your luck changes again."

"Not exactly the lesson I had in mind," Baird said dryly, "but . . . whatever."

"Which reminds me." Cassandra fished a copper (well, mostly zinc) coin out of her purse. "I think I have something that belongs to you."

"My lucky penny!" Gus beamed with joy. "Now I *know* I'm going to win big again . . . one of these days."

Stone sighed and shook his head.

"Take care of yourself, Gus."

"One half of King Solomon's Carpet, over to you."

Baird dropped her end of the rolled-up carpet fragment onto the Annex floor in front of Jenkins. Stone did the same.

"Sorry about the skid marks," she added.

Jenkins shrugged. "Few items in the Library are still in mint condition, Colonel, including yours truly."

"I don't know," she said. "Looks to me like you're holding up pretty well, considering the mileage."

Jenkins arched an eyebrow. "I'll strive to take that remark in the spirit with which it was intended." He nudged the inanimate carpet with his shoe. "An unexpected addition to the

Library's collection. I'll have to find precisely the right home for it. Perhaps the Enchanted Textiles wing, cross-referenced to the Middle Eastern Studies section? Who knows? Someday we may even be able to acquire the other half of the carpet . . . in due time."

Baird wasn't inclined to worry about that now. A hot bath and a good night's sleep were calling her name. "So that's it then? The Djinn is gone forever?"

"Scattered to the four winds, as I understand it," Jenkins said. "I believe we can safely strike Aladdin's Lamp from the list of loose magical objects once more. At some point, I suppose, I should inform the Court of Smoke of the outcome of your investigation . . . if and when I get around to it."

"I leave that to your discretion." Baird's stomach growled, reminding her that she hadn't eaten in hours. "Say, are there still any of those doughnuts left?"

" 'Fraid not," Ezekiel said, "but I might be able to remedy that situation."

"Don't even think about it." Baird decided a bath could wait until they had all properly celebrated their victory. "Stone, Cassandra, Ezekiel, Jenkins, you up for a doughnut run? My treat."

"Don't have to twist my arm," Stone said.

"Mine, either," Cassandra said, "especially if we're talking the ones with all the sprinkles on top."

"I imagine shelving King Solomon's Carpet can be put off until tomorrow," Jenkins said. "Far be it from me to let the defeat of the Forty—and the dissolution of a mad Djinn—go unfêted."

"What he said," Ezekiel said. "Although you're not really going to pay for the doughnuts, are you?"

"Watch me."

It was a shame that Flynn was nowhere to be found. Baird couldn't wait to tell him how she and her Librarians had finished one of his old cases for him, ten years after the fact.

The next time I see him, that is.

ABOUT THE AUTHOR

GREG COX is the *New York Times* bestselling author of numerous books and stories. He has also written the official movie novelizations of *Godzilla, Man of Steel, The Dark Knight Rises, Ghost Rider, Daredevil, Death Defying Acts*, and the first three Underworld movies, as well as books and stories based on such popular series as *Alias, Buffy the Vampire Slayer, CSI: Crime Scene Investigation, Farscape, The 4400, Leverage, Riese: Kingdom Falling, Roswell, Star Trek, Warehouse 13, Xena: Warrior Princess*, and *The X-Files*. He is also a consulting editor for Tor Books.

He has received three Scribe Awards from the International Association of Media Tie-In Writers and lives in Oxford, Pennsylvania.

Visit him at www.gregcox-author.com.